PRAISE FOR CR⟨

M000087624

"I started reading *Cracking the Ice* and could not put it down. Jessie Stackhouse's generosity, hope, and intelligence touched my heart.... Usually I go to bed early; however, I kept reading *Cracking the Ice* until I turned to the last page."
>—Joyce Carol Thomas, National Book Award winner

"Hendrickson's debut novel paints a gripping account of a courageous young man rising above evil."
>— Booklist

"*Cracking the Ice* scores the literary equivalent of a hat-trick: funny, harrowing and finally, heartfelt. This book is a winner."
>— Greg Neri, author of
>*Yummy: the Last Days of a Southside Shorty*,
>a 2011 Coretta Scott King Honor book

"One of the most interesting books I've read this year, a one-of-a-kind book."
>— Reading in Color

"A compelling, civil rights tale of a young man's coming of age on the ice. Hendrickson personalizes history with unforgettable characters."
>— Jewell Parker Rhodes, author of *Ninth Ward*,
>a 2011 Coretta Scott King Honor book

"A worthy, if heartwrenching read.... The best of humanity is explored— and some of the worst, exposed."
>— Long and Short Reviews (four stars)

"A must read for every adult and young adult alike."
>— Pete Webster, UNH Hockey Radio Network

"This is a terrific book and I would recommend it to anyone who likes a great story, hockey fan or not."
>— Dan Hannigan, Maine Hockey Radio Network

Also by David H. Hendrickson

Cracking the Ice

Writing as D. H. Hendrickson

Body Check

Writing as David Bawdy

Bubba Goes for Broke

OFFSIDE

DAVID H. HENDRICKSON

Pentucket Publishing
www.pentucketpublishing.com

OFFSIDE

ISBN-13: 978-0692359105 (trade paperback)
ISBN-10: 0692359109 (trade paperback)

Author's Note

Although Lynn is a real city with its streets and landmarks accurately depicted, this is a work of fiction. Other than clearly identified public figures and historical incidents, all characters and events portrayed in this book are fictional and any resemblance to real people or incidents is purely coincidental.

For dramatic effect, Lynn English High School is described as including ninth grade, which is true today, but was not yet the case in 1967.

To my wonderful son, Ryan,
the greatest five-nothin', hundred-nothin' ever.

OFFSIDE

DAVID H. HENDRICKSON

CHAPTER 1

Saturday, July 15, 1967
Plainfield, Maine

I like football best of all.

Not so much throwing it, but running with it, running faster than anyone else and faking so guys can't even put their fingertips on me in two-hand touch. That's the best of all.

That, and daring the quarterback to throw the ball so far that I can't catch up to it, then proving he can't. It doesn't get any better than that.

But our hick town is too small to have a football team. We're too small for everything.

I'm almost fourteen years old, going into the ninth grade, and I have to go to the next town over, Grainville, just to attend school or play sports. And even though Grainville High takes kids from Plainfield, Beaumont, Eagle Creek, Moose Junction, and Oxbow, it still isn't big enough for a football team.

Up here in Aroostook County in the northern tip of Maine, it's mostly just trees, farmland, and cows. More cows than people, in fact.

Plainfield is so small there isn't even a single stoplight. There's an Amoco gas station and Mabel's General Store on opposite sides of Main Street at the center of town, but that's pretty much it. I suppose

I shouldn't call it a hick town because that means I'm a hick, but geez, what else do you call it?

Heaven, I guess. At least that's what I'll be thinking a few months from now when I'm living in what feels like Hell, and football is the only thing that's keeping me sane. But for now, it's just a teeny, tiny hick town.

To be fair, though, at least Grainville has baseball, basketball, and track. Right now, our Babe Ruth team is playing against the Fort Fairfield Devils, one of the best teams in the league. I stride to the plate with the bases empty and one out.

"Now batting for the Grainville Mustangs, Rabbit Labelle," the PA system announces through static-filled, tinny speakers. "Rabbit Labelle."

I look out to the fence beyond the gap between left field and center where advertisements for Mabel's General Store and the Ashland Rotary Club are painted in white on the green background. I'm not going to hit the ball over that fence. I'm no Willie Mays or Carl Yastrzemski or Tony Conigliaro. But if I hit the ball in that gap, I'll get at least a double, maybe a triple. And every once in a while, the ball hits a warped board between the ad for Mabel's and the one for the Rotary and it caroms funny, right past the outfielder and by the time he's chased down the ball I've got an inside-the-park home run.

The pitcher for the Fort Fairfield Devils, a tall left-hander with lots of pimples and a mop of black hair sticking out from beneath his cap, has been tough on us the first time through the lineup. I led off with a single and stole two bases, but he struck out three guys straight to get out of it in the first inning and has allowed only a walk since. He's probably six inches taller than I am—everyone seems to be taller than I am, even most girls my age—but he's got no chance against me. Not to brag or anything, but I just *know* I'm going to get a hit and score.

"Come on, Rabbit," Coach Beaupre cheers, clapping his big meaty hands together and then slapping his enormous gut. "Get us going."

I hear more cheers from our side of the metal stands, including from my parents, but I tune them out. I push the blue, plastic batting helmet down hard on my head, tap the far side of home plate with my bat, and take my stance.

It's just me and the lefty. Me and the ball.

I rip the first pitch, a fastball on the inside corner, on a line to left field, and race toward first base. The left fielder picks it up on two hops and quickly fires it in to second base as I take a wide turn. If he'd fumbled the ball or tossed in a lazy floater, I might have taken second, but it's a good throw, so I retreat to first.

Nothing wrong with a single. I'll get to second quickly enough.

"Way to go, Rabbit!" I hear my father yell above all the other cheers from the stands. He misses lots of my games because he's a really important executive in his company and has to work late and on the weekends. But I can tell he's really enjoying this one.

I smell the freshly cut infield grass. I slap my hands together, feeling the grit of dirt between my fingers. I adjust my cap.

This part is the fun. I'm going to steal two more bases on Lefty and there's nothing he or his catcher can do about it.

He can throw over to try to keep me close. He and the catcher can try a pitch out. But none of it is going to make any difference. I'm going to be on third base before Lefty can say Carl Yastrzemski.

I take my lead, bouncing on my toes.

Lefty throws over and I dive back. The first baseman, a tall, gangly kid, slaps the tag down hard on my hand. It's way too late, of course, but the hard tag didn't seem intended to try to get me out. On the next throw over, he ignores my entire outstretched arm and hand, instead slapping me across the face with his glove and the hard ball.

I wince, the left side of my face stinging, and lay there for a second. I smell the leather and oil of his glove and taste the grit of dirt on my lips. I ask for time from the umpire and brush myself off. A cloud of dirt surrounds me.

I look at the first baseman, who is grinning. None of it was an accident. A part of me wants to tell him that with teeth as crooked as his, he shouldn't be smiling or even opening his mouth. But I decide on a better revenge.

I try to look intimidated and say, "Cut that out," so softly that the first-base umpire doesn't hear a thing. I hold my hand to the stinging side of my face, playing up how wounded I must be.

Inside, though, I'm grinning, and that inside grin grows even broader when The Jerk laughs and says, "Try to stop me, squirt." He pounds his mitt with his fist. "The great Rabbit Labelle is just a baby."

I take my lead, then add to it. I've got Lefty's timing down and I've got The Jerk thinking about how hard he's going to slap me this next time.

As Lefty starts his throw over, I take off. Not back to first base but for second.

I'm flying, my legs barely touching the ground, and I get ready to slide into second while the shortstop waits for a throw that he knows isn't even going to be close. I can see it in his face.

As I slide, I see the shortstop's eyes widen. He dives toward right field, but the ball sails past him.

I pop up and race for third base, looking at Stevie Lafontaine, the kid in the third base coach's box, for a sign of whether to take off for home. He's just holding his hands high, telling me I don't need to slide. But I knew that. I glance over my shoulder and see the center fielder firing in toward home. I round third in case the throw is wild, but the catcher fields it cleanly and I retreat back to the base.

I decide not to dust my uniform off. I kind of like the dirt. I kind of like everything. If baseball were always like this, I'd like it almost as much as football.

Lefty takes the ball from his catcher, looking rattled. I look over at The Jerk on first base. He's staring at me, so I grin at him and then do something that maybe I shouldn't.

I wink.

The first baseman flushes. I've embarrassed him.

Good. Maybe next time he'll show better sportsmanship. I feel a little guilty, but not too much. I didn't start this.

Rattled, Lefty gives up hits to the next five batters, including a home run by my best friend, Donnie Boudreau, that makes it a 6-1 game. We never look back.

*

We get back home and Mom heads to the kitchen while Dad grabs the newspaper and plops in the tan lounge chair next to the sofa in the living room.

"Dad, let's play catch," I say, trying to stop him before he puts his feet up on the hassock and gets comfortable. "I'll go get the football."

To be honest, it's more fun playing with Donnie, but I'm not sure he's home and my parents don't like me running up the phone bill calling my friends. Besides, it takes a couple minutes to bike over to his house and I've only got an hour before we have to leave.

But there's another reason, too.

When I was little, my dad and I used to play catch in the backyard all the time. He wasn't as pudgy then and could run around a little without getting all out of breath. We'd both throw touchdown passes to each other. We'd toss the baseball around, too, with him giving me grounders, pop flies, and line drives that I'd have to dive for.

These days, though, he's working so much that we hardly play together at all. I suppose that's normal for someone like me who's about to turn fourteen. After all, I'm not eight anymore. It is more fun to play with my friends. A lot more.

But it still was nice when my dad and I did all that stuff together, and he wasn't so serious all the time. This week, he worked late every night, then missed my cross-country race this morning.

I crossed the finish line more than a minute before everyone else in my age category, but he wasn't there to see it.

So I figure maybe he wishes the two of us could be playing together more often. Tossing the football around in the backyard would at least let him make up for him missing my race this morning.

But I'm wrong about that.

"Aren't you forgetting your Summer League basketball game?" he asks, looking up from his newspaper and pushing his dark-rimmed glasses to the bridge of his nose. He looks at his watch. "We'll be leaving in an hour."

"Yeah, plenty of time to play."

He sighs heavily and shakes his head. "I don't have your energy, Rabbit." He runs a hand through his black hair. "I don't think anybody does. I just can't keep up with you."

I don't understand adults sometimes. How much energy does it take to throw a ball around? All he's done for the last three hours is sit in the stands at the baseball field and clap his hands every now and then. How hard is that?

But I'm not going to beg.

If he doesn't want to play catch, that's fine with me. I didn't really want to play that much with him anyway.

"There's more to life than sports," he says, sounding defensive, as if he feels guilty at turning me down. "Life isn't just one big game. I swear, sometimes it seems like you're thirteen going on three."

"I'll be fourteen next month."

"Okay, so you're fourteen going on three," my father says. "Or fourteen going on four. All you think about is sports. Sports, sports, sports."

"It's what I like," I say with a shrug.

"Maybe it's time to start liking some other things, things more important than sports," he says.

I'm tempted to say, "Like what?" but I don't fall for that trap, especially since my mother has appeared at the living room entrance. She's wearing a white apron over her light blue dress. I suppose she's kind of pretty in a mom kind of way, never wearing makeup or flashy jewelry and always wearing plain-looking clothes and tying her long, brown hair up in a bun. But right now, I'm not liking the look on her face. It's clear whose side she's on.

"I do well in school," I say. "Just about all A's. And I read lots of books."

"All of them about sports," my mother says, making it official. They've ganged up on me.

"Not all of them," I say.

"Just about."

I still want to say, "Who cares?" and point out that lots of kids my age don't read at all. Since when is it a bad thing to read about sports? Doesn't she take me to the library every two weeks to get all those books?

I really don't understand my parents.

But I understand them well enough to know that my mom is about to tell me to go clean my room. I can see it on her face. As if cleaning my room is supposed to stop me from being fourteen going on four. As if it's supposed to stop me from being obsessed about sports. As if I'm going to fall in love with having a neat desk and having everything picked up off the floor and I'll want to do that all day.

It doesn't make any sense, but that's how parents are sometimes. I think the room cleaning is just to keep me busy and out of my mom's hair most of the time and my dad's today.

But I see that look on her face and before she can say anything, I take off for the front door. Kind of like taking off for second base on Lefty.

I say over my shoulder, "I'm going over to Donnie's," and slam the door behind me. I add, not sure if they'll hear me, "I'll be back in an hour," but I don't stick around to be sure. I hop on my red Schwinn three-speed bike and pedal away as fast as I can.

And with that I'm gone. It's my best stolen base of the day.

CHAPTER 2

Donnie Boudreau answers the door. He's a good seven or eight inches taller than me and has big broad shoulders from doing all his farm chores. He can beat just about anyone at arm wrestling and has already started to shave, which makes the rest of us jealous.

Donnie and I have been going to school together since kindergarten. His father's farm extends all the way to our house. In fact, our house sits on a corner of what used to be the Boudreau's property, so we live about as close to each other as anyone can out here in farm country. Donnie's been my best friend for as long as I can remember.

"My mom's making me clean my room before the game," Donnie says with a grimace. He's on the basketball team, too, and is a really good rebounder. Time after time, he'll outmuscle the other team for the ball, pass it to me, and I'll outrace everyone down court for a layup. An easy two points.

"My mom was going to do the same thing," I say. "I got out of the house just in time. What is it with mothers and clean rooms? It's like a disease."

"I heard that, Rabbit Labelle," says a voice from over Donnie's shoulder. Mrs. Boudreau is behind Donnie. I feel my face turn hot.

"I didn't mean—"

"Come in, Rabbit," she says, and reaches out to rumple my dirty blond hair like she always does. Mrs. Boudreau is thin and wears her dark hair tied up in a bun like my mom and most of the other mothers in Plainfield. She's wearing a plain yellow dress and a flowered apron. "Do you need a ride to the game?"

"No," I say. "I was hoping Donnie and I could play catch. We have almost an hour, but Donnie says he's got to clean his room so..." I shrug and try to give her my best smile. "I guess I should go back home."

"Hold on there," Mrs. Boudreau says with a roll of her eyes. "I suppose it'll be okay for you two to play if Donnie promises to clean up his room tomorrow."

"Yes!" Donnie shouts like a prisoner just set free and lumbers up to his room to get his football.

We run around back behind his house, past the barn with its weathered siding and faded red silo with the word "BOUDREAU" near its peak. A rooster crows from inside the chicken coop behind the barn. There's a faint smell of manure, not as bad as when it's been spread in the fields, but it never quite leaves the air until the winter.

I race ahead along the dirt road that extends to the back of the Boudreau farm, holding one arm aloft. I'm probably twenty yards away when Donnie hits me with a nice pass that nestles softly into my fingertips. I throw a pass back to him that he promptly drops.

"Butterfingers!" I yell, and we both laugh.

We get to the part of the field where we can play. It's about half the length of a real football field and not quite as wide. The Boudreau farm stretches in all directions, with a fenced-in area where about twenty cows are grazing, and beyond that some corn and lots of potatoes. Lots and lots of potatoes. A scarecrow flitters in the breeze.

This is the best place for playing football in the whole town, even when the manure is thick in the fields and the air is ripe with the smell. Those times of the year, it's thick everywhere and you just have to get used to it.

That's not a problem this afternoon, though, and with the sun beating down from a cloudless sky, Donnie throws me a pass. We're about twenty-five yards apart and I easily catch it.

But I didn't come over here just to throw the ball back and forth. I want to run, to feel the breeze in my face. I want to dive for the ball and catch it with the very ends of my fingertips.

I say that to Donnie, but he says, "Shouldn't we just toss it around instead? I don't want to get tired for the game tonight."

"I never get tired," I say. "Quit being such a baby."

"I'm not a baby."

"I think you need to get your mom to change your diaper."

Donnie laughs. "I'm not a baby."

"Prove it!"

And he does, throwing me a ball I have to race for and dive until I'm stretched out as far as I can just to reach it. The ball floats into my hands, and all we can do for a few moments is whoop it up.

No, it doesn't get any better than this.

*

We win the basketball game with Donnie muscling down the rebounds, as usual, and me scoring on the fast break. But on the drive home, my dad says words that send shivers up and down my spine. He and my mom are sitting in the front seat of my dad's silver Plymouth Fury and I'm sitting in the back behind my mother, so he glances sideways so he can see me out of the corner of his eye while he drives.

"Rabbit, we need to talk about something," he says in a tone that tells me I'm not going to like what he has to say. "Your mother and I have been wondering."

He pauses and my mother jumps right in, turning all the way around to look over the seat back, her soft brown eyes filled with concern.

"We think you may be doing too much," she says. "You've always been a bundle of energy, but today you had your cross-country race in the morning, your Babe Ruth game in the afternoon, and your basketball game tonight. It's too much, even for you. You must be exhausted."

"No!" I say. "I feel great! I've got *tons* of energy left. Honest! If you don't believe me, pull the car around the back of the house when we get home and leave the lights on. Dad and I will play catch."

"The mosquitoes will eat you alive."

"No they won't," I say. "They can't catch me."

My mother grins and my father snorts with laughter.

"They'll catch me!" he says.

"You need to run around more," I say. "You're always talking about how you need more exercise."

This time it's my mother snorting with laughter.

"Don't change the subject," Dad says. "This isn't about me. It's about you."

The look on my mom's face grows serious and her hand grips the seat back so tightly it turns white. "We've got to cut something out of your schedule. It's just too much."

"No!" I say. "It's only because today was Saturday. Summer League basketball is only twice a week. Cross-country races aren't even every week. It's usually boring in the summer. There's never anything to do. Today was great! I wish every day could be like this!"

Her shoulders slump, kind of like the point guard from the other team tonight when I blasted past him for my third straight layup.

"The only way it could have been any better," I say, "is if we had a football team."

Shaking her head, she sinks back into her seat and stares ahead. Finally, she glances over to my dad and says, "Your turn. See if you have any better luck."

And they both break into laughter.

I join in. Any kid likes to see his parents happy, but my mother looks especially pretty when she's laughing. Not Marilyn Monroe or Raquel Welch pretty. She's a mom, not a movie star. But her eyes seem to twinkle and her teeth flash so white when she laughs. It's nice.

We almost make it back home with everyone happy.

Unfortunately, my dad always has the radio on in the car, turned down low so we can talk, and all of a sudden a news report comes on.

Something about some riots in a place called Newark. I've never heard of the place, but it seems pretty significant to my parents because all of a sudden they stop talking and my dad hunches over the radio speakers so he doesn't miss a word, all while keeping his eyes on the road. From my seat in the back, I can see my mom leaning forward, too.

"Turn it up!" I say because I can only barely make out a few words.

My parents look at each other and my father just shakes his head.

"Please?" I say. "I can't hear it."

Neither of them reaches for the radio. I stare at the back of my mother's head, and as if she senses it, she turns and whispers to me.

"This isn't for kids," she says. "It's adult stuff."

It feels like a slap across the face. *This isn't for kids.*

I hate it when they say that. What do they think I am, ten years old? I'm practically fourteen! And if they think I don't know about *adult stuff*...they're wrong.

But I can tell this is a battle I'm not going to win so I strain my ears while looking out the side window, pretending not to care.

I hear the radio announcer say something more about Newark and people dying and then Plainfield. *Plainfield!* That's where we live! I can't keep quiet. The words just rush out of my mouth.

"What's happening in Plainfield?" I say, and Mom turns all the way around again.

"Not our Plainfield," she says. "Plainfield, Maine is just fine. It's Plainfield, New Jersey, where there are problems."

"Everything is fine, Rabbit," my father says firmly and shuts off the radio. "The place where the problems are...well, we wouldn't live there."

Mom opens her mouth to say something and then gives Dad a sharp look.

"Like I said, this is something for adults," she says. "Mind your p's and q's and think about something else."

Then she looks at my Dad as if he's done something wrong, as if whatever is happening in Newark and that other Plainfield is his fault.

CHAPTER 3

My mother says something funny on the drive home from my next baseball game. Not ha-ha funny, but odd funny. Strange funny. What-do-you-mean-by-that funny.

It's Tuesday and Dad is working late again so he isn't there. By the time I come up to bat in the last inning, I've already hit two doubles and a single, and stolen three bases. I'm up with two outs and the tying run, Stevie Lafontaine, is on second.

I just know I'm going to knock him in.

I'm hotter than Carl Yastrzemski, the player on the Red Sox they call Yaz, the best hitter in the American League. He might even get the Triple Crown this year, which happens when you lead the league in batting average, home runs, and runs batted in.

On the first pitch, I hit a screaming line drive right at the third baseman. He sticks up his glove as he ducks and I'm sure it's going to fly right past his head and maybe even get past the left fielder because it's a screamer, a ball I've pounded as hard as I can. If it gets past the left fielder, I might even get an inside-the-park home run for the game-winner.

Instead, the ball smacks loudly right into the middle of the third baseman's glove, a miracle because he's got his eyes closed, his head tucked behind his arm, and he looks like he's about to pee his pants.

But the ball lands dead in the middle of his glove.

He opens his eyes wide and looks around, trying to figure out why the parents on his team are cheering. He doesn't realize he's caught the ball, or rather that the glove has somehow caught the ball with no help at all from him.

But then he sees it in his glove and a look of absolute astonishment comes over his face. His jaw drops and his eyes bug out. Then all of a sudden, he pulls his hand out of his glove, shakes it, and yells, "Ow!"

It would be funny, like something you'd see on a Saturday morning cartoon, except that I've just made the last out of the game.

I stand halfway down the first baseline, staring at the third basemen, not believing my eyes.

But it's true. We've lost, and I made the last out of the game.

After we shake hands with the other team, I head to where my mom is standing next to the metal fence, and we walk to the car.

I feel so bad. I've let the team down.

"You had a great game, Rabbit," Mom says, squeezing my shoulder. She has a kind face and right now it's filled with compassion, but I barely notice.

I mumble a half-hearted response.

"You hit a rocket there," she says. "The fielder just got lucky. It happens sometimes. You can't get a hit every time up there. Not even that Yastrzemski fellow on the Red Sox can do that."

If I didn't feel so bad about making the out, I might even laugh that Mom is talking about the Red Sox. They're the team everyone is calling the Cardiac Kids because they're so exciting with lots of come-from-behind wins. But a year ago she barely knew the Red Sox existed.

Instead, I just nod and buckle myself into the front seat. I can feel the dirt from the infield on my face, but I don't bother wiping it off. I can smell my own sweat, but I don't care about that either. I don't care about anything.

I made the last out.

Mom talks a lot as we drive back to the house, and I nod to keep her happy until she says the funny, but not funny ha-ha, thing.

"Rabbit?" she said, glancing over at me quickly with a nervous look in her eyes. "How much do you like it here in Plainfield?"

My head, which was bowed while I chewed the bottom of my lip and stared at the black floor mat, looks up.

"Why?" I ask.

"I'm just asking."

"I like it. I've got good friends and everyone is nice…well, except Old Man McDougall."

Behind our house is a wooded area that goes on for miles until you hit Old Man McDougall's apple orchard. Lots of times Donnie and I run through those woods, up and down the hills as we kick up old fallen leaves, then we step on the large rocks that cross a stream right before the orchard starts. We've never taken any of Old Man McDougall's apples, but we've heard all the stories about how the old man sneaks up on kids who steal his apples and shoots them in the butt with his BB gun, then calls the cops. So Donnie and I just run out there and on a hot sunny day catch some shade underneath the trees for a couple minutes before we head back.

"You've had problems with Mr. McDougall?" my mom asks.

"Not really," I admit. "But he still seems like a cranky old man."

"He's not that bad," she says. "Just don't take his apples."

"I don't. I don't even like apples."

Mom nods, and a distracted look comes over her face.

"What's going on?" I ask.

"Nothing."

"Then why are you asking if I like it here?" A terrible thought hits me, and I feel a sudden, cold stab of fear. "Are you and Dad getting divorced?"

Mom recoils in shock, blinking in surprise. "No, of course not. Why do you say that?"

"You're sure?"

"Of course."

"Then why are you asking if I like it here?" I look at her and though her cheeks are flushed, I don't know if that means she's angry or upset or what. "Is it because one of you is going to leave here and live somewhere else?"

She shakes her head vigorously. "No. Absolutely not." She draws in a deep breath. "But...well, I wasn't supposed to talk about this without your father being here."

"Talk about what?"

"I'm not supposed to—"

"*Talk about what?*"

Mom looks at me with concern. Without realizing it, I've almost been hollering. "I'll tell you as soon as your father gets home."

*

"We need to talk to Rabbit," she says to my father as soon as he steps inside the front door, before he even gets to set his briefcase against the wall, loosen his tie, or take off his suit jacket. Instead of going up to my room, I've been sitting downstairs in the living room, pretending to read my library book, a biography about Joe DiMaggio, but all I've been able to think about is what's going on.

"Talk about what?" he asks cautiously, cocking his head as he steps into the living room.

"About *you-know-what,*" she says and gives him the eye.

I'm about to explode. I know, just know, that they're getting divorced like Richie Leblanc's parents, even though it doesn't make sense. Mom and Dad seem pretty happy together. They argue once in a while, but not often.

An angry look comes over my father's face. "You promised to wait—"

"I slipped just a little," Mom says, spreading her arms out, palms up. "I was just trying to gauge what his reaction would be and..."

I can't hold it in any longer. "*Will you just tell me what's going on?*"

Dad looks startled, but Mom nods and steps beside him. "Your father has an opportunity at work. A promotion."

I wait for the full explanation.

Mom and Dad look at each other.

"If I take the promotion," Dad says, "we'll need to move. Down to a big city outside of Boston. It'll be a big change for all of us."

I look at him and then at Mom. "You two aren't getting divorced?"

Dad looks stunned. "Of course not. Marie, what did you—"

"I tried to tell him," she says.

"We're not getting divorced," Dad says firmly and puts his arm around my mother to prove his point. "But we'll be moving—*if* I take the promotion, that is—we'll be moving to a big city called Lynn."

My head spins.

Plainfield is the only place I've ever lived. All my friends are here. Donnie Boudreau...Scooter Seavey...Jimmy Chaisson...I go through all of the names. It's a long list.

I'll have to say good-bye to all of them.

"Your mother and I have discussed this a lot," Dad says, glancing sideways at her. "We're not sure if I should take the promotion. There are a lot of problems in the big cities now. It's not necessarily a good place to raise a boy."

"Why not?" I ask, although I feel like saying, *Then don't go!*

"There are problems."

"What kind of problems?"

"Well, among other things, in the big cities there are...well...Negroes."

"Andre!" Mom exclaims.

My father throws his hands up in the air. "How do you think I should explain it? There are race riots breaking out everywhere—"

He stops.

"What your father means," she says, "is that there are lots of problems right now between white people like us and Negroes, or black people as they prefer to be called now."

"We don't have those problems up here," Dad says, "because everyone up here is white. Everyone gets along."

I think of how some players on the baseball and basketball teams farthest away from us call us Frogs because so many of us here are French.

And how Jimmy Chaisson got in a fight with one of them and called the kid a dumb Mick, which is what he said you should call the Irish.

But as my parents look closely at me, I say nothing.

"We'll be going from a tiny town of a few hundred people where everyone knows everyone to a big city of about a hundred thousand," my father says. "And Boston isn't far away and it has millions."

"This promotion is a big one for your father," Mom says, "But we're going to do our homework about Lynn before we make the move. We're going to make sure it's the right choice for the family."

"What kind of homework?" I ask, my head still swimming but spitting out questions fast and furiously.

"Well," my father says, and he cracks a weak grin, "we'll make sure your school has a football team."

That sounds good, but it's the only thing that sounds good about moving, and I can think of lots and lots of bad things. Especially leaving my friends. But as bad as I'm thinking things might get, I never imagine how awful they'll really become, and how I'll need football to hold my life together.

CHAPTER 4

I lay on my bed, the room in almost total darkness, unable to get to sleep. A slight cooling breeze flows through my open window. Outside, crickets chirp loudly in the fields. The clock on the nightstand shows that it's past midnight, and I'm still tossing and turning. I turn toward the window. I turn away. I face up toward the ceiling and count the tiles.

All I can do is think.

My Dad is going to take the promotion. He and Mom can talk all they want about doing their homework about Lynn and "weighing the pros and cons," as they like to say, but he's taking it. I can see it in his face. He's worked too hard for it, all the nights he's stayed late even if it meant missing my games and all the work he's brought home in his briefcase. The promotion is his reward. He wants it so bad he can taste it.

But I can tell that Mom is scared and she really doesn't want to go. She's never lived anywhere but here. She grew up in this house. She went to the same school I go to. And when her parents died way back before I was born, she took over the house.

This is home.

She got really mad when Dad told me that Lynn would have a football team, saying that he wasn't playing fair, that he was "stacking the deck." He said he was just joking, and maybe he was, but I think he wants this promotion so much that he figured he'd get me on his side that way.

I can't get out of my mind all the friends I'll never see again.

Ever.

I can't imagine that. In baseball, I've always scooped up a hard ground ball and thrown it to Donnie Boudreau at first or flipped it to Stevie Lafontaine at second where we'd turn the double-play. Dennis Martel has always been on the mound, throwing his unhittable curve ball, making guys duck out of the way as they've seen it coming at their heads, only to have it break over the plate, earning a "*Steee-rike!*" from the umpire.

When I've played basketball, there's always been Donnie grabbing all the rebounds for our team and passing the outlet to me. Or in the half court, me lobbing it down to him after he's posted up a guy he can score on. When we've played each other one-on-one, he's been the one ready to block my shots, forcing me to move farther away from the basket and either make the shot or sucker him into coming out for me. Then I blast past him for a layup.

I'll never again play flag football or two-hand touch with the guys in Donnie's field out beyond the barn and chicken coop, sometimes hearing the cows moo while we're whooping it up. Everyone else will still be playing, but not me. They'll be having a great time, just like always, and Mrs. Boudreau will bring out cold lemonade after they've been playing for a while and they're all sweaty and have grass stains on their clothes.

I always had more grass stains than anyone else because I'd try to dive for everything. But I won't have any grass stains at all. I'll be living in the big city with everything concrete and dirty brick and asphalt.

All the best things in my life...gone.

No more runs through those back woods all the way to Old Man McDougall's orchard. Donnie will have to run there himself. Or with whoever his new best friend will be.

It makes me feel so sad. Donnie. Jimmy Chaisson. Scooter Seavey. All of them. I thought we'd always be together. Well, maybe not when we're fifty years old. I mean, I'm not an idiot. I know people grow up and sometimes friends go off to different places. Jimmy says he can't wait until he's old enough to go over and fight in the Vietnam War and kill some Japs like his dad did in World War II. Donnie laughs at him and says there aren't Japs in Vietnam, but Jimmy says all gooks are the same and he can't wait to kill 'em. He's only afraid the war will be over before he gets old enough to fight.

But Vietnam or college or a job somewhere else have always seemed as far away as Pluto. I thought we'd all be together until we got to Pluto.

Now that isn't going to happen, and it's because of me.

Even Diane Durnall, who sits two rows in front of me in school and is so pretty with her long black hair and bright smile. I think she likes me, but I guess I'll never find out for sure. I won't even get to say good-bye to her—not that I'd want to do, of course—because I'm sure we'll move before the school year starts again in September.

As much as I love football, and as neat as it'll be to finally put on a uniform and play, I'd rather keep my friends. It's also a little scary heading off to a big city. What'll it be like? I'm not afraid of all the black people there unless there are riots. I've always been able to get people to like me. Why should the color of their skin make them any different?

*

"It isn't just the color of their skin," Dad says the next day at breakfast when I ask about it. The smell of bacon fills the air. We're sitting at the dining room table, my father at one end and my mother, still wearing her white apron, at the other. We're eating fried eggs, English muffins, and crispy bacon. I cut into one of the egg yolks and let its juices spread across my plate, then swish my English muffin in it and take a big bite. I follow that with some crunchy, tasty bacon. This sure beats Cheerios.

"They're *different*," my dad says. "They just are. They're not like us." He hesitates. "They hate us."

"Maybe they have reason to," Mom says.

Dad shoots her an angry look. He's wearing a suit like he always does for work. I guess that's what executives always wear. This one is his gray one with a white shirt and a blue tie.

"Well, if it's so dangerous," Mom says, "maybe we shouldn't move."

"I didn't say it's dangerous," Dad says, sounding annoyed. "I just said that they hate us."

"But—"

"We'll find a nice, white neighborhood and it won't be a problem," he says. "End of story." He cuts his hand sideways through the air, which is his way of saying the discussion is over.

But I can't help asking the question. "So there are white neighborhoods separate from black neighborhoods?"

"Yes," Dad says.

"Why?"

He hesitates. "There are a lot of reasons."

"Like what?"

"We should talk about this tonight," he says, glancing at my mother and looking flustered. "I need to get to work."

"C'mon, tell me," I say. "I'll walk out to the car with you."

He clanks his fork onto his plate, shakes his head, and takes a deep breath. He leans forward on both elbows. "It's simply best if people stay with their own kind. White people prefer to be around other white people. The same for blacks."

"I don't get it," I say. "I don't care who I'm around."

He purses his lips, glances at Mom, then back at me. "You're just not old enough to understand," he says, and he must see my dislike for those words because he quickly adds, "Besides, most blacks are poor. They can't afford to live in the nice, white neighborhoods. The houses cost too much for them. So even if they wanted to live with us—which they don't—they can't because they don't have enough money."

"Why are most of them poor?" I ask. I've long since stopped eating my breakfast. We usually talk about sports, mostly the Red Sox. We've never talked about stuff like this.

Dad looks to my mother for help.

"Eat your eggs, Rabbit," she says.

"Why are most blacks poor?" I repeat, and shovel some egg into my mouth.

"Well," he says. The word hangs in the air for what feels like a long time. "Okay." His eyes dart from me to my mother and back. "You can't repeat this to your friends, and after we move—"

"*If* we move," Mom says quickly.

Anger flashes in my dad's eyes, then is gone. "If we move," he says, and gives her a look that seems to say, *there, are you happy?* He looks back to me. "You certainly can't repeat this down in Lynn near any black people. That would cause problems."

He pauses and I nod.

"Most people won't say it out loud," he says, "but black people just aren't as good as us. They're not just different; they're inferior, intellectually and otherwise."

That doesn't seem fair. I look to Mom for confirmation, but she looks away, her face flushed.

"And lots of them are lazy," Dad says.

I think about the only blacks I know, athletes I see on the black-and-white TV in our living room. George "Boomer" Scott, Joe Foy, and Reggie Smith on the Red Sox. All the black players on the Celtics, especially Bill Russell. Jim Nance and Houston Antwine on the Patriots. They don't seem lazy to me.

And what about Jackie Robinson? I've read books about him and what he had to do to break the color line in baseball. He seemed anything *but* lazy or inferior. In fact, I've sometimes dreamed of being another Pee Wee Reese, the white player who befriended and stood up for Jackie Robinson. I think that would be great, something really heroic to be proud about.

But I stay quiet and let Dad keep talking.

"So they don't get good jobs," Dad says. "In fact, lots of them are criminals. Like the ones who've been rioting in Newark and Plainfield and in other places. Plainfield, New Jersey, I mean. Not here, of course. Burning buildings, destroying property, killing people." He shakes his head. "They're animals. So it's best that they keep to themselves. Let them burn their own neighborhoods down."

"Andre," my mother says sharply. "I think you've gone too far—"

Dad stands up. "I've really got to go," he says, and gives me a hug. He grabs his briefcase and, after a quick peck on the cheek to my mother, he dashes out the door.

After the door slams shut, I say to my mother, "That doesn't seem fair."

"It's complicated, Rabbit," she says. She looks away. "I don't necessarily agree with *everything* your father said, but he's a very smart man."

"What if I'd been born black?"

"You couldn't have," she says, her cheeks again turning rosy.

"I know that," I say. "Geez, Mom, I'm not ten. I know that because I'm your son, the son of you and Dad, I have to be white. But what if I were the son of black parents? What if I were black? I—"

"You couldn't be black," Mom says firmly.

But she's missing my point. "What if I *were* black," I say. "Does that mean I wouldn't be as smart as I am now? Could I even be a criminal?"

"Rabbit, stop it! You aren't a *criminal*," my mother says, a threatening look in her eyes. "Enough of this silly talk! You aren't black. You're white. Now I don't want to hear another word of this nonsense. Do you hear me?"

"But—"

"*Do you hear me?*"

I look down at my plate. All that's left on it are a few crumbs from my English muffin. "Yes."

"Okay, then," she says. "Clear the table and then go clean your room."

"Aw, c'mon," I say.

"You heard me."

"What difference does it make if my room is clean or not?" I say. "I bet Carl Yastrzemski had a messy room when he was my age."

"And when you're done cleaning your room, get outside and mow the lawn."

"Aw, geez," I say.

"Don't you sass me, young man," she says. "Now get going. Skedaddle." She waves her hand in a shooing gesture.

What a lousy day this is shaping up to be. I'd almost rather be going to school.

CHAPTER 5

I clean my room, mow the lawn, and then rush over to Donnie's house before Mom thinks of more chores for me to do. It feels like I've escaped from that prison—what's the name of it?—Alcatraz. Geez.

I can't tell whether Mom is upset about us moving or about me asking questions about black people. Probably both. But she sure is cranky these days. I figure I'm going to stop asking her questions because she just gets all flustered and then to shut me up she gives me as many chores as she can think of.

Maybe if I never ask a question again about blacks or being black, I'll never have to do another chore. Ever. I'll be like the smart rats Mr. Perrault talks about in Science class, the ones that get shocked when they do something bad, like going down the wrong alley in a maze, so they stop doing it. I'm no genius, but I can be that smart.

So I ask Donnie my questions as we head out to his backyard, each of us with a football tucked under our arms, hoping enough of the other guys in the neighborhood come over to start a game.

"You ever think about what it would be like to be black?" I ask.

Donnie looks at me like I'm crazy. "You mean like…a Negro?"

"Yeah, only my mom says they prefer to be called blacks now."

Donnie stares at me. "How's she know that?"

It's a good question. How does she know? She doesn't know any more of them than I do. "I don't know."

Donnie just shakes his head.

"Maybe she read it somewhere," I say. "What difference does it make?"

Donnie shrugs, then looks at me suspiciously. "Why are you asking?"

I don't want to tell him that my dad is getting a promotion and we're probably going to have to move. That we're *definitely* going to move even if Mom and Dad won't admit it. They can argue about it all they want and Mom can be unhappy about it all she wants, but Dad isn't saying no to that promotion.

But for now, that's my little secret, almost as secret as Donnie swearing me not to tell about the time a couple years ago he wasn't feeling good in his stomach and couldn't make it back to his house before he crapped his pants. I never told anyone 'cause it was a secret. But I can't tell him about this even if he won't tell anyone, because Mom says that Mrs. Boudreau may be a nice person but she's a gossip and if you tell her something, the whole town knows.

I don't want the whole town to know that we're leaving, and Mrs. Boudreau might find out from Donnie. Plus, I guess I don't want to admit it to myself. If I actually say it out loud to Donnie, then it really is the truth.

So I only say part of the truth.

"My dad was talking about black people rioting in another Plainfield," I say. "Not our Plainfield, but Plainfield, New Jersey. That's south of New York City."

"I know where New Jersey is," Donnie says. "I'm no Allen Richter." Allen Richter is the dumbest kid in our class. He doesn't know *anything*. If the teacher calls on him, sometimes it's even fun to guess what dumb thing he's going to say. I mean, I know that isn't nice, but it can be funny. Even Allen thinks so.

"My dad says that black people aren't like us," I say.

"Of course they're not like us," Donnie says with a frown. "If they were like us, they'd be white."

"What I mean is that he says they aren't as smart as us and they're like…lazy and stuff."

"Yeah, so what?"

"Do you think that's true?" I ask.

"Must be," Donnie says. "That's what my dad says, too."

"It just…doesn't seem fair."

Donnie shrugs. "Who cares?" Then he gets a look on his face that says that he's just gotten an idea. "Is it fair that you're faster than everyone else in town, faster than anyone we play in baseball or basketball?"

"But—"

"Is it fair that we're both kind of smart and Allen Richter is so dumb?"

I don't say anything to that.

"Is it fair," Donnie says, "that Diane Durnall is so pretty, but Joanie Bergeron is fat and ugly?"

Donnie's mention of Diane Durnall catches me off guard.

"Diane is really pretty," I say, feeling a warm grin creep across my face.

"And she likes you, not me," Donnie says. "Is that fair?"

*

Back home, I wander into the living room and spot the previous day's *Bangor Daily News* on the coffee table atop the *Wall Street Journal*. We're way too far out in the boonies to have daily delivery, so my father brings the papers home from work.

Each night, I devour the sports pages, poring over the articles, the box scores, and the statistics while listening to the Red Sox broadcast on my small transistor radio. It's tuned to WEGP, 1390 AM, where Ken Coleman, Ned Martin, and Mel Parnell announce the games. Coleman has been my favorite since the night in April when rookie lefthander Billy Rohr took a no-hitter into the ninth inning. I was sitting on the edge of my seat, eyes glued to the radio, the newspaper long since set aside, and Coleman made the call. Tom Tresh hit a long fly ball to deep left field and the no-hitter seemed a goner for sure, but then Coleman cried out, "Yastrzemski goes back and makes *a tremendous catch!*" Coleman was practically screaming. I'd never heard an announcer sound so excited, before or since. Rohr lost the no-hitter two batters later, but I can still feel the excitement crackling through that static-filled broadcast.

Other than the sports pages, I only read the funnies. I ignore the front page headlines about what the President and Congress are doing or how the Vietnam War is going or whether the economy is going up or down. None of that interests me.

Until today.

A front page article about race riots in Detroit catches my eye and I pick it up.

CHAPTER 6

Dad takes the promotion, of course. I knew he would. He calls me in from outside and tells me to sit down at the dining room table. He has a serious, grim look on his face as he takes his seat at the head of the table. Mom sits at the other end, her eyes puffy and bloodshot.

"We'll move before the start of the school year," he says. "Down there, ninth grade is the first year of high school, so you'll be starting fresh like everyone else. Your classmates will be coming from different junior highs, so on that first day of classes it won't be like everyone knows everyone else except for you. Everyone will be seeing lots of strangers they never saw before. It'll be perfect timing."

Perfect? I don't think so. Perfect timing would be never.

"We won't be leaving until your Babe Ruth and Summer Basketball League playoffs are over," my father says. "You won't miss anything there. We're trying to make this as easy for you as possible."

I look to Mom and her eyes begin to water. In a shaky voice, she says, "Your father has assured me that you'll be safe. We'll all be safe."

"I'm going down there tomorrow to look for a house," he says. "I'll find us something nice in a safe neighborhood." He glances briefly at Mom. "There's an elementary school that's almost completely white. Pickering Junior High isn't too bad, either. But the high schools, Lynn

English and Lynn Classical..." He shakes his head. "They both have about the same number of blacks and Puerto Ricans. You'll have some of them in your classes. There's nothing I can do about that."

Even though I knew it was coming, my head is spinning at the news.

"It'll be an adjustment, Rabbit," he says. "I can't tell you that it won't. We have a peaceful little town here where everyone knows everyone else. And everyone is pretty much like everyone else.

"We're going to a big city. You're not going to know everybody. You're not going to want to know everybody. There'll be some good things and some bad things. But if there's anything that frightens you and causes you any kind of problems at all, you let your mother or I know and we'll take care of it."

I can't answer. I feel a lump in my throat that just won't swallow. So I just nod again.

"You'll be fine, Rabbit," he says and reaches out and squeezes my shoulder. I don't have to look at my mom to know that she's crying. I hear her sniffling and blowing her nose even as I keep my eyes on my dad. "In fact," he says, "You'll do *great*."

I wish I was so sure.

CHAPTER 7

I'm only sad about moving, not scared, until our Scout troop goes on a campout a little over a month before the move. We pitch our pup tents deep in the woods, hike up and down McDonald Mountain, and get attacked by clouds of mosquitoes so thick we wonder if they're going to carry us across the border into Canada. We use our mess kits to cook ourselves burgers and then make s'mores out of marshmallows we've toasted over the fire, putting them between graham crackers along with Hershey's chocolate bars. Donnie burns his first two marshmallows because he leaves them too close to the fire, and then makes a game of burning the rest on purpose until Mr. Marshall gets mad at him and tells him to knock it off.

At night, with the sky dark and the stars and the moon bright in the sky and the crickets chirping so loud we wonder if they'll keep us awake all night, we gather around a bonfire. We build it in an open area with no overhanging branches so we can pile on the logs and let the flames leap higher and higher, over my head for sure and maybe even Mr. Marshall's. As the logs crackle and snap and the smell of the burning wood floats over us, we sing a few songs and then sit down on the ground Indian-style and tell stories.

That's when I get scared.

Not when Donnie tells the one about the murderous psycho with the hook. That story is spooky the first time you hear it. It's about a guy and his girlfriend making out in a car at night and they roll up the window because they've heard a news report about a psycho with a hook for one arm who's on the loose and she's scared. The next day, in broad daylight, they find the detached hook stuck in the window.

Maybe that one even gives you the chills the second or third time, but I've heard it so many times it makes me feel more like laughing than screaming.

What spooks me out and gives me goose bumps even though it's hot and muggy and we all smell of sweat is when Randall McLeod tells his story.

"This really happened, not like the stories I make up," he says as an owl hoots in the distance. No one ever calls him Randy. He's not a Randy kind of kid. Strictly Randall, two years older than everyone else in the troop. "It happened in New York City, where the Empire State Building is? It's the biggest city in the world, you know?"

Randall is kind of fat. His mother says that isn't true, he's just big-boned, but he seems fat to me. He doesn't play sports, but if he played baseball and hit a home run, it might take him a couple minutes to get around the bases. He breathes loud and always smells of sweat, not just now when in the flickering light of the bonfire you can see the under-arm stains on his scout's uniform. Still, he's a good kid, and no one tells better stories.

"My cousin Joey is about our age and lives down in Portland," Randall says. "His dad, my Uncle Art, decides he wants to see the Red Sox play the Yankees in Yankee Stadium just once in his life. He wants to see 'The House That Ruth Built,' which is what they call Yankee Stadium because of Babe Ruth playing there and all that.

"So Uncle Art drives down there with Joey and after they do some sightseeing, they head for the stadium, which is in what they call the Bronx. It's a bad place with lots of muggers and stuff, but Uncle Art parks a long way away from the stadium because he figures it's cheaper that way. He doesn't like to spend money on *anything*.

"Everything's fine, even though the Red Sox lose, until they go to leave and can't find the car. He parked so far away that they get lost. Next thing you know, they're surrounded by ten of the scariest-looking guys you ever saw. A gang, all of them wearing leather jackets with the same logo. I think it was something like the Diablos."

Richie Leblanc jumps in. "They were Puerto Ricans?"

"No, no," Randall says, looking annoyed at getting interrupted.

"Negroes?"

"No, they were white," Randall says, wiping beads of sweat off his forehead. "But tough. Mean. Scars on their faces. Cigarettes hanging out of the corners of their mouths. You know. Like in the movies. These guys get arrested as often as they take a leak."

Randall looks around as if challenging anyone else to interrupt. None of us says a word. Finally, he continues.

"So Uncle Art puts his arm around Joey and pulls him close, like he's protecting him, and says, 'Can I help you guys?'"

"One of the guys in the gang, a short, skinny kid with lots of pimples on his forehead, says to their leader, 'Hey Carlos, he wants to help us,' and they all laugh. But Carlos, who has long black hair slicked back, just pulls a switchblade out of his jeans pocket and flicks it open—*snap*!" Randall motions with his hand as if he's got a switchblade in it and he's just flicked open the blade.

Richie Leblanc interrupts again. "I thought you said they weren't Puerto Ricans. That's what a name like Carlos is. It's a—"

"They're not Puerto Ricans!" Randall says, glowering. "Carlos can be...I don't know...Italian. He's not Puerto Rican! None of them are. Now will you let me tell the story?"

Richie shrinks back and says nothing.

"So Carlos, who probably is Italian," Randall says, glaring at Richie, "he takes the cigarette out of the corner of his mouth and then touches the tip of the switchblade to a spot between his teeth, as if he's got a piece of food stuck there and always uses his switchblade to take care of it.

"Now Uncle Art is the cheapest guy I know. In church, he just pretends to put money in the offering plate, but he really doesn't. His hand is always empty. I've seen it. But now he says, with his voice all shaky and stuff, 'I'll give you all my money. Just don't hurt us.'

"The gang laughs and the short, skinny kid with the pimples says, 'Of course you're going to give us your money. It's just a question of what else.' And as he puts his hand out to Uncle Art, the rest of the gang laughs again, all but Carlos, who just keeps picking his teeth with his switchblade, holding his cigarette down to his side.

"With his eyes bugging out, Uncle Art pulls his wallet out of his side pocket. He usually puts it in his back pocket, but he put it in his side pocket just for this trip because he heard that makes it safer from pickpockets and New York City is loaded with them. But he's losing that wallet anyway. He hands it over to the kid with the pimples and the kid announces how much money is inside.

"Carlos, who hasn't moved an inch, suddenly lifts his cigarette and with a quick cutting motion aimed at Uncle Art and Joey, slices off the glowing tip with his switchblade. The tip flies through the air, glowing bright, and hits Joey in the chest. Joey yelps, brushes it away, and starts pissing his pants.

"The gang starts laughing and laughing, everyone but Carlos. Uncle Art says, 'That's all the money I have.' He turns his pockets inside out, showing nothing but a handkerchief, the ticket stub for the elevator to the Empire State building that he was keeping for a souvenir, and his car keys.

"Carlos finally speaks. 'No lighter?' He gestures toward his unlit cigarette that now is only about half its original length. The other half, the lighted half, is at Joey's feet. 'What am I supposed to do now?'

"Uncle Art gulps. 'I don't have one. I don't smoke.'

"Carlos stares at him. 'Well, that's unfortunate.'

"The gang laughs and the kid with the pimples says, 'Unfortunate for you, buddy!' and they all laugh again.

"Carlos puts the unlit cigarette back into the corner of his mouth and says, 'So what are you going to do for me since you can't even give me a light?'

"Uncle Art spreads his hands, still holding the car keys in one of them. 'I've given you all our money,' he says. 'If I had a lighter, I'd give you that, too.'

"Carlos smiles and says, 'Yes, you would. You certainly would. But since you don't have a lighter, toss me those car keys.'

"Uncle Art blinks. 'The keys?'

"The kid with the pimples laughs and says, 'You got a hearing problem?' Uncle Art gulps and shakes his head.

"Carlos says, 'I didn't think so. I thought you heard me right.' He nods. 'So where's the car?'

"Uncle Art spreads his hands. 'I don't know. Honest to God. We parked in some parking lot, went to the ballgame, and then got lost on the way back. I tried to save money parking a long way from the stadium and now I can't find. Honest to God, I don't know where it is.'

"All the gang laughs and laughs. Even Carlos, who laughs so hard the unlit cigarette almost falls out of the corner of his mouth. They laugh like it's the funniest thing they ever heard. Finally, Carlos says, 'Then I guess those keys aren't going to do you no good.' Uncle Art doesn't say anything, so Carlos says, 'So toss me the keys.'

"Uncle Art, who by now is close to pissing his pants just like Joey, says in a dry and cracking voice, 'But we live in Maine. If I give you the keys, how are we going to get home?'

"Carlos looks at his switchblade and then at Uncle Art, then again at the switchblade and Uncle Art. Before Carlos looks at the knife one more time, Uncle Art tosses him the keys. Carlos catches them like one of the Yankees catching a lazy fly ball. He flips them to the kid with the pimples. Carlos gives him a nod, and the kid grins and strolls to the nearest sewer grate about thirty feet away. He dangles the keys in the air theatrically, like he's on Broadway or something, and drops them.

"They clatter for a second on the grate and then drop out of sight. As Uncle Art's eyes bug out, Carlos says, 'I guess you're walking home.'

"The gang all laughs and after Carlos says, 'Let's go,' they all stroll down the street, laughing and clapping each other on the back without once looking back."

Randall looks around and spreads his hands, signaling the end of the story. Just to be sure, he adds, "The end."

"What a great story!" someone says.

"Cool!"

"Did that really happen?"

All around the bonfire, guys are praising Randall. The ones next to him are slapping him on his back.

But I sit there, my mouth dry and my palms moist, unable to speak.

So that's what the big city is like. Switchblades and gangs.

That's what I'm moving to. Not New York City or the Bronx, but close enough.

Soon, I won't be hearing the sounds of crickets or owls hooting or a bonfire snapping and crackling as it reaches to the sky. I'll be hearing the clicking sound of a switchblade.

CHAPTER 8

After the camping trip, I don't ask my parents about switchblades and gangs, although I do ask my mom, "Is Boston like New York City, like the Bronx?"

It's Monday morning, Dad is at work, and we're in the kitchen. I'm standing next to the refrigerator in my T-shirt and shorts. She's between the sink and the stove, wearing her white apron and beating eggs to make French toast.

"The Bronx?" She looks at me quizzically as she adds milk to the eggs. "Why are you asking about the Bronx?"

I don't want to repeat Randall's story, so I just say, "It's part of New York City, where the Yankees play. I was just wondering."

"I don't know about the Yankees," she says. "But I suppose the Bronx and New York City are like Boston. Boston is smaller, of course. I don't know, maybe half the size. Or maybe even a third, I'm not sure. But compared to Plainfield, I suppose Boston is very much like New York City. Millions and millions of people. Huge by comparison. Gigantic."

I nod and don't say anything.

"But we're going to Lynn, not Boston," she says, dipping a piece of bread in the egg-and-milk liquid and dropping it in the already sizzling frying pan. "Lynn is about half an hour outside of Boston and nowhere near as big. There aren't millions of people there. More like a hundred thousand. Still huge compared to Plainfield, but not even close to the size of Boston or New York City."

I don't want to use the word "gang" and certainly not "switchblade" so I say, "What about the people there? Are they more like New York City or Plainfield?"

Mom wipes her hands on her apron and puts her hands on my shoulders. "Maybe not exactly like New York City, but a lot closer to that than Plainfield. Around here, almost everyone except us is a farmer, so your friends are getting up at dawn to help milk the cows or feed the chickens or whatever chores they help out with. Your new friends in Lynn won't be like that." She draws in a deep breath. "There are going to be blacks and...and Puerto Ricans. Is that what you're concerned about?"

But that isn't at all what I mean. I want to know if there'll be guys like Carlos, picking his teeth with a switchblade, and the kid with the pimples on his forehead, saying things like, "Of course you're going to give us your money. It's just a question of what else." I can hear his laughter as he says it, as if he's right there in the kitchen next to us.

But I can't ask that, so I just let my mother go on.

"Even though we're moving to a nice neighborhood," she says, "you're going to have to get used to seeing other kinds of people. I'm sure you're worried about going to school with blacks, but the high schools are still mostly white. It shouldn't be too bad."

My mother takes her hands off my shoulders. She flips the French toast.

"Listen, I don't share all of your father's views about blacks," she says. "He may be a little...well, too harsh. But I'm as scared of them as your father is, especially with all the rioting that is going on elsewhere. But there have been no riots in Lynn, and Boston has been pretty good, too. Don't worry. You'll be safe."

But I'm not worried about the blacks like my mom is. The only ones I know are the sports heroes I've read about. Maybe it'll be different when we get to the big city. I might get plenty scared then about the blacks and Puerto Ricans, but right now I'm worried about Carlos and his switchblade.

"Your father wouldn't be moving us there if it would be putting us in serious danger," my mom says.

I wish I could believe that. His heart is so set on his promotion he's almost like a dog that sees a piece of steak and can't take its eyes off it, licking his chops and drooling all over the place. My dad isn't really drooling, but he might as well be. If full-grown tigers walked the streets of Lynn, I think he'd convince himself that the tigers weren't really there or that if they were, they never got hungry.

He loves me, but I think, in a way, he loves that promotion even more. Maybe that's not fair. In fact, I'm sure it isn't. But he's taking us away from Plainfield, pretty much the safest place on Earth—or at least it's always felt that way to me—and he's dragging us with him to the big city, where tigers of some kind walk the streets. White tigers like Carlos and black tigers and Puerto Rican tigers.

My mother can say that we'll be safe, but what does she know? She's never been to Lynn. She's never lived anywhere but Maine. She might not even know what a switchblade is. I'm sure she's never seen one.

Except for the couple of times we've driven all the way down to Boston to see a Red Sox game—usually once a year—I bet she's hardly even seen a black person or a Puerto Rican. And those times, as soon as she's spotted one, she's turned around from the front seat of the car and told me to lock the back doors. If one of them is in my class, maybe even sitting in the seat next to me, I'm not going to have a door to lock.

"Could you take me to the library?" I ask all of a sudden.

*

After we eat breakfast and wash and dry the dishes, Mom drives me to the library in her light blue Ford Fairlane, looking pleased for the first time in a while. Usually, it's her idea to take me instead of the other way around. I like reading if I can't be playing sports, but usually I'm playing. This time, though, I'd have ridden my bike all the way if she couldn't take me, even though the library is over five miles away in Grainville.

The library is tiny even though it's shared between Plainfield, Grainville, and a couple other towns, but I find what I want—two special books I'd have never even thought of checking out just a month ago. I add books about Willie Mays, Jackie Robinson, Bob Cousy, and Mickey Mantle—my usual kind of selections—and put them on top before I go to the checkout counter. Old Miss Smith, her hair white and her face all wrinkled with a thick pair of glasses far down on her nose, records my choices, looking at me with eyebrows raised at the two special books at the bottom of my stack.

She leans forward so close I can smell her talcum powder and Listerine mouthwash. She whispers, "I know you're moving soon. Don't forget to return these before you leave."

"Yes, ma'am," I say and move the two special books back to the bottom of the pile.

Mom has gotten a couple books herself, and we head out to our car. I slide into the front seat, which is mildly hot in the early morning summer sun even though we left the windows rolled down.

"What did you get?" she asks, turning on the radio to WEGP.

"The usual," I say, trying to sound nonchalant. "Sports stuff."

When we get home, I race up to my room, dump the other books on my desk, and open the first special book, *The Cross and the Switchblade*.

*

It's worse than I thought. *The Cross and the Switchblade* is about New York City, not Boston or Lynn, but it scares the living daylights out of me just the same. It tells the story about some preacher who deals with a gang called the Mau Maus and their leader, Nicky Cruz. They don't just pick their teeth with their switchblades. They use the knives in ways that make my heart pound and my hands shake. They stab people just because they're in a rival gang or are "on their turf."

Some of them die.

I can't stop reading, skipping over the religious stuff so I can learn more about the kind of gangs I might soon have to protect myself against.

For the first time in my life, I don't want to go to Babe Ruth practice that afternoon. *Who cares about baseball*, I think. I never thought I'd ever think those words, except compared to football or basketball, never thought I'd rather read a book than play any sport. But I do.

I go to practice anyway, tucking *The Cross and the Switchblade* underneath my other library books so my mom doesn't see it. At practice, though, I can't concentrate. I barely notice the smell of the freshly cut grass or Richie Leblanc's body odor. As Coach Beaupre pitches batting practice to one player after another, I don't hear the crack of the bat from my position at shortstop. Instead, I hear the clicking of the Mau Maus' switchblades and imagine Nicky Cruz holding the razor-sharp tip of one to my neck.

Balls that I'd normally scoop up easily are getting past me and once, Jimmy Chaisson rips a line drive that almost takes my head off.

"What are you doing, Rabbit?" Coach Beaupre hollers. "Get your head in the game!"

Any other time, I might have thought, *this isn't a game, it's a practice*, and made a private joke of Coach's little error while making sure I didn't make another one of my own. But all I can think now is, *who cares about games? They don't matter compared to getting stabbed by the Mau Maus and left bleeding and dying in a dirty, big-city gutter.*

After practice, I go behind the backstop where all our bikes are lined up in a row, but Jimmy Chaisson catches up to me first. Jimmy is kind of average everything: height, weight, and strength, except that he has red hair and freckles.

"What was your problem today?" he says. He's laughing, as if there's nothing more important than baseball.

I wonder if I should tell him about switchblades and gangs and stuff like that, but quickly decide not to. What does he know about that kind of thing? He's just a dumb kid like me, thinking there isn't anything worse than dropping a fly ball or missing a free throw. Or not paying attention during Babe Ruth practice.

So I just shrug my shoulders.

"You want to come over my house?" he says. "Donnie and a bunch of the other guys are busy so I don't think we'll get a game going, but we can still toss the football around."

I shake my head. "Not today," I say. "I'm busy, too."

His jaw drops open. Usually I'd make some kind of crack that he better close his mouth before all the bugs in Plainfield fly inside. Not a real knee-slapper, but the kind of thing we say to each other all the time. Instead, I say nothing.

He looks at me funny. "What are you doing that's so important?"

I suddenly feel hot in the face and suspect I'm turning red. I sure can't tell him that I won't play because I'm reading a book. That would be embarrassing. So I lash out.

"What are you, my mother?"

He recoils like I slapped him.

"Geez," he says.

I feel bad, so I scramble to think of what to say. He's about to turn away when it hits me.

"It's moving stuff," I say, and in a way, that's not a lie. I might not be packing yet or anything like that, but reading *The Cross and the Switchblade* is all about moving. It's about getting prepared so I don't end up bleeding my guts out in a gutter.

The explanation seems to take the sting away from Jimmy. He nods and gets a sad look on his face, which always seems to happen when I remind my friends that I'm leaving.

"That's too bad," he says, and I'm not sure if that means that it's too bad I'm moving or that I have to do moving stuff or just that I won't be playing catch with him.

And now I feel sad, too.

"Yeah," I say, and hop on my bike.

I pedal hard, but it still feels like forever before I'm propping my bike against the wall inside the garage. I race up to my room, noting the smells of tomato sauce as I go, and before I know it, I'm back in the world of Nicky Cruz and the Mau Maus.

Far sooner than I'd like, Mom calls me down for dinner. At first, I barely even hear her, but then her voice gets loud and insistent.

"*Rabbit!*" she hollers. "*Dinner!*"

"Just a sec," I call down, wanting to finish the page. Actually, I want to finish the chapter, or even the book, but at least the page.

"Now!" she yells. "Wash your hands and get down here immediately!"

I mutter softly and put the marker in my book and slide it back into the bottom of the stack. I wash my hands and stomp down the stairs.

My mother looks at me and frowns.

"Are you all right?" she asks, and when I get close, she presses the back of her hand against my forehead.

I just nod.

Dad isn't here. Looks like he's working late again.

"You don't have a fever," she says, "but you look pale and you spent most of the day in your room. Are you sure you feel okay?"

Again, I nod.

"Cat got your tongue?"

I shrug.

She cocks her head. "Is something wrong?"

I shake my head.

She sighs. "You're upset about us moving, aren't you?"

I am, though for more reasons than she knows, so I shrug again and nod my head. It seems the answer most likely to stop the questions.

"You'll miss your friends," she says, putting her arm around me, "but you'll make new ones. Loads of them. Maybe better ones, you never know."

I wonder if my new friends will be Lynn's version of the Mau Maus.

A grim look comes over her face. "Your father won't be home for a few hours, so it's just the two of us." She glances at the clock on the wall. "Again."

I pile spaghetti on my plate and put lots of sauce and three large meatballs on top. I eat quickly and quietly, which disappoints Mom. She keeps trying to get me to talk, but we really don't have anything to talk about.

CHAPTER 9

The next morning, I stare at the red-and-white For Sale sign centered on the thick, green lawn and feel like ripping it out and stuffing it in the trash. But that won't help anything. We're moving even if we can't sell the house. Dad says the company will take care of it.

I hate his company. But that doesn't help either.

So I ride my Schwinn three-speed over to Randall McLeod's house on the other side of town. It's about three miles away, so I'm sweating pretty good by the time I get there. The lawn is overgrown with two junk cars parked on the right side of it next to a falling-down fence. The yellow paint on the house is chipped and peeling.

I put the kickstand down and leave my bike in the pebbled driveway. I walk up the rotting wooden stairs. I press the doorbell, but no one answers. I press it again and then knock on the door.

Finally, Mrs. McLeod answers. Her hair is all straggly and her face is pale except for a bruise on the right cheek. Her eyes are bloodshot. She squints. "Rabbit Labelle?"

"Hi, Mrs. McLeod," I say. "Is Randall home?"

"What are you doing here?" she says, which doesn't sound very friendly, but maybe she's just surprised because except for Boy Scouts, I never spend any time with Randall. He doesn't play sports and he's been attending Grainville Regional High School the last two years while I've still been in junior high. We really don't have anything in common.

"I want to talk to Randall," I say.

"You selling anything?" she asks with a frown. "'Cause we ain't got no money."

"No," I say quickly, then decide to tell her just enough to let me see Randall. "I want to talk to him about one of his stories."

A look of disgust comes over her face and she wrinkles up her nose like I stepped in a dog turd and am about to track it inside. "Him and his stories." She shakes her head and opens the door, letting me in. "He's in his room, downstairs in the basement."

"Randall!" she hollers, announcing my presence. "You've got a friend here to see you."

I walk down the creaking stairs to a dank basement that smells faintly of mold and Clorox. Randall looks at me in astonishment from where he sits on his unmade bed with a book in his hands. Behind me in the far corner, a washing machine chugs away on a load of wash. An old desk rests against one wall and a battered dresser against the other. Randall looks around as if surveying his room and his face turns crimson. He sets down his book and climbs off the bed.

"What are you doing here?" he says.

I laugh. "You sound like your mother."

A look of hot anger flashes across his face and then is gone. "I just… you just…" He wipes sweat off his forehead.

I finish the thought for him. "I know, I never come over. Too busy playing sports, I guess."

He nods.

When the silence becomes uncomfortable, I point to the book, which I can now see is from the library, and ask, "What are you reading?"

He grins slightly and says, "It's a mystery by a guy named John D. MacDonald. There's a whole bunch of them starring a beach bum in Florida named Travis McGee."

"A beach bum?"

"Yeah, he does things for people and they pay him. It's kind of hard to explain, but it's really good. You should try one. The library has all of them."

"Is there sports in them?" I ask.

"Ummm…no," he says.

I hesitate. "Switchblades and gangs?"

"What?"

I shift on my feet and repeat myself.

Randall looks at me funny, then says, "No."

I nod, knowing that I'll never read the books he's just recommended. But I don't want to hurt his feelings by telling him that, so instead I say, "That's kind of why I came over."

"What do you mean?"

"Your story about your Uncle Art," I say. "The one you told at night when we went camping. About the gangs with switchblades down in New York."

Randall brightens. "You liked it?"

"Well, I don't know if 'like' is the right word," I say. "It scared the crap out of me."

Randall grins. "That's what we were doing, telling scary stories. I just figured I'd tell a real one instead of the dumb boogeyman ones everyone else was telling. And of course, the guy with the hook."

I force a laugh. "Yeah, the hook."

"Like, who hasn't heard that one a million times," Randall says.

I hesitate. "But about the gangs and switchblades….well, I was kind of wondering what else you know about them."

"Me?" he asks, and actually turns around and looks to see if someone else is in the room. "I've never lived anywhere but Plainfield." The look on his face says that he wishes he lives somewhere, anywhere, else.

I shrug. "I just figured if you knew the story about your Uncle Art, you might know other stuff like that."

He shakes his head. "There's maybe a couple of books I've read that have gangs in them, but that's not really what the book is about."

I nod, unable to hide my disappointment. I can see from Randall's expression that he feels bad he can't help me.

He suddenly says, "Where are my manners?" He points to the foot of the bed and says, "Here, sit down," and he plops himself down on the opposite end, right on top of his pillow. He nods over at his desk and says, "I've only got one chair."

I sit on the bed and say, "This is fine," but I wonder if I should just leave instead. If Randall doesn't know anything about gangs and switchblades, there's not too much for us to do. There isn't a football, basketball, or baseball in sight.

But I give a try.

"I was wondering...do you think there are gangs with switchblades in Boston just like New York?"

He considers the question and says, "I suppose. I mean, they're both big cities. New York is bigger, that's all." A look of realization dawns on his face. "Oh, I get it. You're wondering because you're moving down there pretty soon."

"Yeah."

"But you're not moving right into Boston," he says. "You're going to Lynn. That's a lot smaller."

"Yeah, but it's a lot bigger than this cow town," I say. "A hundred thousand people."

"That's big," Randall says. "Huge, compared to here. But it isn't millions like Boston or New York. So it might be different. Probably is," he says hopefully before his face clouds. "Although..."

"Although what?" I say, my palms suddenly as sweaty as Randall's forehead.

"Well...it probably doesn't mean anything."

"What doesn't mean anything?"

"Forget it. It's stupid."

But I can see from Randall's face that he doesn't think it's stupid at all. It might be important.

"*What?*" I say, louder and more forcefully than I intended.

"Well," Randall says with a sheepish look. "There's this saying about the city you're going to. About Lynn. I don't know who I heard it from. Maybe Uncle Art. It probably doesn't mean anything. It's just funny."

"Tell me!"

"Okay, okay. It goes like this," he says. "*Lynn, Lynn, City of Sin. Never come out, the way you went in.*"

I'm stunned speechless. My father sure never said he was taking us to the City of Sin. *City of Sin?* There had to be gangs on every street corner.

"I think the last part is supposed to be dirty," Randall says, leaning forward and speaking in barely more than a whisper.

I blink. "What do you mean?"

Randall flushes. "You know about...you know...you know about the birds and the bees, right?"

"Sure," I say, feeling a bit insulted. "I'm not as old as you are, but I'll be fourteen soon. I'm not ten, for crying out loud. Geez."

"Sorry," he says. "I didn't mean anything by it."

I nod sullenly.

"I just didn't want to have to explain things to you," he says, and makes an "O" with the thumb and index finger of one hand and then pokes a finger from the other hand inside and raises his eyebrows.

We both break into laughter, although mine retains a nervous undertone that I can't quite shake. When we stop, I frown and say, "So what's dirty about the second part?"

"*Never come out, the way you went in,*" he says, leaning forward again. "I think that's about sex."

"It is?"

"I think Lynn has a lot of..." His voice falls into a whisper. "...a lot of prostitutes." He gives me a look.

"It does?" I ask in astonishment.

"It must," Randall says. "*Never come out, the way you went in* means when you have sex with one of the prostitutes, you don't come out the same. You know, like you get VD and stuff."

I feel my jaw drop. I'm so shocked I can't even speak.

So this is where my father is taking me.

CHAPTER 10

I bike home, thinking about *Lynn, Lynn, City of Sin. You never come out, the way you went in.*

Prostitutes. Venereal disease. Gangs. Switchblades.

What else?

Well, my dad has already told me that one. There are black people who are going to hate me before they even know me. Probably gangs of blacks, all with switchblades. And Puerto Ricans.

It's hot outside with the sun high overhead, but I don't think that's why I'm sweating bullets. Today, I'd give Randall McLeod a run for his money in the sweat department. I no sooner wipe it off my forehead and onto my pants than the moist beads start forming again.

If I had any doubts before about whether Lynn actually had gangs with guys like Carlos in them, picking their teeth with their switchblades, they're gone now. Lynn may not be the size of New York City or even Boston, but you don't earn the slogan *Lynn, Lynn, City of Sin* and *not* have gangs.

I can't believe I'm leaving Plainfield for a place like that. I mean, Pittsburgh is known for its steel. Nashville for its country music. And Boston, I guess, for its beans.

But I'm going to a place whose reputation is for prostitutes and venereal disease.

I tromp up the stairs and flop onto my bed. I bury my head in my pillow and start to shake. What am I getting into? If I weren't almost fourteen, I think I'd start to cry.

Fourteen seems old compared to when you're ten or eleven or even twelve. But it doesn't feel old enough to go to *Lynn, Lynn, City of Sin.*

I wish Randall had never told me about it. I can't even get myself to just call the place "Lynn" now. It's at least "Lynn, Lynn City of Sin." I wish he'd never told me about his dumb cousin Joey and Uncle Art and their trip to New York. About Carlos and switchblades.

But is that really true? I'd be happier now, that's for sure. I wouldn't feel this cold sweat all over me.

But I also wouldn't be prepared. Isn't that the Scout motto, *Be Prepared*? Maybe by knowing what I'm getting into, I can be prepared for it.

I wonder if I should buy a switchblade to protect myself. But where would I get one? Would Randall know? Nah. He knows books, not weapons. How do I find one? How would I pay for it?

I'm sure I'll be able to buy one in the City of Sin. With prostitutes and gangs on every corner, there'll be someone selling switchblades.

I roll over on my bed and sit up. I've got to get something else on my mind before this drives me nuts, so I dig the other book out of my library stack. It's called *Black Like Me.* I'd gone to the library looking for a book on switchblades and *The Cross and the Switchblade* was the first one I spotted in the card catalog. In the same way, *Black Like Me* was the first one I found about black people. Other than all the sports books I've already read, of course.

So I start reading. At first, I still can't concentrate because of all the other stuff rattling around inside my brain. But pretty soon I get into the book. It's a true story about a white guy who makes himself look black through some kind of treatments to see what it's like and how he's treated. It happened eight years ago, back in 1959, and it's down in the South, in New Orleans, so it isn't like it's going to be down in Lynn.

Lynn may be south of Plainfield, Maine, but it's not The South, where black people—or Negroes, as the book calls them—can't go to the same stores or sleep in the same hotels or use the same bathrooms as white people. At least they couldn't in 1959. Lynn won't be like that. There won't be bathrooms marked "White" and "Colored." But in *Black Like Me*, the man who is made to look like a Negro can't even be friendly and offer a white woman a seat on the bus near him.

I wonder what it would be like if I were black here in Plainfield. Would my teammates on the baseball and basketball teams treat me the same way? Would they even want me on their team? Would Donnie still be my friend or would his mother, who is always so nice to me, be afraid of me and not even let me in her house?

I feel like my head is about to explode. Things were a lot easier when all I had to do was hit a baseball, steal a base, or sink a jump shot. Suddenly, my life is filled with all this confusing and scary stuff, all because we're moving to *Lynn, Lynn, City of Sin*.

I'm so lost in my thoughts and in the book that I don't even hear the pounding of footsteps up the stairs until they reach the top of them and Donnie appears in the doorway. I don't have time to hide the book or do anything but just stare.

"Your mom said you'd be up here," he says. "Whatcha reading?"

"Nothing," I say, shutting the book so the back cover faces up and the title isn't visible. I push it off to the side on the bed so my body shields it from his view.

Donnie grins and raises his eyebrows. "What, is it dirty?"

"No," I say.

"I betcha it is," he says. "That's why you're trying to hide it. Let me see."

"No!" I say as he puts out his hand.

Donnie jumps on my bed, landing on top of me like it's Pig Pile time and reaches for the book. I hold it away from him. Next thing you know, we're wrestling with each other and I'm losing. Donnie's bigger and stronger than I am—*everyone* is bigger and stronger than I am and Donnie's bigger and stronger than just about everyone—so after just a little grabbing and grunting and me smelling his bad breath in my face, he gets the book.

Donnie jumps off the bed and holds it up triumphantly like a split end with a football after he's caught a touchdown pass.

"Got it!" Donnie says, and then looks at the cover. He frowns. "What's this?"

I can't explain so I don't even try. I just lie there on the bed staring at him.

Donnie's eyes widen just a little as a look of dawning understanding comes over his face. "I got it." He grins. "It's got to have lots of dirty parts in it because it's about black people! It must be really dirty. Tommy Flanagan says that Negroes have—" Donnie lowers his voice to a whisper "they have sex all the time. It's in their blood. It's why their…their dicks are bigger than ours. Tommy says if you want a dick as big as a Negro's, you just need to have sex all the time."

I burst out laughing and Donnie joins me.

"So where are the dirty parts?" Donnie says, glancing at the book. "This must be *loaded* with them."

I shake my head. "There aren't any."

"Come on! I'm your best friend. How'd you hear about it? Tell me!"

"There aren't any dirty parts," I repeat, and feel the warmth of a flush coming to my cheeks that has nothing to do with the wrestling we've just done. I figure I could tell him that at least there aren't any dirty parts in what I've read until now, unless you count the part where a guy tells the pretend Negro that his shaved head will be popular with the ladies because it means he's high-sexed, whatever that means. But saying anything like that won't help.

"There aren't?" Donnie says, astonished. "Really?"

I nod and look away.

"So why are you reading it? Is this guy a basketball player or something?"

"No," I admit.

Donnie looks at me like I'm some kind of bug, like he doesn't even know me.

I can't think of anything else, so I say, "You want to go out and play catch?"

Donnie grins. "Now *that's* more like it!"

He puts the book on the center of my desk and I don't think to move it back to the bottom of my stack. We grab my football off the dresser and head outside.

CHAPTER 11

When I come back inside because Donnie has run home for dinner, Mom gives me a funny look but doesn't say anything. I don't find out what that look is about until Dad comes home. For once, he isn't working late and we're eating together. It's stuffed peppers, not exactly my favorite, but I don't hate it, either. Not like liver and onions or spinach. I just wish Mom would let me eat only the juicy meat inside and discard the peppers, but I lost that battle a long time ago.

I can tell something is up by the way they're both looking at me. Mom's eyes are full of concern and Dad's face looks grave. For a brief instant, I allow myself a flash of hope that we're not moving after all. Perhaps the promotion has fallen through. But that would be like believing in Santa Claus or the tooth fairy.

I plunge my fork into a stuffed pepper the size of a baseball, slice it open with my knife, and cut a bite-sized chunk of meat. I scoop up some mashed potatoes with it and shovel it into my mouth.

I don't look up. If my parents aren't going to tell me Christmas has come early and we're staying right here in Plainfield where we belong, then I don't want to look at them. I cut another chunk out of the stuffed pepper, wondering for a silly second or two if gang members use their switchblades to cut their meat. It's an absurd thought and I know that right away, but somehow I can't get rid of the image of Carlos picking his teeth with his switchblade and then plunging it into one of Mom's stuffed peppers.

"Rabbit," she says, and I'm forced to look up. She glances at my father and her face flushes. "Your father has something to talk to you about."

He looks surprised, as if he expected my mother to relate the big news. He stares at her for a second or two before clearing his throat and speaking.

"We know this move is going to be tough on you," he says.

But you don't care, I think. *At least, not enough to do anything about it, like give up your stupid promotion.*

But I don't say anything. I just wait.

"Your mother noticed something in your room," he says. "She wasn't prying. It was accidental. But she couldn't help notice a couple of your library books. One about Negroes and the other one called *The Cross and the Switchblade*."

I think back to Donnie putting *Black Like Me* back onto the desk and leaving it out there for my mother to see. I'd made a point of always putting the two special books at the bottom of my stack so they wouldn't be so obvious, but I hadn't paid attention to him leaving it out in the open. Those two books aren't exactly like having the kind of dirty pictures that some of the guys talk about at school, but I hadn't wanted to face a conversation like this.

My father waits for me to respond, but I say nothing. I dig into the mashed potatoes that still have plenty of butter sitting on top and shovel some more into my mouth. I usually like mashed potatoes, but right now I don't taste a thing.

"We don't want you to worry," my mother says. "Our new house will be in a nice neighborhood."

"I've been assured there isn't a single Negro living on either our street or the surrounding ones," my father says.

I want to tell my father that he sounds almost as bad as the Southern white people in *Black Like Me*, at least the parts I've read so far. If I were black, why shouldn't I get to live in the nice neighborhoods, too? That is, if there really are nice neighborhoods in Lynn. Maybe they're all bad and it's just that the ones they keep the black people in are even worse. I bet none of their neighborhoods are as nice as ours in Plainfield with guys like Donnie, Jimmy, and Scooter.

"And as for this *Cross and the Switchblade* book," my mother says, "Lynn isn't going to be like that. It isn't New York City. It's just—"

"*How do you know?*" I say, almost shouting the angry words.

My mother recoils and her eyes widen. My father's face clouds over and his jaw sets. He stabs a finger at me. "Don't you *ever* talk to your mother that way!"

I never have until now, at least not that I can remember. But I just couldn't help myself. And I can't help myself now.

"I'm sorry, I didn't mean to be…" The word *uppity* from *Black Like Me* pops into my mind, but that isn't what I want to say. I shake my head in frustration. "…I didn't mean to be disrespectful, but Mom, you've never been to Lynn. How can you possibly tell me what it's going to be like there? You don't know."

My mother looks at me in shock. "What has gotten into you? How *dare* you sass me like that, young man!"

"I'm not sassing you," I say. "I'm sorry if the words are coming out all wrong." I make a final attempt to get back on their right side. "You're a great mom," I say, and something in her face softens. Her shoulders, tight and rigid before, relax, at least a little. "But isn't what I say true? You're just guessing. You're *hoping* everything will be all right."

My mother stares at me, still in shock. Silence hangs in the air for what feels like forever. Finally, she blinks furiously, and with her voice shaking, says, "Your father knows about Lynn and that's good enough for me. That makes it good enough for you, too. He went down there and checked out the city and bought us a nice house. He's been very concerned about you and has done everything he can to make this work out. You should be grateful for all he's done for us!"

Grateful? Did she really say that? My shock at the ridiculousness of her words renders me speechless.

"You'll be fine," my father says, trying to make his voice soothing. "It'll be an adjustment for you. It won't be like Plainfield, I'll give you that. But I'm sure you'll find that Lynn is a lot nicer than you think. Give it a chance."

"*Lynn, Lynn, City of Sin,*" I say, the words slipping out of my mouth before I realize it. As my mother's jaw drops and my father's cheeks flush, I say, "It doesn't sound very nice to me."

Both of my parents sit in a stunned silence that stretches long enough for me to hear the clock on the wall behind me loudly go *tick... tick...tick.* Finally, I break the silence.

"And that isn't all," I say. "It gets worse. *Lynn, Lynn, City of Sin. Never come out the way you went in.* That last part is supposed to be about having sex with prostitutes and getting VD."

Mom gasps. Her hand shoots up to her mouth. Her eyes are wide and her face turns ashen. "Rabbit!"

My father looks ready to explode, his face beet red and his hands clenched into tight, trembling fists hovering just over the white tablecloth. For a brief moment, he's so angry he can't even speak. Then it all gushes out.

"That's not fair!" he shouts. "That stupid phrase! It just isn't fair at all!" His eyes burn holes in me. "Where did you hear that?"

I shrink back from him even as I hear his admission of guilt.

"You knew!" I yell back. "You heard it, too. You're sending us to the *City of Sin* and you don't care!"

He leans across the table and slaps my face.

"Andre!" my mother shrieks. "What are you doing? The two of you!"

I burst into tears, not because of the pain, because it really doesn't hurt that much. It only stings. But he's never slapped me before. He's given me spankings, the last couple years with his belt, but everyone's dad does that.

But this...he's never done this before.

I run from the table, hearing my father say something about disrespect, and I bound up the stairs, taking them two at a time, relieved that I don't hear anyone following me, only my parents arguing below.

I duck into my room and slam the door. I stare at it as I back away until my rear end bangs into the bed. I gasp for air. Downstairs, my parents shout at each other, loud enough for me to hear every word. Then my mother bursts into tears. My heart pounds inside my chest as if it's about to explode, hammering far harder than it does after I've raced around the bases for a triple or sprinted up and down the basketball court five or ten times.

More shouting downstairs.

I realize I'm not just crying a little. I'm bawling like a little baby. But I barely feel ashamed.

Mostly I'm scared.

Just like a little baby.

CHAPTER 12

My mother comes up to my room half an hour or so later, knocks on the door, and steps inside. Her eyes are puffy and bloodshot from crying. She sniffs and dabs her red nose with a handkerchief. I'm lying on my bed, staring at the ceiling, my hands tucked behind my neck.

While my parents argued downstairs, I couldn't do anything but look at that ceiling with its one baseball-sized water stain in the far left corner and wonder if they're getting a divorce after all. Maybe my father can take his promotion down to *Lynn, Lynn, City of Sin* all by himself and leave my mother and me up here in Plainfield where we belong.

Am I a bad son for hoping, at least a little, that happens? I don't want to go to Lynn; I want to stay right here. But my father sure wants to go. It's like he can't think of anything but that stupid job of his.

So let him go.

He'll be happy there and if he divorces Mom and leaves us, then—*never come out the way you went in*—he can even have some prostitutes and get VD.

Yuck. It's disgusting to even think about, but it would teach him for leaving us.

And if there are guys like Carlos and Nicky Cruz and gangs like the Mau Maus, well, maybe they'll be making my father piss his pants just like Randall's cousin Joey. It would serve him right. I feel guilty for even thinking this, but I can't help it.

"Rabbit," my mother says from just inside the doorway to my room, and I feel even more guilty for hoping Dad leaves us because I know it would break her heart. She looks at me through those bloodshot eyes and tries to smile. "Are you okay?"

I want to tell her I'm not okay. Not unless we can stay in Plainfield. Not just her and me. Dad, too.

But I just nod.

She comes into the room and sits down on the foot of my bed. She rests a hand on my leg.

"Your father and I love you very much," she says. "We'd never do anything to knowingly hurt you."

She waits, seeming to want me to say something, but I stay silent.

After a few seconds go by, she says, "Your father is convinced this is what's best for us. This promotion is important." Her eyes, which have been locked onto mine, look away. "Not just for him but for you, too. You're going to want to go to college some day and that's terribly expensive. We'll need the money from the promotion to be able to pay for it."

She gives my leg a squeeze. "Besides," she says, "there's a big, wide world outside of Plainfield. Outside of Maine. You're going to want to experience it." She forces a grin. "Aren't you always saying that you're almost fourteen now and we should stop treating you like a little kid?"

She waits for a response, so I give her one. "And you and Dad say I'm thirteen going on three."

That stops her, but only momentarily. "That's because all you're interested in is sports. There's more to life than just playing games." She stiffens her shoulders. "I'm sure this move will help you mature more quickly into a fine young man."

"Maybe a dead young man," I mumble.

My mother's eyes flash with anger. "Listen to me. Just stop that talk right now. I'll have none of it. Your father assures me you'll be fine."

I say nothing.

"He's a wonderful father and a great provider for this family," she says.

"Then why did he keep *Lynn, Lynn, City of Sin* a secret?" I say. "He knew and he didn't tell us!"

My mother recoils, then winces just a bit. I've hit a nerve.

"He…he felt it wasn't a fair picture of the city," she says. "He didn't want to alarm us. He wants us to give Lynn a chance. If it's really that bad, and I mean really dangerous, then we'll find some other community nearby that's safe. Your father will just commute into Lynn. He wants to avoid that after all the hours he's spent commuting over to Presque Isle every day and then all the way down to Bangor every other Friday. It's been a real drain on him. But he'll do it in Lynn if our safety is ever at risk. He's promised that."

I say nothing.

"Okay?" my mother asks.

It isn't okay, but the only way to end this conversation is to agree. So I nod.

Mom smiles. "Don't forget, Lynn schools have football."

I nod again and try to return her smile. But I don't feel it. Not at all.

CHAPTER 13

My last few weeks in Plainfield fly by. We win the Summer League basketball playoffs without hardly being tested, but only finish as runners-up in the Babe Ruth playoffs. Jimmy O'Shea, a dark-haired kid from Ashland who's close to six feet tall and has got to weigh about 175 pounds, just wipes us out. He's so big, he throws a fastball that seems like it's past you as soon as he lets it out of his hand. A couple parents even say we should demand to see his birth certificate, but nobody does. We get only three hits and lose 2-0. I get two of the hits, both singles to right field, but Jimmy O'Shea strikes me out in the fourth inning. It's my first strikeout of the year. It's a lousy way to end the season, but I guess you can't win every game.

I guess it's also a lousy way to end my time in Plainfield. It's hard knowing that I'll never see my friends again, that I'll never put on the Grainville baseball or basketball uniform again. We'll never go to Mabel's for an ice cream, three scoops of it piled high on a sugar cone.

I get sad about that, but try not to think about it and just keep busy, doing stuff like playing football in Donnie's backyard with the rest of the guys. But it's hard not to think about leaving here when you're packing your things into boxes and writing on them in thick, black Magic Marker: *Rabbit's Room*.

About the only good thing is how the Red Sox are doing. They'd been in second place, a couple games out, ever since a ten-game winning streak in July. Now, a seven-game winning streak has lifted them into first place for the first time since April. Pretty amazing for a team that a year ago finished in next-to-last place.

But even that good news comes with a sad ending. In the game that kicked off the seven-game streak, Tony Conigliaro, their cleanup hitter, got beaned with a fastball. Hit right below the eye. Knocked him unconscious. A fractured cheekbone, a dislocated jaw, and a damaged eye. They carried him off the field on a stretcher.

Tony C. already had twenty homers and sixty-seven RBIs. Only Yaz was better. Now he's out for the rest of the year. Maybe forever.

If the Sox had any chance at all with him, those chances are over now. Down the toilet. The Sox may be in first place, but there's no way they can stay there without Tony C. in the lineup.

It's over. Just like Plainfield.

*

The day before we leave, Donnie and I run through the back woods one last time all the way to Old Man McDougall's orchard. For reasons I can't explain, I yank one of the apples off the tree even though everyone says Old Man McDougall will appear out of wherever he's hiding and shoot me in the butt with his BB gun.

I don't care. Let him shoot me. I take the apple and, with my best Jim Lonborg fastball, hurl it against the tree trunk. It smacks loudly and bits of it fly all over.

Donnie looks around, probably thinking *he's* going to get the BB in the butt for my actions, but Old Man McDougall never shows up and we run back to Donnie's backyard one last time. On the way, I stop on the fifth of the seven small boulders jutting out of the water that we use to cross the stream. I unzip my fly and pee in the water.

I really don't have to go that bad and don't pee very much, which gets Donnie looking at me funny even though he wasn't watching. He could tell from the sound, I guess.

I'm ready for him to ask why I did that, but he doesn't say anything, which is good because I don't really know why.

We go back into his house and Mrs. Boudreau is waiting for us in the kitchen. There's a plate on the counter stacked high with chocolate chip cookies. The aroma of her baking fills the air, making my mouth water. She's gives us both a big cookie off the top of the plate.

"Straight out of the oven," she says with a smile and she's right. It's still warm, with the chocolate chips still half melted.

"Thanks," I say, and she hands me a bag filled with more cookies.

"For the road," she says, and a sad look comes over her face. She looks like I feel. "We're going to miss you, Rabbit," she says. "You've been a good friend to Donnie."

I nod, the mouthful of cookie still in my mouth not tasting quite so good anymore. *Lynn, Lynn, City of Sin* has ruined even Mrs. Boudreau's cookies.

I finally realize that I need to say something so I mutter my thanks and something about Donnie being a good friend and appreciating all the snacks she's made for us. It sounds stupid and as gooey as those melted chocolate chips, but it's the kind of thing you need to say, especially to adults.

"Well, I gotta run," I say to Donnie and his mother, and before things get any more gushy, I whirl and fly out the door.

*

The moving truck arrives early the next day, the words *Ace Moving—We Do It For You!* stenciled in bold across the sides in bright red and black. My father says that the company is paying for the three movers—two skinny guys and a red-faced chubby one—as well as an extra premium for one of them to drive Mom's car since she doesn't like to drive long distances.

My father is so proud of that. His company loves him so much.

Good for him.

Donnie comes over and we toss the football around half-heartedly. I don't feel like running around and diving like usual. I don't really feel like anything at all. So we just throw the football like a bunch of tired adults who don't have energy for anything more, just like my father, back when we'd play catch.

The time comes to get into Dad's car, the silver Plymouth Fury, and pull away from our house. I don't really know what to do with Donnie. I'm sure not going to hug him or anything silly like that. And I'm not going to shake his hand like a couple stupid adults would.

So I just say, "See ya," and he replies with the same.

I give him a wave from the back seat as we leave and he waves back. Then our family is off, leaving Plainfield for the last time.

Mom is in the front seat crying softly while my father drives. All I can think of is how very much I hate him.

CHAPTER 14

It's hours on the turnpike before we leave Maine, the static-filled radio stations going in and out. It's a warm, but not hot, August day and there's a strong breeze flowing through my father's half-open driver-side window. He's doing all the driving, of course, and has left the moving truck far behind.

We cross from Maine into New Hampshire and soon after that into Massachusetts. I've been trying to read copies of *Sports Illustrated* piled on the seat next to me, but now I find myself reading the same sentence over and over.

When I see the green sign with white letters that announces Route 129 Lynn, my heart starts beating faster and my palms become sweaty. I swallow hard as the white sign on the right announces:

Entering Lynn

Established 1629

Never come out the way you went in.

I don't know about sex, but I'm sure I won't be leaving Lynn the same way I'm entering. I'm going to be worse, much worse. If I even get out alive.

Almost immediately, we slow down for traffic and stop at our first light. Behind us, a car horn sounds, long and loud.

Hooooooonnnkkk!

As we drive along Lynnfield Street, I'm stunned at how tightly packed together the houses are, one right on top of the next, leaving hardly any room to breathe. My chest tightens and my palms grow moist.

The air smells funny, too. It's not so much what it has that shouldn't be there, but rather what it's missing. Except when the manure gets really ripe in the fields, the clean and crisp air in Plainfield smells of all the trees and brooks that surround it. You can take in a big gulp of air and what seems like pure oxygen flows through your body. Here, though, the air smells like dirty concrete, if that makes any sense, and car exhaust.

Pine trees and babbling brooks versus dirty concrete and car exhaust. Tough choice.

After driving past a dirty brick fire station on the left, we stop at Shop Kwik, a convenience store on the right that has seven or eight cars in its parking lot. While my father gets each of us a bottle of Coca-Cola, I pick out a Baby Ruth from the rack of candy bars, gum, and mints below the counter. I wait for my parents at the back of a line of four people and spot a shocking title at the top of the adult-sized magazine rack.

Playboy.

A dark brown square of plastic covers all but the title, but it still takes my breath away. Could that really be the dirty magazine I've heard guys talk about, a magazine with pictures of naked women inside? It's hard to believe that such a thing would be right here out in the open even with something covering all but the title. That would never happen in Plainfield.

But I guess that's part of a place where you...*never come out the way you went in.*

We walk back out to the car, and with a nervous grin my father hands me my bottle of Coke. I take it without saying thanks.

Union Hospital comes after that on the right and it's huge. The light brown brick building goes on for what looks like a couple football fields. I suppose its size shouldn't surprise me. I figure it's only a matter of time before I arrive there in an ambulance because someone like Carlos or Nicky Cruz will have stabbed me.

I instinctively touch my chest. No wounds yet. The only stitches I've ever gotten is when I cut open my foot on a clam shell once when I was a little kid and we were at some beach.

"Just a couple more streets from here," my father announces, pushing his glasses to the bridge of his nose. "It's not too bad, don't you think, Rabbit? Pretty nice, actually. I heard Rico Petrocelli, the Red Sox shortstop, lives only about a mile from here."

I find that hard to believe. Why would a player for the Boston Red Sox live here?

My father points to the sidewalk where four boys my age are walking along, talking to each other, dressed in T-shirts, shorts, and sneakers not much different than mine. A sliver of fear shoots through my chest. Are they part of a gang? They don't look like it. There are no gang colors like the Mau Maus wore in *The Cross and the Switchblade*. I can't see any weapons either, but that doesn't mean anything. A switchblade fits easily in a pocket. Any dope knows that.

"Have you noticed that we haven't seen a single Negro yet?" my father says as I swivel in my seat to watch the four boys. "Not on the streets and not in the Shop Kwik. I told you this is a nice part of the city we're going to be living in." He glances back at me and although he doesn't say it, I know what he's thinking. *It's not at all like that horrible little saying about Lynn that you threw in my face.*

When I don't reply, my mother chimes in. "I think your father's right." Something in her voice sounds like she's trying really hard to believe this but still isn't convinced herself. "There are no wide open spaces. All the houses seem so close together, but it seems nice."

My father looks hopefully in the rearview mirror, seeming to want my approval. It's almost as if he *needs* my approval.

Well, he isn't going to get it.

I say nothing.

Disappointed, he glances at my mother and raises his eyebrows.

He makes a right turn onto Allston Street. We go past a fenced-in house on the right with rose bushes lining its yard, then up a small hill and turn left into a paved driveway in front of a medium-sized, tan-colored house. It's got a tiny, yellowing lawn in front. Weathered, wooden fences separate it from the houses on both sides. The house next to ours on the left has a rusted-out junk car on the lawn.

But what strikes me the most is how I've gone from a place where I rode my bike to our next door neighbor to here, where I could easily throw a football from the neighbor on one side of our house to the one on the other. There's no room at all. Like when you're sitting in a row of seats with fat people on both sides, their elbows sticking into your ribs.

We climb out of the car and my father beams with pride. He points, not to the house in front of us but to the other side of the street, which is an entirely wooded lot.

"See the lot over there, Rabbit?" he says, and starts walking in that direction. "I thought it would make you feel comfortable, like you were back in Plainfield. The road dead ends after two more houses right up there." He points to the end of the street. "No one has developed that side of the street because it slopes off steeply, and I guess the drainage isn't very good or something like that. It's one of the few undeveloped lots in the city. Trust me, I spent a lot of time looking for something like this. It's pretty rare."

He looks at me, all smiles, as if he expects me to jump up and down for joy. I have to admit, it's a whole lot better than I feared. I didn't expect to ever see a tree again or a stream or anything like that. But it's not like I'm still going to have Donnie, Jimmy, Scooter, and the rest of the guys around.

My father waits, so I give him a grudging nod. He responds with more enthusiasm.

"Look at it," he says. "You've got about five houses' worth of wooded area. Down at the bottom of the hill, there's a little pond. The real estate agent said kids play hockey there when it freezes in the winter. What do you think of that, Rabbit? That'll be a new sport for you to try."

"How wonderful!" my mother says, standing next to my father now.

Hockey? I've never played hockey before in my life. I can barely even skate. Maine has cold winters, especially in Aroostook County, which is as far north as you can get. It's much colder than here in Massachusetts, so wherever there's water, there's ice. But no one plays hockey there. The winter sport is basketball. I was the starting point guard for the Grainville Mustangs, one of the stars, in fact. I'm not going to give that up for a sport based on skating. It might be fun to play around with, though. The few times I skated, it felt good to be gliding along the ice. But for me and everyone I've ever known, winter means basketball.

"What do you say to that, Rabbit?" my mother says.

I nod some more. I seem to be nodding a lot.

She leans forward slightly, clearly expecting me to say something, so I mumble, "Thanks."

A satisfied look comes over my father's beaming face and he breathes in deeply. He looks as if he hit a grand slam to win the game in the bottom of the ninth with two outs.

"Do you want to run down there for a bit before we open up the house?" he asks. "We've got time. I'm sure the movers are at least fifteen minutes behind us."

My hatred for my father is melting, but I'm not ready to give him the satisfaction of watching me run through those trees down to the pond. He isn't going to win that easily. This still isn't like Plainfield, and not just because my friends aren't here. This wooded area may be rare for Lynn, but it still isn't like the back of Donnie's house where we ran probably a mile or so through the woods before we got to Old Man McDougall's orchard. You could go sideways, too, and the woods just went on and on.

Not like here where this little area is only as wide as five houses and doesn't go back far at all. I can see the backyards of the next street over. The whole thing isn't much bigger than the size of a football field.

I figure I'll check it out later. Without my parents hovering around, expecting me to say that I was wrong about this place and they were right.

"Nah," I say. "Later."

Again, my father's face shows disappointment. "Well," he says, "let me show you the house." We turn onto a brick walkway, but bypass the steps to the front door, which my father points to, and curl around to a side door, which he also identifies, and then to the backyard.

It's tiny. The white fence on both sides of the house extends here along the back as well. Over the fence, on the other side of it, there's someone else's backyard, presumably from the next side street over. It feels like we're inside a tin of sardines. Everyone is stacked on top of everyone else. There's no room at all to play catch or do anything.

Most of the backyard is made up of a metal swing set on the right and what seems to be a garden area on the left. The swing set includes two swings and a slide that reflects the sunlight into my eyes. It might be okay if I were a five-year-old.

My father sees my reaction. "We'll sell the swing set. And unless your mother wants to try a garden, we'll grass over that area, too. It'll give you more room to play."

"Don't bother," I say, and anger flashes in my father's eyes.

"Damn it, Rabbit," he snaps, his face turning red. "You're not even trying."

"Andre," my mother says soothingly and touches his arm. "It's a big change. Give him some time."

My father purses his lips, shakes his head, and breathes air in loudly though his nose, his nostrils flaring. He clenches his jaw. He takes in another long breath of air through his nose, then heads for the side door.

We go inside and he points out all the obvious stuff in the still-empty house. The kitchen, the dining room, the front room, the cellar downstairs, and the bedrooms upstairs. He spends extra time on my bedroom, which looks like any other empty room without the furniture. When the movers get here and everything gets unpacked, I guess it'll look the same as my old bedroom.

Except it won't be the same.

"This cost a lot more than our old house," my father says, as if trying to convince me of something. "Everything costs a lot more down here. You wouldn't believe the car insurance. It's outrageous."

I come so close to saying, *Then why did we even come here?* I want to say it. A part of me screams to say it.

But I keep quiet.

The movers arrive and soon I'm unpacking all my boxes, hating this place all over again. I don't care if there are a few trees and a pond on the other side of the road.

I don't belong here and I know it.

CHAPTER 15

W e've been here for three days and I haven't seen any gangs or prostitutes yet, but I also haven't met any friends. A girl my age named Amy lives two houses away, but what am I going to do with a girl? I've never even seen her outside her house except one time when she was walking with her mother out to the car.

There are some boys, most of them only ten or eleven, who play street hockey down at the base of the hill. Each of them uses a hockey stick with a white plastic blade on the bottom and their puck is a special orange ball that doesn't bounce much. They mark off the two goal areas on the street with chalk and seem to have a lot of fun. Since Allston Street is such a small side street with only eight houses before it dead ends, there's almost no traffic, so they rarely have to stop and step aside to let a car pass.

But I only watch them from my own front lawn, six houses up the street and up the hill from where they play. I don't have a street hockey stick. I don't even know the rules, although it does look pretty obvious. But I've never played before and would look foolish getting beat by a bunch of ten-year-olds. That would be so embarrassing. I can't remember ever getting beat in sports even by older kids. Sure, the team I'm on has lost games, though not very often, and I haven't batted 1.000 in baseball or hit every shot in basketball. Nobody does. But I've always been one of the best players, if not *the* best, out there. I've certainly never been the worst.

But it's getting boring not having anyone to play with, so I go down to the street hockey game, carrying my football. The eight kids—a goalie and three other players per side—just keep running and passing and shooting as if I don't even exist until a car turns into the street and they have to stop to let it go by.

The nearest one, a dark-haired kid who's probably twelve but still several inches taller than me, says, "Who are you?" He doesn't say it in a threatening or especially unfriendly tone, although it's certainly not the kind of welcome I was hoping for.

I swallow hard and say, "My friends call me Rabbit. I live up the street." I nod in the direction of my house.

"Rabbit?" the kid says with a frown as everyone clusters around us. Almost all of them are sweating profusely, their hair damp with sweat, beads of it forming on their foreheads or trickles of it sliding down their cheeks. "What kind of name is 'Rabbit'?"

"It's a nickname," I tell him. "People have called me that for as long as I can remember," I say, deciding not to point out that adults and even my parents use that name for me. "Because I run fast, I guess."

The kid looks down at me. "Like you're some kind of Bobby Orr off the ice?"

"Who?"

They all look at me in astonishment. The kid who's been asking me all the questions scowls and says, "You don't know who Bobby Orr is?"

I shrug and feel the heat rising in my face. "I just moved here three days ago. I don't know anybody around here yet."

Around me, they all erupt in laughter. Behind me, I hear, "What a nimrod!" and others add similar remarks.

The dark-haired kid shakes his head. "Bobby Orr isn't some kid around here," he says with a disbelieving shake of the head. "He's on the Bruins. He's only the best defenseman in hockey. Probably the best *player* in hockey. What's wrong with you?"

I feel myself redden even more. Here I am talking to a bunch of ten-year-olds, or close to it, and they're making me look like a fool. But how was I to know? I've always skipped the hockey stories in *Sports Illustrated*, and the Maine newspapers never covered the sport.

"Where'd you come from?" another kid asks. He's the shortest one in the group, shorter even than me, with red hair and lots of freckles. A smirk comes over his face and he adds in an exaggerated Southern drawl, "From way down South where they don't have no ice? Just like Gomer Pyle?"

A couple of them laugh until the dark-haired kid says, "You dumb-ass!" They all fall silent and he continues. "Does it sound like he's from the South? Is that the kind of accent you hear?"

The redhead's face colors, making the freckles blend in a bit more. He glares at me, angry, as if this is all my fault.

I look around the circle all about me, looking for a friendly face. Although only the little redhead seems openly hostile—I don't see anyone slipping a hand into the pocket of their shorts or jeans for a switchblade—nobody looks specially friendly, either. Mostly, I'm just looking at faces that can't believe I don't know who Bobby Orr is.

"I come from Maine," I say finally. "Way north in Aroostook County. There's plenty of ice up there. Lots more snow than you ever get down here. But no one plays hockey."

"What, you just play with yourself?" the redheaded kid says, and they all laugh. I start to wonder if maybe this is a gang after all, just a younger one that may not be as scary as the Mau Maus.

My mouth has gone dry so I lick my lips. I hold the football up, half expecting this gang to take it away from me and there'll be nothing I can do about it since I'm so outnumbered. But I still take my best shot. "Anyone want to play catch?"

They just stare at me.

"Or is there someplace to play football?" I quickly add.

"Why would any of us quit playing street hockey with each other just to play catch with you?" the bigger, dark-haired kid asks.

I shrug. I guess it was a dumb question. It just never happened like this in Plainfield. Everyone always wanted me to play with them and play on their side. If guys were picking teams, I was always the first one chosen.

"Come on," another kid says. "Why are we wasting our time talking to this nimrod? Let's get the game going again."

And so they all turn away, all of them without even a backward glance except for the dark-haired kid who seems to want one last look at someone stupid enough not to know who Bobby Orr is.

*

I stay in the house for most of the next few days. It's bad enough to get humiliated, but even worse when it's by a bunch of little kids. From our house, I see them playing down the street, yelling and taking big sweeping shots and racing after the ball, but I'm not about to join them. I already look like an idiot. I'm not going to make it worse by trying to play with them. They'll either laugh at me and turn me down or let me play and *then* laugh at how bad I am. What's the point?

Besides, it's a stupid game, with the orange ball hopping over their sticks all the time. Not at all as good as football or basketball. Maybe it could be better than baseball with all of its standing around and doing nothing. But for now, street hockey is my least favorite sport. I'd rather jump rope with little girls. At least they wouldn't laugh at me.

So I spend my last few days before school starts getting my room all set the way I want it. My bed is in the corner away from the door; Patriots and Celtics pennants hang above it on the two walls. One for the Red Sox hangs over my desk along another wall and a couple bookcases line the other wall.

At night, I listen to the Red Sox games, broadcast on WHDH, 850 on the AM dial, by Ken Coleman, Ned Martin, and Mel Parnell. It's part of the same Red Sox broadcasting network that I listened to back in Plainfield, complete with the same static drowning out parts of the play by play even if it's at a different end of the radio dial.

If I close my eyes, Coleman's familiar, deep voice describing the Cardiac Kids takes me back to Plainfield. Sometimes that makes me feel better; most of the time, though, it makes me feel even more homesick.

But I still listen. Hey, they're the Cardiac Kids. I thought they were dead when Tony Conigliaro got beaned and knocked out for the year, but their big hearts are still beating.

During the day, I read the new *Sports Illustrated,* and then Stan Musial's biography. But because I want to be out there *doing stuff,* I find myself rereading the same paragraph over and over. I sort my Topps baseball cards for the fifteenth time, getting no enjoyment out of the bubble gum smell they still hold. Back in Plainfield, I'd sometimes even hold the cards up to my nose so I could smell them and it would make my mouth water for a stick of that pink gum. I could almost taste its sweetness with that smell.

But not now.

That night, Mom makes cheeseburgers with macaroni and cheese, usually one of my favorites, to try to cheer me up, but it doesn't work. The two of us eat alone at one end of the dining room table because now my father is working even later than he did back home, back in Plainfield. I mean, I know Plainfield isn't our home anymore, but it still feels like it. I think it'll always feel like home and this horrible city will always feel as foreign as Afghanistan or Bolivia.

Mom looks unhappy, taking each bite slowly, looking at me.

"It'll get better, Rabbit," she says.

But it doesn't.

CHAPTER 16

On the first day of school, I put on a pair of black dress pants and a long-sleeved dark blue shirt, take two quarters for lunch from my mother, and head for the door, not sure if she's going to grab me and give me a hug or what.

To my dismay, she follows me out the door and starts to walk me to the bus stop as if I'm just starting kindergarten. This is my first day of school in *Lynn, Lynn, City of Sin*, but it isn't my first day of school ever. I'm not five years old.

So before we leave our brick walkway with its yellowed grass on both sides, I stop and speak up.

"I'm fine," I say. "You don't need to walk with me."

"That's okay," she says. "I want to see you off for your first day. Make sure everything is okay."

My heart sinks. "Everything will be fine," I say. "Really." I don't feel that way at all. I just know it'll be even worse if I show up with my mother acting like I'm five years old.

"I know," she says with a phony brightness that matches my own. "But I'll feel better watching you get on the bus myself."

I stop walking and it's several steps before she realizes it and turns to face me. She blinks, as if confused.

"I'm not a baby," I say.

"I know you're not," she says. "You're getting to be a fine young man." Her smile looks frozen, as if she's ducked her head in the freezer for too long.

"I don't want you to come with me," I say louder than I intend. She recoils, looking stunned. "I'm fourteen years old," I say. "They'll laugh at me if I can't even walk to the bus stop by myself."

She nods and tries to smile. "Of course. I'm sorry." But she looks like she's going to cry.

"Mom, don't do this," I say, pleading with her.

She puts a hand to her mouth. "I'm worried about you, Rabbit."

Join the club, I think. I haven't spotted any switchblades yet, but I've only seen the younger kids on my street. What's waiting for me today has my palms moist and my heart pounding.

"I'll be fine," I say, trying to muster a conviction I don't really feel.

"Of course," she says, kisses me on the forehead, and races back up the steps and into the house without looking back. I know the reason she didn't look back. She was bawling her eyes out.

Oh well, I think. *That got the day started out on the right foot.* I walk most of the way down Allston Street, the cool wind in my face, then turn right onto Parker Hill Avenue and cut up and down the hill on out to Lynnfield Street, the busy main drag.

I slow down as I near it, not sure which pocket of kids I should join. The girls are on the left in two large clusters so I turn to the right where there are four smaller groups of boys. The two closest are the youngest ones, including all of the boys who were playing street hockey, presumably waiting for the Pickering Junior High bus. Even though these are the only familiar faces, they aren't friendly ones, and I'm certainly not going to wait with junior high kids.

Standing furthest away are four older boys, all but one of them smoking, their hands cupping their cigarettes to shield them from view. They look scary as anything. Every one of them is equipped with a switchblade, I am sure.

Next to them is a group of five boys who look younger than the toughest group but older than the younger ones.

Swallowing hard, I walk up to the five boys, who eye me with suspicion. They're all taller than me by at least three or four inches. The tallest, who's got me by at least eight inches, has black hair, as does another whose face is covered with pimples. Two have light brown hair, and one blond.

"Hi," I say. "My name is Rabbit. I just moved here."

"Junior high bus waits over there," says the blond-haired kid with a nod of his head toward the street hockey players.

"I'm in high school," I say. "Just starting. Ninth grade."

"You're in ninth grade?" he says. "What are you, one of them geniuses that skip a couple grades? You look like you're ten."

"I'm fourteen," I say, and try to smile. "I'm short. That's all."

A girl from across the street laughs loudly, and I turn quickly toward her. She's pretty and is wearing a short blue skirt with a light yellow blouse. I stare at her, sure she's laughing at me, until I realize that she and her friends don't even know I exist.

"Like what you see?" the blond kid asks. I turn back to him, see the smirk on his face, and feel my face grow hot.

The tall, dark-haired kid jumps in. "Did you say your name was *Rabbit*?" he asks in disbelief. "What kind of name is that?"

One of the light-haired kids pretends to be Elmer Fudd pointing a gun at Bugs Bunny, and they all laugh again.

I wonder if I should start using my birth name, David, but only schoolteachers have called me by that name. And no one has ever made fun of it before.

"I play sports," I say with a shrug that I hope conveys a confident nonchalance even while I feel like a criminal suspect being questioned by Sergeant Joe Friday on the *Dragnet* TV show. "I'm quick, so they call me Rabbit."

"You play sports?" says the tall kid, frowning. "Which ones?"

"Basketball, baseball, and track," I say. "And I want to play football, but they didn't have a team where I lived."

"Basketball and football?" the tall kid says. "A squirt like you?"

"I was the top scorer on my basketball team. Led the team in assists, too." When the kid gives me a look like he doesn't believe me, I grin and add, "But I didn't get many rebounds."

He nods. "I led the freshman team in scoring *and* rebounds last year. I'm sure I'll lead the JV team this year, then play varsity as a junior. You'll hear about me."

"What's your name?"

"Rick Cassidy," he says.

"Maybe they'll let me play for the JV team if they need a guard," I say. "I've played against older players all my life."

Rick's face clouds over and I can tell right away I've said the wrong thing. I realize too late that he's taken this as an insult. Since he didn't play up on the JVs, who do I think I am to think that I might?

"This ain't no hick town up in Maine," he says. "You'll be lucky if you make the team."

I shrug.

"How tall are you?" he says.

"About five feet," I say, feeling uncomfortable. I'm four feet, eleven and one-half inches, but I'm not about to say that.

He leans closer and in a lowered voice asks, "Did you play against many blacks?"

"No," I admit. I didn't play against a single one. Never even saw one anywhere near Plainfield.

"Almost half the players on the freshman team last year were black," he says. "Some teams we played against were all blacks. They'll be just as quick as you, as tall as me, and can jump right through the ceiling. You'll be lucky if you can get your shot off."

I nod, not knowing what else to do. What could I say in response to that?

"You're not even gonna make it to basketball season," another kid says. "Not if you're playing football. Guys like Jessie Stackhouse are gonna crush—"

Rick Cassidy holds out his hand, stopping the other kid with a shake of the head and a curious hint of a smile on the corners of his lips.

I'm touched by this stunning act of kindness. I hadn't thought Cassidy liked me at all. In fact, he seemed to hate me, but here he was, keeping the other kid from getting me too scared of the biggest bruisers on the football team.

The buses arrive before we can say another word, both of them yellow with black lettering on the side: LYNN PUBLIC SCHOOLS. The only difference is the banner on the front of one says PICKERING and the other ENGLISH.

We file onto the bus. It's about a third full, the girls all in the front and boys in the back. I hope to sit with Rick and talk some more about sports, but he sits with his friends and I'm left to a seat by myself two thirds of the way back. The toughest kids are all the way in the back. Smoke from their cigarettes fills the air even though they've opened the windows. I feel their eyes on me, but say nothing.

It's an uneventful ride until we get to the school, other than the smoke stinging my nostrils and making my nose run. It's a good thing I've got a handkerchief in my back pocket.

The bus pulls into a half circle in front of the huge, gray, concrete building, three stories high and wider than a football field. ENGLISH HIGH SCHOOL is etched on the façade sitting atop four classical-style columns that straddle the three red front doors. A scraggly tree, barely ten feet tall, spreads its branches off to the left; bushes line the full width of the building.

Everyone in front of me files out except for two older girls, one blonde and one brunette, both pretty and wearing astonishingly short skirts. They're still finishing their cigarettes.

When I step into the aisle, strong hands grasp onto my shirt from behind and hurl me back into my seat. I look up at an angry, red-haired older boy towering over me. A cigarette dangles from his lips. His skin is pockmarked with acne.

"Give me your lunch money, squirt," he says.

My heart thunders in my chest. I can't swallow.

He backhands me hard across the face, knocking me up against the windows. My cheek stings where he hit me and my eyes water. I look to the front of the bus and see that Rick and all the other kids I talked to have already stepped off.

"You hard of hearing, punk?" the big kid says, glowering as he grasps the seat backs and lowers himself to within inches of my face. Ugly blackheads dot his nose. His breath smells of cigarette smoke. "Give me your money."

I reach into my pocket and hand him my two quarters.

He pockets them, a smug look on his face and, after dropping his cigarette to the floor and stubbing it out, saunters down the aisle along with the rest of his friends. They look down on me with disgust as they pass.

"Easy money, eh Smitty?" one of them says, and my tormentor grins and nods.

Smitty.

I've been wondering for weeks who my Carlos or Nicky Cruz would be. Now I have my answer.

Smitty. Last name: Smith. Red hair.

I wait until everyone else is almost off the bus before I get to my feet, my legs shaking.

"C'mon, hurry up," the squat, bald bus driver says. "Put the goddamned cigarette out and get out of here. I ain't got all day."

I manage to get down the aisle and look outside, relieved to see that Smitty and his friends, perhaps Lynn's version of the Mau Maus, aren't waiting for me.

I'll go hungry today, but at least I won't hear the flick of a switchblade and feel cold, sharp steel against my throat.

CHAPTER 17

I go to the wrong first period class. It's a stupid mistake, but my head is spinning, and not just because the big kid slapped me around and took my lunch money. Even if I forget about that, which is hard, I can't get over how huge this school is.

Back in Grainville, one small, two-story brick building housed all the students from grades seven to twelve and that included several of the surrounding towns. But here, the gray corridors go on forever, lined by green lockers and filled with more students and teachers than I ever could have imagined.

There must be close to two thousand students here. That's more people than in any city or town in Aroostook County except for Caribou and Presque Isle. The sounds of laughter and conversation fill the hallways as everyone bustles from their homeroom class to first period. It feels so loud and busy and crowded. I guess I'm like the country bumpkin on his first visit to New York City who just stands and gawks at all the tall buildings and all the people everywhere. Lynn English is just so *huge*.

Most of the students are white, maybe nine out of every ten, but it still feels strange to see blacks and Puerto Ricans walking the same hallways with me. I don't think of it as good or bad; it's just different. A few times, I catch myself staring before I quickly look away.

My father talks like the blacks are dangerous, but it wasn't a black kid who beat me up on the bus and took my lunch money. Mostly, they seem to keep to themselves, walking and talking with each other. Which, I guess, is okay. If I were one of them, that's what I'd probably do.

But what I really can't take my eyes away from is the girls and their short skirts. I mean, skirts more than halfway way up to…to…well, you know. I can't take my eyes off them. No girls up in Plainfield dressed that way. Miniskirts. Wow. I try to keep my eyes off them, but next thing I know I'm staring again.

So I don't know if it's because I'm just so overwhelmed by all the girls' pretty legs or all the students filling the hallway or maybe I'm just a dumb hick who got slapped around and gave away his lunch money, but I go to the wrong first period class. I don't realize the mistake until the teacher, Mr. Lombardi, finishes reading off the roll call and I'm not on it.

In fact, it takes me a little longer than that because I'm thinking of the Green Bay Packers. As soon as I heard the name Lombardi, I thought of Vince Lombardi, the coach of the Green Bay Packers, who won the first Super Bowl last year, easily beating the Kansas City Chiefs. So I'm daydreaming about how great it would be for the Packers coach to be at the front of the class talking about the team's season and about the "Packers sweep," in which the offensive guards pull out and form a wall of blockers, and about his top players, especially quarterback Bart Starr. The Packers are one of my favorite teams after the Boston Patriots and the New York Giants.

All of a sudden, I jerk out of my football thoughts and realize my name hasn't been called. I pull out of my shirt pocket the white index card that holds my schedule, stare at it for a brief moment, and realize my error. I've gone to my Monday first-period History class in room 212, just like it says on the schedule card, but today is Tuesday. Of course, school always starts the day after Labor Day, a Tuesday. Everyone knows that. I know that. But somehow with my brain spinning away like a top, I went to my Monday class.

I jump out of my seat, explain to the startled Mr. Lombardi what I've done, and dash out of the room and down the long, empty hallway for my real class. An older teacher pops out of one classroom and I almost crash into her, but I make a spinning move like O. J. Simpson does at USC, stopping on a dime and whirling 360 degrees around her and I'm back at full speed again, looking back over my shoulder to shout my apologies. She calls out something about a hall pass, whatever that is, but then falls silent, and the echo of my footfalls fills the corridor.

I'd be happy with my move if I weren't so embarrassed at having to make it in the first place. Instead, as I open the door to the right classroom, I feel like the hillbilly that I am, too stupid to go to the class for the right day.

The teacher, Mr. Sipowicz according to what's written on the upper right corner of the blackboard, glares at me from where he's standing, a piece of chalk in his hand and half a sentence written on the board. He's got thick glasses with black frames and gray hair cut so close to the scalp it can't even be an inch long. He looks at me like I'm a bug.

"I'm sorry, I really am," I say, out of breath after my sprint down the hall. "I went to my Monday class instead of my Tuesday class." I feel hot and foolish as Mr. Sipowicz glares at me for a few more seconds.

"What's your name?" he finally says.

"Rabbit," I say instinctively, and then correct myself. "David Labelle, I mean."

Mr. Sipowicz consults some piece of paper on his desk, glares some more, and then points me to an empty seat near the back on the far side of the room, next to a black girl. I go behind everyone, but several of the boys and a couple girls turn around to look back at me and what I see in their faces shocks me.

I'd thought that "what a clodhopper" would be written there, but instead I see just the opposite. They're looking at me with admiration. A few of them smile and one boy with long, golden blond, curly hair, gives me a nod and a grin.

I realize after a brief delay that they think I did this on purpose, that it was a scam to cut the first ten minutes of class and get away with it. I want to say to them, "No, that's not how I am!" but even a hayseed too stupid to go to the right class can see that's not the thing to do.

So I smile back, albeit a bit sheepishly, and slide into my seat. I rest my arms on the light-brown, hard-plastic writing surface and glance around. Based on everyone's reaction to me, I feel like a king.

What a strange, strange place.

CHAPTER 18

On the way to my third-period History class, one of the guys who was so impressed with me, Jimmy Keenan, drops the bombshell. He has blue eyes and curly, golden-blond hair that the girls clearly adore. He is, of course, about six inches taller than me and outweighs me by at least forty pounds.

He also seems to have trouble getting serious about anything. But as we walk together down the gray and green hallway that feels a mile long, we look like two cool, popular guys, and I feel that maybe things won't be so bad after all.

"I was wondering," I say, "who do I see about playing on the football team?"

"You?" he says with a big grin. "Are you serious?"

"I may be small, but I'm fast. I want to play. When are tryouts?"

Keenan gives me a curious look, one with an eyebrow raised in disbelief. "You're kinda late," he says. "We've been practicing for two weeks. And a few captain's practices in the summer."

My jaw drops.

"No teams wait until the start of classes," Keenan says. "If they did, they'd be behind. All the schools start practicing two weeks before Labor Day, which is the league limit. Everyone knows that."

"I didn't know," I protest. "I'm not from around here."

We keep walking past the endless rows of green lockers. When we'd first stepped into the hallway, my eyes had gone quickly to some cute girls in miniskirts, but they might as well not even be there now. My heart is thumping and I'm hearing none of the surrounding buzz of conversation and the outbursts of laughter. I'm hearing only Jimmy Keenan's words.

"Didn't your junior high practices start before the first class?" he asks. "Even by a day or two?"

I feel myself redden, my skin suddenly so hot it's like I'm next to a furnace. "I, um…didn't play in junior high." As Keenan looks at me as if I'm some kind of bug, I continue. "We lived in a tiny town. It didn't have a football team. Just not enough players. So I've never played on a team before, but when we played in the backyards, I was the best player there. I'm really fast and can dive and catch any pass you throw me."

"Let me get this straight," he says, shaking his head. "A little guy like you, practically a midget, who's never played football before, is going to come here from the boonies in Maine where you were *great* playing in the backyard—" his voice drips with sarcasm "—where you never had to deal with a guy twice your size drilling you into the ground, and you're gonna miss the first two weeks of practice and still make the Lynn English Bulldogs? Are you insane?"

There's nothing I can say so I just shrug my shoulders, feeling embarrassed and almost as foolish as Keenan thinks I am.

"Football ain't like the con game you pulled about saying you went to the wrong class so you could show up late," he says. "No one *likes* those two weeks of Summer Suicides. They're brutal. We're practicing twice a day and it can be hotter than hell. The two worst weeks of my life.

"Lots of guys quit the team then. Said it just wasn't worth it. I almost thought about it myself and I'm a really tough guy." He looks at me as if to determine whether or not he has to prove that. Apparently deciding he doesn't, he continues on. "But Coach McDonough says it gets rid of the weaklings, the ones who are only trying to be on the team to get popular." Keenan grins. "You know, to be able to nail some cheerleaders."

I feel my face growing hot, but somehow manage to get out a few words in my defense. "I'd have gone if I knew."

"Coach ain't gonna buy that," Keenan says. "I'll show you where his office is at the end of the day, but he's probably just going to toss you out on your scrawny midget ass. He's going to say that if you cared enough about being an LEHS Bulldog, you'd have found out one way or another. I guarantee he'll use one of his favorite phrases: 'Excuses are for losers.'"

*

"Excuses are for losers, kid," Coach McDonough says. We're inside his office, next to the gymnasium, and his good-sized butt is up against a plain, old oak desk. He's a big man, not much over six feet tall, but wide and beefy, like an offensive lineman, and with a ruddy complexion. "If you really cared about being a Lynn English High Bulldog, you'd have found out one way or another."

I'm struck by how Jimmy Keenan was able to predict the coach's reaction almost word-for-word. But Coach McDonough keeps going.

"Those two weeks help me and my staff separate the wheat from the chaff," he says. "They don't call them Summer Suicides for nothing. It's brutal and I make sure it's that way. The team gets stronger when you eliminate the weak. You think I can let a pipsqueak like you get away with missing my two weeks of hell and then just start practicing as if nothing happened? What kind of message does that send to the team, to the young men who gutted their way through those two weeks while you were vacationing at some Camp Jamboree?"

"Sir, some of those two weeks we were still in Plainfield, up in northern Maine, six hours away," I say. "But I'd have somehow gotten down here, if my parents let me, if I'd only known."

Coach McDonough stares at me. "What position did you play in junior high?"

My face burns as if I'm in Hell itself, and in a way, that's exactly where I am. I wish that the ground would open up and swallow me.

"We didn't have a team in Plainfield," I say and Coach McDonough erupts in laughter and waves his hand in a shooing-away gesture. But I keep going, unwilling to quit like those kids who didn't love football enough to make it through two-a-days in the summer heat. "But I was the best player up there on my basketball and baseball teams and a bunch of us played football all the time in the back yards. No one could stop me. Just give me a chance."

"Kid, you've been wasting my time," Coach McDonough says. "Now you're insulting me, telling me that because you were better than your four or five little hick friends you can somehow compete down here with the big boys. Here with men."

I stand there and realize I'm trembling, like a rabbit trapped by a fox. Or something even bigger.

"I'm doing you a favor by telling you to wait until next year," Coach McDonough says. "Maybe you'll go on a growth spurt. Work out. Bulk up. 'Cause right now, you'll just get killed out there."

He stares at me, and a part of my brain wants me to say, *They can't hit me if they can't catch me.*

But my mouth won't work. It feels like it's glued together as I look up to the coach, noticing for the first time that his dark hair has a white patch the size of a golf ball on the right side, almost as if he was painting his house and didn't clean up afterward.

"How big are you?" he asks, and before I can try to answer, he says, "I'll bet you're five-nothin', hundred-nothin'."

I have no idea what he's saying and just gawk at him.

"You're five feet tall, if you're lucky, and I'll bet you aren't even a hundred pounds," he says. My heart sinks. I'm four-eleven and a half. That last fraction of an inch has been taking forever to arrive. And he's right, I'm ninety-seven pounds.

"Close enough, sir," I say. "But I'm fast. Just—"

McDonough laughs. "Five-nothin'. Hundred-nothin'. Lotsa guys on this team will be almost twice your size. Bruiser McKinley's over six feet tall, more than two hundred pounds. And mean. What do you think's gonna happen when he tackles you? Christ, you're not even a meal for him. You're just an appetizer."

He flicks his hand. "Go on, get out. Come back next year. Or check out the Chess Team instead. I heard they've got openings." He chuckles.

Feeling almost as if my life is in the balance, I make one last try.

"Please give me just one practice," I say. "If you don't see what you need to see, then I'll thank you for the opportunity and come back next year. Just one."

"I don't—"

"But if you see enough to give me another day after that, then I'll be back out there again working hard for the team. Just one practice at a time. You're risking nothing and you might be getting a player who surprises you, who helps this team."

Coach McDonough stares at me. "Kid, you got balls. I'll give you that." He rests his hands on the desktop and drums his fingers. Then he startles me by yelling out, "Callahan!"

Another coach wearing a gray LEHS Bulldogs T-shirt and beige slacks rushes in. Coach McDonough introduces him as Coach Callahan, the JV coach, and explains my situation. Coach Callahan is much smaller than Coach McDonough, probably a former running back instead of a former lineman, and younger, too, maybe not even thirty. He has brown hair and a mustache.

"I'm gonna give him a shot," Coach McDonough says to Coach Callahan. "One practice, maybe only five minutes, until you decide you've seen enough. He sticks around as long as you see some potential. He's gone as soon as you say so."

A huge smile breaks out over my face and I can barely contain the whoops of euphoria.

"Thank you!" I say with a barely controlled shout.

"Five minutes," McDonough cautions. "That's probably all you'll last. But you'll get your shot." He draws in a deep breath. "I don't suppose you brought a mouthpiece, gym socks, a jock strap and a cup today, did you?"

I shake my head no, afraid that he'll rescind his offer. "But I could—"

"Go around the corner and you'll see the team manager, Luke Scanlon. Have him issue you a locker and a full supply of equipment. Make your mouthpiece tonight and come tomorrow ready to play."

"Thank you, sir!" I turn to Coach Callahan. "Both of you!"

I want to rush out of the office before he changes his mind, but Coach McDonough asks, "What's your name?"

"Rabbit," I say, then curse myself. I should just skip my nickname for now. Maybe forever. But it's too late now. "It's David Labelle, but my friends all call me Rabbit."

"Rabbit," he says, shaking his head. He looks at the other coach and rolls his eyes. "You ever hear of Wonderland?" he asks me.

I blink. I've been to amusement parks, but I'm not sure if any of them have been called Wonderland. "I, um…"

"'Course not, you just got here," he says. "It's a dog track in Revere. People bet on the dogs, greyhounds, that chase a mechanical rabbit around the track. They never catch it, of course, but when they're being trained, they catch real rabbits and tear them to shreds." He points to the locker room. "You better hope none of those greyhounds in there catch you."

CHAPTER 19

Dad's actually at dinner that night, which would be nice if he weren't so intent on congratulating himself for it, making sure that I know he "cut out early" to hear firsthand how my day went.

It's hard to believe that I used to have fun with him, that he was the kind of person who could even have fun.

He's seated at the head of the table, still wearing his suit and tie. My mother sits opposite him and I'm in between. Family photographs of the three of us smiling hang on each wall, but only two of us are smiling now.

I'm still euphoric over the way I talked Coach McDonough into at least giving me a chance. But I am concerned that Coach Callahan is really only going to give me five minutes and then kick me off the field.

Mostly, though, I don't want to give my father the satisfaction of seeing me happy about the football team. I still hate this place and, of course, he's the reason I'm stuck here.

So instead, I dump the lost two weeks of practice on him.

"I probably have no chance at all," I say, shoveling a huge slab of meatloaf on my plate to go with a huge mound of mashed potatoes. I'm starving after having no money for lunch. Then I put lots of gravy on the potatoes and smear catsup on the meatloaf. "I barely talked the coach into giving me a five-minute tryout tomorrow."

"Five minutes?" my father says, his voice going way up in pitch, so he sounds almost like a girl. He pushes his glasses back up to the bridge of his nose. "That's ridiculous! Since when are tryouts only five minutes? I'm sure you must have misunderstood."

"Nope," I say. "The problem is that the team has already been practicing for two weeks."

"But school only started today."

"Doesn't matter. The league says you can start practicing two weeks before Labor Day, so everyone does it. Two-a-days. The practices are so tough, so many kids quit that most years they don't even have to make cuts."

I look at my dad. "If you'd asked about the football team when you enrolled me, they would have told you."

My father looks defensively to my mother. "How was I to know? Whoever heard of high school teams practicing in the summer? It never even occurred to me to ask."

"Coach McDonough says if we cared enough, we would have found out," I say, and stab a piece of meatloaf and shove it in my mouth.

"But that's…that's preposterous!"

I feel the tiniest bit of guilt for dumping this on him, but it's *really* tiny. A microscopic amount of guilt. It's my father's fault that I'm stuck down here while Donnie and the rest of the guys are still in Plainfield where they, and I, belong. So as far as I'm concerned, all the blame goes to my dad.

"I was lucky to get any chance at all," I say. "He's given me tomorrow's practice, but he said I might last only five minutes."

"That hardly seems fair," my mother says.

I eat my food without replying, hoping the silence screams at my father.

"Well, give it your best shot," he says quickly. "It's the best you can do." Clearly realizing that football isn't going to win him the brownie points he'd hoped for, he switches the subject. "What about the rest of your day?"

I'm not going to tell him, or my mother, about my problems on the bus. It's just too embarrassing. Besides, what could they do? I'm just going to ask for twice as much money tomorrow and hide half of it. But for a brief moment, I wonder if I should tell them just to make my father feel more guilty for what he's done. Even though I know there's no way we'll ever move back to Plainfield.

But I chicken out.

"My classes are going to be so easy, I'm going to have trouble staying awake," I say, and shovel a big scoop of mashed potatoes into my mouth. They taste great, and I follow that mouthful with some more meatloaf.

"This place sure has piqued your appetite," my mother says.

My father cuts her off. "Just because you didn't get any homework in your first day doesn't mean it's going to be easy," he says in that cautionary don't-get-too-big-for-your-britches tone.

"I know," I say. "It isn't that."

"What is it?" my mother asks. She smiles and asks in a playful tone, "Aren't the kids in your classes smart?"

"Not really," I say, surprising her. Her eyebrows raise and her mouth drops just a little. All of a sudden, I wish I'd kept quiet. But it's too late now—I've opened a can of worms, as she would say—so I keep going. "They mostly goof off as much as they can. They don't seem to care a whole lot."

"Kids are goofing off? In your accelerated courses, too? English and French?" my father says, stopping a forkful of meatloaf an inch away from his mouth, then setting it down. He's angry, clamping his jaw down tight. "I find that hard to believe. Those kids should be the cream of the crop."

His nostrils flare as his eyes bore into me. He isn't angry at the other kids for goofing off; he's angry at me because he doesn't believe me. He thinks I'm lying about the whole thing, trying to ruin his great plan for us here in the City of Sin.

"English and French don't seem very accelerated to me," I say. "Especially French. It's only French II."

"French II?" my mother says, "In the ninth grade? You took that last year. Or was it the year before?"

"That's what I'm saying. It's all stuff I already learned the last two years."

"In all your courses?" my father says, staring at me in disbelief, as if he hasn't heard a word I've said.

"Pretty much."

"That isn't what they told me a couple months ago."

I shrug. I think about being mean and saying he must have done a lousy job checking out the wonderful Lynn schools, just like he failed to find out about football practices, but figure I'll let him come to those conclusions himself.

"You're sure?" my mother says, leaning forward as if to make sure I hear her. "Maybe you misunderstood. It's only been one day."

"I'm sure. The teachers all talked about what they were going to cover this year," I say. "I'm not going to have to do a thing."

My father's fork clatters on the table. "Well," he says, glaring at me as if it's my fault. "We'll see about that."

*

Early the next day, he drives me to school. We head straight for the principal's office, the clicking of our shoes on the tile floor echoing loud in the empty corridor. I look around, hoping no one I know sees me, and am relieved to see something finally has gone right.

We step inside the waiting area. Wooden benches line the two closest walls. A long metal counter separates us from the inner half where the principal's and vice-principal's offices lie, each one with a secretary outside of it at a desk, furiously typing on her typewriter. My father steps to the counter and clears his throat loudly. The closest secretary looks up and offers a weak smile.

"Can I help you?" she says.

"I hope so," my father says with a frozen smile even weaker than hers. "I need to talk to the principal. My name is Andre Labelle and this here is my son, David." He puts an arm around me. I want to pull away but know that would be a bad idea. "He began classes yesterday and there seems to be some mistake."

"What's the problem?" the secretary asks. She's about ten years older than my mother, and has gray hair and the beginning of wrinkles on her face.

"David is a smart boy, but it sounds like he's been placed in classes with all the…um, with all the *less gifted* students. I came down here less than a month ago and was told that David could qualify for the top classes in English and French and the second-level ones in History, Math, and Science. Instead, he's enrolled in a watered-down curriculum that will see him repeating course material he covered last year or even the year before that."

I shift uncomfortably on my feet as the secretary—Miss Dunbarton, according to the black name plate on her desk, looks at me.

"What's his name again?" she asks, and my father tells her.

"Oh yes," she says, and offers a tight smile. "You're from Maine." She says it the same way someone tells you that you've stepped in dog poop. "Up in Aroostook County, right?"

"Yes," my father says, tight-lipped.

"One minute," Miss Dunbarton says. She steps to the principal's office and knocks on the oaken door just below the black sign that proclaims: Mr. Saunders, Principal. She ducks her head in and whispers something.

She pops back out again and says, "Mr. Labelle? Mr. Saunders will see you now." She turns to me. "David, please have a seat on one of the benches."

I sit on the bench and wonder if one of my classmates will come in and look at me again with mistaken admiration, thinking that I'd gotten in trouble already on just my second day. Before even homeroom. That would cement for good my bizarre reputation as a troublemaker. But I'm left on the bench for almost no time at all.

My father emerges from the inner office, smiles at me, and winks. I can't believe he actually winked. I'm not a ten-year-old, although he seems to have trouble remembering that. It's so embarrassing.

A thin, white-haired man with an angular face whom I assume is the principal, Mr. Saunders, pokes his head out and hands a file folder to his secretary. "Jeanie, please type up a new schedule for the young man and a short memo of explanation to his teachers." He gives me a wry smile. "David, I hope this is the last I see of you this year."

Not knowing what else to do, I smile back.

When we get back out into the corridor, I look at the card that shows my schedule. It's completely changed; not one class the same.

"It's really rather insulting," my father says, breathing loudly through his nose. "The school records hadn't arrived yet from Plainfield, so they just assumed that you belonged in the lowest tier classes."

I can sense he's going to tell me why, but wants me to ask so I do. "Why?"

"Because this is almighty Massachusetts," he says. "They think they're so smart and people up near Plainfield are just a bunch of red-neck potato farmers. As dumb as dirt." He fixes me with a stare. "Don't you *ever* let them think that of you."

CHAPTER 20

Since I'm not supposed to be dumb as dirt, I make sure I go to the Wednesday first-period class, accelerated English, arriving very much on time. I feel even more awkward and conspicuous entering a new classroom today than I did yesterday, sticking out like a sore thumb, as the saying goes. Most of the other students went to some junior high school together, either Pickering or Cobbett, and then they also met each other again yesterday. I hand the teacher, Miss Minter, the note from the principal's office, and she nods, points me to a seat at the corner of the back, and goes to a side closet to fetch me a textbook.

She's old, with gray hair and lots of wrinkles, and wears glasses. She speaks in a gravelly voice, but seems nice. She introduces me to the class and then jumps right into a discussion of passive verbs. Unlike yesterday, I'm learning new things right from the beginning.

It's a smaller class, only nineteen students, compared to about twenty-five in most of the ones I was in yesterday. I notice right away that its composition is an even bigger change. I'm only the seventh boy, surrounded by a dozen girls. All of us are white except for one black girl in the front row who doesn't seem to look anywhere but down at the book on her desk or up at the board and Miss Minter.

Only a few of those students follow me to my next class, History, so I'm meeting a whole new group of strangers. Some of my classmates are shy and don't say anything and others talk mostly amongst themselves, but a few act friendly, especially Jeff Goodwin, a wise-cracking redhead with freckles who reminds me of Jimmy Chaisson even though he's far louder and more boisterous. Also, Paul DiSimone, who's so quiet he can't get a word in edgewise with Jeff. And Anna Levesque.

"Who do you have for Math and Science?" Anna asks from the seat on my left while we wait for History to start. She has short blonde hair, glasses, and a pretty smile.

I shrug. "I don't know." Only the room number is shown on my schedule. I hand it to her and she smiles.

"You're with us in those classes, too!" she says. "That's great! Mr. Robinson in Math seems really good. The Science teacher, Mr. Tempkin, is a little strange and kind of boring, I think, but he isn't too bad."

I nod, feeling tongue-tied, and try to smile but feel foolish. What can I say? "Good," I manage and immediately feel my face turn hot. Could I have come up with a more stupid, awkward response? Probably not if I tried.

But Anna just smiles. She seems like the nicest person in the whole school. Everyone in my new classes are at least okay—there aren't any thugs like the ones on the bus—but Anna tops them all.

"Do you play an instrument?" she asks.

"What?"

"An instrument. Like a trumpet or saxophone or the drums."

"Oh, sorry," I say. "No."

"Too bad," she says. "I'm in the band. I figured if you played something, I could introduce you to everyone."

"Thanks," I say, really feeling grateful for this kindness. I shrug, suddenly wishing I played *something*, so I could be in the band with her, too. Not because of anything gushy, but just that she's acting so nice to me. She's the kind of person you'd want to be around.

A sudden burst of inspiration hits and I finally ask a question that just might let her know I'm not a total hayseed who can't even carry on a conversation. "What instrument do you play?"

She brightens. "The flute. I started on the clarinet but switched to flute two years ago."

"Are you any good?"

"No, I'm awful." But as she says it she laughs in a way that tells me she's actually pretty good, and I join in on the laughter.

"What sports do you play?" she asks.

"All of them, but I like football most of all," I say. "I missed the practices before classes started, but I'm trying out for the team this afternoon."

Anna's face clouds over. "*You're* trying out for the football team? You're kidding." Her eyes widen and her cheeks flush as she realizes that she's accidentally insulted me, at least a little. "I mean…I'm sorry…it's just that—"

"I know, I'm short," I say, feeling a little embarrassed because the words came from this nice girl, but not so much, really. I've been hearing it for as long as I can remember. "But I'm fast. My friends call me Rabbit."

"Rabbit?" Anna asks, cocking her head to the side a little bit, clearly thinking it's a pretty odd nickname.

"Yeah," I say, and it strikes me that my *old* friends called me Rabbit, but no one calls me that here—except for my parents, that is, and they don't count. I don't really have any friends anymore. I was starting to make friends with Jimmy Keenan, but that's not very likely now that I'm not taking any classes with him.

Anna must be able to see something in my face because she starts to say something, only to be drowned out by the bell signaling the start of class. But she leans a little closer and as soon as it stops, she softly says, "Good luck in football practice…*Rabbit*."

We both grin broadly. A warm sense of happiness—or perhaps it's relief—fills my chest. I may still be little, but for at least a few seconds I feel like I'm six feet tall.

I've made my first true friend in the City of Sin. I never, *ever* would have expected that it would be a girl.

CHAPTER 21

Everything feels enormous on me: the shoulder pads make me look like I might actually have muscles; the ancient helmet is huge, wobbling on my head even with the chinstrap as tight as I can make it; and the high-top cleats may be the right size, but since I've never worn high-tops or cleats, they feel gigantic as I clomp across the pavement of the school's back parking lot to the practice field.

It's unseasonably hot for early September, an extension of a summer that isn't willing to give way to fall just yet. I smell the stale sweat baked into my equipment by all the boys that preceded me into this position, but especially with the helmet. Unlike the hard plastic versions everyone else is wearing, I've been given a beat-up, old leather relic that seems like it dates back to the days of Red Grange and no facemasks.

I wonder if the equipment manager, Luke Scanlon, an unpleasant fat kid with lots of pimples, gave me this edition to humiliate me. Perhaps it's been given for the last fifty years to the kid who everyone knows is going to get cut.

The field is massive, like everything else here, the well-trampled grass stretching out for what has to be at least a quarter of a mile, if not more. In the distance, well past our far goalposts, soccer players are warming up, running and jumping and kicking their black-and-white balls back and forth.

I get in the back line and we do stretches and calisthenics to loosen up. The varsity captain, Jake O'Meara, leads us through jumping jacks, push-ups, and sit-ups. Everyone chants as we do them: *One! Two! Three!* It sounds cool except that my voice is high and squeaky compared to the older players.

The varsity players become easy to spot, not just because they're so good but also because they got the better plain white practice jerseys. For a while, at least, everyone is going to practice together, a possibility that makes me gulp when I see a couple of the hulking beasts towering over me. But we aren't doing any contact drills yet, so I'm still alive.

When we do sprints, I finally get a chance to shine, even with my clippity-cloppity cleats on. In my group, I either finish first or not far behind a couple of the varsity players. Mr. McDonough notices this and screams at his stars.

"You gonna let that little shrimp beat you?" he hollers. "Quit dogging it, Joyce! You, too, O'Meara! I'll send the both of you down to the JVs where you belong!"

The two who must be Joyce and O'Meara give me dirty looks when we get back in line, like I was trying to show them up, but hey, I'm just trying to impress the coaches. Why wouldn't I run as fast as I can?

Five minutes pass and then another five. None of the coaches have kicked me out yet.

Even though I'm just five-nothin', hundred-nothin'.

Finally, the coaches separate out the players by position, taking the lineman to one area to work on some drills, and leaving the rest of us to work on passing. Seven quarterbacks take turns throwing passes to the rest of us, who as running backs, tight ends, or receivers can all be expected to catch the ball. We start out by just going deep as fast as we can and then switch to post patterns—running straight, then cutting toward a pretend goalpost.

I would have expected this to be where I could really show that I belong on the team, hopefully being in the position to have to dive and make a fancy catch.

Instead, I miss the first three passes.

I can't understand it. I've always felt like there was glue on my hands and if I could touch the football, I could catch it. And that's how it was in the back yards in Plainfield.

But that isn't how it is on the Lynn English High School practice field with big, clunky shoulder pads making it suddenly more awkward to lift my hands over my head to catch a pass. Far worse, though, is that when I turn to look for the ball, I can't see it. It's like a hand is over my eyes. All these other kids played junior high and most of them probably played Pop Warner football before that. For me, all this is new. I've never worn a helmet before and that's causing me problems.

"Catch the ball!" hollers Coach Callahan after I miss another pass. "You look like Stevie Wonder."

And that's the problem. I just can't see the ball. It's not like I've got problems with my eyes. I've had 20-20 vision since my first eye test. But with all this equipment on, I'm just like that blind musician, my hands groping for a ball I can see one second and then not see the next.

Coach Callahan comes over to me. "You may be fast, kid, but you can't catch worth a damn." He swears to emphasize his point. "You gotta focus on the ball. Watch it into your hands. Not flail around for it like Stevie Freaking Wonder!" He mockingly flaps his hands to make his point. "Miss this next pass, and I'm cutting your ass."

But as if to rescue me, Coach McDonough changes the drill, making half of us who were trying to catch passes into defensive players. I move to defensive back and things go better for me there. I may be having trouble seeing the ball, but I can certainly see the player I'm supposed to cover. I'm not a total Stevie Wonder.

Almost every time, I stay with my man, stride-for-stride, even against the big varsity kids, which makes me feel a little better. Sometimes, it's a weak quarterback throwing the ball and the pass doesn't even come close to the potential receiver. But when it does and I'm covering one of the kids who's maybe only six or seven inches taller than me, I usually break up the pass. One time I even have an interception right in my hands only to have the receiver whack my helmet, trying to catch the ball himself, and it crunches down over my eyes and I drop the ball.

The only time I'm overmatched in this drill is when the varsity captain, Jake O'Meara, is throwing the ball and one of the tall varsity receivers has a foot or so on me in height. O'Meara lofts the ball high into the receiver's hands and I can jump all I want to try to break it up, but I can't even come close.

But I'm not trying to make the varsity, and I'm hoping Mr. Callahan has seen me stay stride for stride with every one of the varsity players. Well, except for one. A black kid that I hear other players call Willie beats me every time. But he's six feet tall, looks like a senior, and is getting past everyone who tries to cover him.

He's so good, I wonder why he isn't captain. Jake O'Meara may be the quarterback and is very good, but it seems like Willie is even better at what he does.

Finally, they separate out the varsity and JV teams, sending us down to the far end of the field. There are about twenty-five of us and I'm definitely the smallest kid on the field, but I'm relieved to see none of the biggest players have followed us.

But Jessie Stackhouse has. He's black, close to six feet tall, probably weighs one-seventy or one-eighty pounds, and hits like a freight train. He's clearly the most intimidating JV player and I get a first-hand example on the second set of contact drills.

The "run to daylight" drill involves four players: an offensive lineman, a defender—either a defensive lineman or linebacker—and a running back and quarterback. The quarterback, who doesn't really do much at all in this drill, just hands off the ball to the running back. The offensive lineman takes on the defender, one-on-one, and tries to drive him in one direction or another, opening a hole—"daylight"—for the running back to take.

The first time I do the drill, it's boring. The offensive lineman overpowers the defender, pushing him way off to the right, and I just run right straight ahead.

Boring.

In a game, I'd run like crazy until some other defender caught me or I scored a touchdown, but in this drill, there are no other defenders, so I could have walked "to daylight"—heck, I could have even crawled—with the size of the hole the lineman opened.

The second time, though, Stackhouse is the defender and he tosses aside his blocker easily. I try to fake him to the left and go right, but he has none of it. As he wraps his arms around me, he lowers his helmet and drives it into my arm, where I've cradled the ball.

The fierce impact of his helmet on the ball pops it up in the air, and though I flail for it as Stackhouse drives me into the ground, it bounces away.

"Gotta protect the ball!" Coach Callahan screams as I head to the back of the line. "If you can't protect the ball, you can't play!"

My ears burn even as my body reverberates from the shock of the big hit. I wonder if this fumble will be my final straw. All those missed passes put me on the cutting line. This probably pushed me over.

*

I sit on the wooden bench in front of the gray metal locker that was assigned to me, wondering if this is the only time I'll ever use it. I had my shot. Did I blow it or will I get another chance tomorrow? I guess I'll just keep coming back until one of the coaches tells me to stop.

I pull off my shoulder pads, feeling tired and discouraged, and hook them on a hanger below the eye-level top shelf where I put my helmet. There are a dozen rows of these gray lockers, each with about thirty of them facing out one way and another thirty on the backside of them facing the other.

Bruiser McKinley, the huge, mean senior that Coach McDonough warned me about, clomps toward me, still fully dressed except for his helmet. Grass stains smear his foul-smelling uniform. He's a starting varsity lineman on both the offensive and defensive sides of the ball. He's got some belly fat that jiggles as he walks, but powerful rippling biceps. Sweat plasters his stringy black hair to his scalp and drips off his face.

He towers over me and slams his helmet against my locker.

I jump.

"Move over, kid," he says, his voice deep and gravelly.

Startled, I slide down a few feet to give him room.

"I said, move over!" he says, his face livid, as if I've insulted him somehow. He slams his helmet against the locker again. "Don't you know anything?"

I blink, not understanding what I've done, and move farther away. He must see the look of confusion on my face so he explains.

"I'm a varsity senior and you're a freshman," he says. "This is my locker." He points to his locker on the other side of the bench directly opposite from mine. "That means you give me ten feet on both sides. This is my space. You keep your scrawny ass out of it."

Gulping, I nod and move fifteen feet away, closer to two JV players whose names I don't know, one white and the other black. Bruiser turns his attention to the other end of the row, shouts some insult to a player, and then laughs. I continue to undress in silence while the buzz of conversation and laughter fills the foul-smelling air.

I grab my towel and head for the showers at the far end of the room. Three older players are lined up on the left waiting for a shower, so I stand behind them.

"What are you doing here?" the black-haired guy in the back of the line says. "Freshmen go over there," he says, pointing to the right where I belatedly see some of the JV players going. "Christ, you don't even have any hair on your balls." He gives me a hard shove and I stumble backwards, my arms windmilling. I fall squarely on my behind, half of my towel landing in a puddle of water. My ears burn at the sound of the older players' laughter. I want to say that I do, too, have hair on my balls, it's just blond like the hair on my head so it's hard to see, but even a fool like me knows that'll just make things worse.

I hang my half-drenched towel on a hook and join the rest of the team's lower class as we get clean by walking through a U-shaped, green-tiled corridor with jet-spray hoses mounted in snaking fashion at varying heights, spraying lukewarm water out of a succession of pinholes. I walk through twice before I feel clean.

No wonder the seniors have confiscated the real showers for themselves.

I use the good half of my towel to dry off as best I can, and then head for Bruiser and my locker at the far end of the room. I'm not surprised at all when an older player whose name I don't even know jumps out of one row and snaps his damp towel at my ass, connects with stinging perfection, and then laughs at my girlish yelp.

Lynn, Lynn, City of Sin? Of course. I'm in Hell.

CHAPTER 22

That night, while lying on my bed staring up at the blank white ceiling, I run through my biggest problems and go one-for-three in solutions.

Not great, but better than nothing.

I can't figure out what to do about Smitty, the big kid on the bus who took my lunch money on the first day. I can't keep giving him the money—or at least, I sure don't want to—but I'll lose every fight I have with him trying to defend myself. I can't beat him.

I wonder, though, if he carries a switchblade.

For all of my worries, I haven't seen a single one of them. Neither have I seen a single prostitute. As much as I hate it here, I wonder if Lynn may not be quite as bad as its reputation. Or as Mom would say, its bark is worse than its bite.

But do I want to take a chance that Smitty just might carry a switchblade after all? Can I take the chance and then wind up in that huge Union Hospital down the street where there's probably a special wing just for switchblade victims?

I decide to ask my mother for a ride tomorrow morning. I avoided the problem today when my father and I drove straight to school to fix my classes. I can avoid it another day if she'll drive me this time. We have two cars and she seems so anxious for things to work out here for me that I'm sure she'll do it. I'll just need to figure out an excuse for why I need the ride.

Maybe I'll be intentionally late. Or maybe I'll just tell her the truth. I don't like either idea. I'll have to come up with something else.

So I'm 0-for-1. Next up, Jessie Stackhouse.

I don't see a solution there, either. He's just really good, really tough. I've got to work on my moves some more, figure out what it will take to make him miss me, and hold onto the ball for dear life when I can't. If I can't beat him for a touchdown or even an extra two yards, I just need to make sure he doesn't make me fumble.

That makes me 0-for-2. Just about right for a country bumpkin like me.

But then I do figure out why I dropped so many passes. And this is big enough, important enough, to make me satisfied to go 1-for-3.

The problem is with that ugly helmet. Not that it's ugly, old, or old-fashioned with its leather exterior. Just that it's so big. Not just big, actually. On my small head, it's *huge*. And because of that—because the fit is the exact opposite of snug—it wobbles when I turn to look for the ball or when I make any kind of move at all. And when it shifts, it blocks my vision for a split second until it returns back to its stationary position.

Because of the helmet, it's as if every time I go out for a pass, I've got Green Bay Packers All-Pro cornerback Herb Adderly putting his hand right in front of my eyes.

It's so obvious that I feel like a total moron for not noticing it right away. But I'd never worn a helmet or any football equipment before. It all felt so bulky and strange, the huge shoulder pads, the clunky cleats, the constant taste of the mouthpiece's plastic in my mouth. And of course, in Plainfield, I'd never been tackled, or had to worry about getting tackled by a monster like Jessie Stackhouse.

Those are the excuses for not figuring it out right away. But they're just excuses. I suspect, no matter what my father says, that I really am just a dumb hick, a *very* dumb one. Even if I'm now taking accelerated English and French.

So the next day before practice, I walk up to Luke Scanlon, the team manager who handed out my equipment. He's standing outside the coaches' offices, leaning against the drab tan-colored wall. I tell him I need a new helmet.

When I explain why, he scratches his big gut and looks down at me like I'm a bug. "Go away, kid," he says.

I blink. What's it to him to get me a good helmet? It's not costing him anything. "But I need a new one," I say. "The one I got is too big for me."

"Yeah, I know," he says. "You look pretty funny out there. Like your head is bigger than your body." But he doesn't move. He just stands there, arms crossed in front of his flabby chest, leaning against the wall.

"But it's making me drop passes—"

"Kid, don't waste my time," he says, and steps so close I can smell onions on his breath. The top of my head doesn't even reach his shoulders. "You ain't making this team even if I give you Gale Sayers' helmet." Sayers is the Chicago Bears running back who led the NFL in rushing last year, and with his kick returns added, set a record for all-purpose yards.

"But—"

"Kid, I'm busy," he says and bumps his big gut against my chest. "Get out of here!"

I walk to my locker, oblivious to everyone around me, my head spinning at the thought that I'm so bad I'm not even worth a proper-fitting helmet.

I put my uniform on, head out to the field, and under the hot sun in a cloudless sky break into a fresh sweat even before the first jumping jack. But when the oversized helmet slides down to block my view on the first passing drill, I don't hold my silence.

"Labelle, get over here!" Coach Callahan hollers, a vein bulging out of his forehead as his face turns red with frustration. "You've got worse hands than a goddamned lineman!"

For a moment, the words get caught in my throat. It's not my way to ever say anything back to a coach, but I know that if I don't speak up, I'm going to get cut.

"Coach," I manage before my throat gets tight and I can't say anything more.

"*What*?" He's furious and the practice has barely even started.

I take a deep breath and force myself to speak. "It's the helmet," I say. "It's too big. It moves around and blocks my view."

He stares at me, hands on hips, and rolls his eyes. "You're telling me *the helmet* is why you can't catch a goddamned pass? Excuses are for—" Then he looks at me more closely. He grabs my facemask and wobbles the helmet around. He shakes his head and swears loudly. "Scanlon!"

Luke Scanlon, the team manager who'd made fun of my request for a new helmet half an hour ago, rushes over from the sideline. He's wearing a gray LEHS T-shirt and matching shorts.

"Get this kid a helmet that fits him," Coach Callahan says to him. "What the hell were you thinking, giving him that monstrosity? It'd be big even for Moose." Moose Mahoney is a huge offensive tackle, easily over two hundred pounds. Not all muscle—lots of flab actually—but huge.

Luke Scanlon gives me a dirty look and silently starts walking toward the school.

"Run!" Coach Callahan yells and the chubby team manager breaks into a labored jog.

"Labelle, get back in line and do the best you can until Scanlon gets back out here," Coach Callahan says.

I run to the back of the line and for the first time in the two practices, I find myself next to Jimmy Keenan. Yesterday, I was matched against him with me playing cornerback to his flanker and I broke up the pass, but we haven't shared a word since my father got my classes all changed.

"Hey," I say, seeing that there are another ten guys ahead of us in line. A word or two should be okay.

Keenan gives me a cold look. "What happened to you? I thought you were pulling another hooky scam until I saw you out here."

"I was supposed to be in different classes," I say. "My parents got them changed."

"Didn't belong with us dummies?" Keenan says without even looking at me.

"It's not like—"

"Least I'm smart enough to know when my damned helmet doesn't fit," Keenan says, and turns his back, ending the conversation.

I think for a fleeting second that back in Plainfield, I couldn't make an enemy. Here, except for Anna, I can't seem to make a friend.

CHAPTER 23

I've made up my mind. I don't care if I get beat up. Unless I hear the click of a switchblade, I'm not giving up my lunch money. I can't imagine that a punch in the face from Smitty will hurt any worse than getting tackled by Jessie Stackhouse.

It's time to stick up for myself and stop imagining that everyone around me is more dangerous than they really are.

I just hope I'm right.

But before I deal with Smitty, I've got something I need to get off my chest with Rick Cassidy, the kid who I'd *thought* was being nice when he stifled his friends' discouraging football comments.

If I'm going to fight, I might as well fight 'em all.

So I walk up to the bus stop, holding three textbooks against my left hip, and make a beeline for Cassidy, who is surrounded by the same four friends who were there on the first day of school. He's talking and the others are in rapt attention.

"What did I ever do to you?" I ask Cassidy.

He can't be bothered to answer my question. He just laughs.

"You knew football practices had already started," I say. "But you couldn't be bothered to tell me. Not only that, but you made sure none of your buddies did either. Just to be a jerk."

The words surprise me. I'd have never said anything like this back in Plainfield. Lynn is changing me already.

Never come out, the way you went in.

But I know I'm right. I've replayed that first day through my head multiple times.

"Maybe I like being a jerk," Cassidy says, confirming my suspicions. "Especially to cocky little midgets like you. What're you going to do about it?"

He takes a step forward so he's right in my face, but since he's close to a foot taller than me, it's his chest that's in my face.

"I'm not doing a thing," I say, and take half a step back. "You can whip me seven days a week, but I just thought we might be teammates some day on the basketball court, so it might be good to clear the air."

Cassidy frowns. "Teammates?" He shakes his head. "Ain't no way we're ever going to be teammates."

"Don't be so sure," I say, and walk away from the group and stand by myself, ten yards away.

The five of them snicker and shake their heads as they look my way.

The bus arrives soon after. As usual, the girls take the front rows while the oldest and toughest boys go all the way back, most of them lighting their cigarettes before they even sit down. I take a seat all by myself as far forward as possible on the right side and wonder if perhaps Smitty will leave me alone.

But the bus has barely taken off when he slides in beside me.

"Missed you the last two days," he says.

I say nothing. My palms feel moist and clammy. My mouth, dry.

"Were you trying to avoid me?" Smitty asks.

My heart hammers as I shake my head.

"I think you were," he says, "but it's okay." He smiles. "You can pay me today for the days you missed. So that'll be a dollar fifty."

I don't move an inch. Every muscle in my body is tensed.

"This time, I'm forgiving you the interest," he says, "but in the future it'll be a quarter for each day you're late. I don't like having to chase after what's mine." He puts his hand out. "Now pay up."

I notice the odor of stale sweat upon him. His breath reeks of cigarette smoke.

I'm even more sure now of my decision not to pay even though I know I'm going to get the tar beaten out of me. Smitty's talk of paying for missed days and interest confirms what I had assumed. He was never going to be satisfied. In fact, for him, the thrill of seeing fear in my eyes was probably more rewarding than the money itself.

Well, he won't see that anymore. Even if I feel terror all the way down to the pit of my stomach.

"I can't," I say in as calm and even a tone as I can manage.

Smitty's eyes narrow. "I don't think I heard you right."

"I can't," I say firmly. In truth, "I won't" is probably far more accurate because I have two dollars in my pants pocket and another fifty cents inside my shoe just in case, but I figure "can't" is an easier refusal for Smitty to hear.

I see him clench his fist, so I get ready.

He pivots and throws a hard left-handed punch at my face. I block it with my forearm, letting my textbooks clatter to the floor.

He winds up again and like a machine gun fires five punches. I've got both my fists raised, trying to protect my face, but he's too big and too strong. I can't block them all.

One punch lands solidly against my cheekbone. The pain radiates all through that side of my face and I realize I'm yelling a mixture of "Leave me alone!" and "Help!" as I flail about, trying to fight back.

Smitty keeps up until one of the girls screams.

"What's going on back there?" the driver yells. "Hey, knock it off!" The bus slows and pulls over to the side.

Smitty gives me one last shove, jumps up from the seat and walks, hunched over, to the back of the bus. The screamer falls silent.

The bus driver stands up and scans the bus, both hands on his hips. He looks about sixty, is bald, and wears glasses. He has a big paunch that hangs over his belt. In a fight, he'd lose to almost everyone on the bus, except for the girls and maybe me.

But the bus has fallen silent beneath his gaze.

As he takes a few steps toward the middle of the bus, I bend over and pick up my books. I run my fingertips across my cheek. I don't think anything is broken and I don't see any blood, but it does sting.

"No fighting on this bus," the driver says. "You hear me?"

No one says a word.

"I'll look the other way if you're gonna smoke the butts," he says. He pats a package of Winstons in his shirt pocket. "I've got the weakness myself. But no fighting."

He stares at every last one of us, stopping for a few seconds at me.

"Piss off, old man!" comes a voice from in back, followed by a chorus of laughter.

The driver pretends not to hear it, heads back to his seat, and we continue on to school in an odd mixture of awkward silence and forced laughter.

When I step off the bus, I rush toward the main entrance, its three doors feeling like a finish line.

But Smitty catches me.

He flings me against a concrete column, its abrasive surface scraping my palm. He grabs my shirt and pins me hard against the column, which is cold and rough against my back.

"You made a very bad mistake," he says, his eyes narrowed. "Very bad. You better have the money tomorrow."

Then he spits in my face, knocks my books to the ground, and heads inside.

CHAPTER 24

By my second-period History class, I've developed a good shiner without knowing it. I can't tell from the stares and smirks sent my way as I walk the hallways from first-period English, because getting stared at and laughed at are nothing new.

But when I walk into History, Anna and Cindy Murphy stop their conversation, gasp, and stare at me with their jaws dropped, and simultaneously ask, "What happened to you?"

Everyone else who's already in their seats, which is about half of the twenty-five students, turns to stare.

"Whaddya mean?" I ask, once again proving what a dolt I am. I hardly needed to be Sherlock Holmes to figure it out.

"Your face," Cindy says. She's a pretty girl with long, black hair, a perfect complexion, and always shows up stylishly dressed. Today she's wearing a flowery blue blouse with gray slacks. Guys are always looking at her because even though she's just a freshman, she has a junior or senior's figure. She doesn't flaunt her chest the way some girls like her might, but it's hard not to notice.

"Your eye," Anna says. "You've got a pretty bad black eye."

"It's awful," Cindy says.

"But you should see the other guy," Jeff Goodwin announces to a smattering of laughter. Jeff is as close to a class clown as we get in the tough courses. He can be a funny guy, but he knows when to be serious.

"How bad is it?" I ask, touching my fingertips to the tender flesh.

"I think you're gonna die," Jeff says.

"Take a look," Anna says, and fishes a small mirror out of her pocketbook, then hands it to me.

I look at myself in the mirror and wince. Puffy, purple flesh circles my left eye, the lid already blackening. I look hideous.

"Don't bother coming to the next dance," Jeff says. "There won't be a girl in the school that'll be seen with you."

"That isn't true," Anna says. Then her eyes open just a little in surprise and her face flushes.

"Thanks," I say to her, both for what she's just said and for the mirror, which I hand back, and slide into my chair.

"You *better* come to the dance," Cindy says.

"You'd dance with Frankenstein over there?" Jeff asks, pointing an index finger in my direction.

"Well," Cindy says with a coy smile, "if I weren't going out with someone."

"Who?" Sue Fitzgerald asks, her gray eyes alive for the first time in the conversation. She's got long brown hair, braces on her teeth, and is wearing a light blue dress.

Cindy just grins broadly. "It's a secret. For now, at least."

"Phil Montague?" Sue guesses.

"It's a secret!" Cindy says.

"It's such a secret," Jeff says, "her boyfriend doesn't even know."

We all laugh, but Sue isn't done yet. "Jimmy Keenan!" she says, and cocks her head, waiting for confirmation.

"I wish!" Cindy says, and rolls her eyes. She nods in Anna's direction. "Anna's the lucky one."

A crimson tinge creeps up Anna's neck and fills her cheeks. She glances at me and then looks away.

"What's Keenan got that I don't have?" Jeff asks with a grin that says he knows the answer.

"How about everything," Cindy says.

"Yeah, tell me about it," Sue says with a wistful sigh.

The bell rings to start class, and Anna gives me an apologetic look. I force a smile that I don't feel.

*

After classes, I hustle down to the gym for football practice. I step through the swinging doors into the locker room and am immediately assaulted by the loudest rock 'n' roll music I've ever heard. The beat seems to make the walls vibrate and the singer is singing words I can't even decipher.

I don't know much about popular music since there weren't many radio stations near Plainfield. In fact, I don't know *anything* about popular music. If I was listening to the radio, it was to catch the broadcasts of the Red Sox, Celtics, or Patriots. I never listened to music, and the only albums in the house were my mother's country music favorites. Patsy Cline, Loretta Lynn, Hank Williams, and George Jones. Oh, and Elvis.

But I don't recognize this music at all.

Later, I learn that this is the team's stereo system that's playing and it'll be like this before every practice. The only reason it wasn't blaring the previous days was because it was in the shop getting fixing, probably from being played too loud.

Over the noise, Scanlon hollers my name. "Hey, *Rabbit!*" he yells with a sneer before I'm halfway to my locker. For him, the nickname is a way to ridicule me, not a way to show any friendship. "Did your girlfriend beat you up? Or was it your mom?"

I turn away, but he yells, "Don't walk away, *Rabbit*. Coach Callahan wants to see you."

Scanlon smirks and waves me good-bye.

My heart sinks.

No.

If they were going to cut me, why didn't they do it after yesterday's practice? Why give me hope all of last night and today that I still had one more practice to prove my worth only to give me the ax now? The timing feels cruel. Sadistic.

My breathing becomes shallow, as if I've just been sucker punched, which is exactly how I feel.

Feeling a bitter taste in my mouth, I push through the swinging doors to the coaches' offices and knock on Coach Callahan's door.

"Come in!" he hollers, and I step inside.

"Whoa!" he says. "What the hell happened to you?"

All I can think of is Scanlon waving me good-bye, so I don't even realize that Coach is referring to my black eye.

"Scanlon said you wanted to see me," I say. And all my emotions come tumbling out. "I know I don't have any experience and I'm little, but if you'll just give me a chance for another couple days, I can show you—"

Coach holds his hand up in a stopping gesture. "What are you talking about?"

I blink, confused. "I thought you were cutting me."

Coach laughs. "What made you think that?"

"Well…Scanlon…um, I don't know."

Coach Callahan leans back in his seat. "Did you get that shiner at practice yesterday?"

The change in topics surprises me. "No," I say. I don't really want to say anything more, so I stay silent.

Coach cocks his head. "Your dad?"

The question startles me so badly, I say more than I intended. "Oh, no!" I say. "Just a kid on the bus. Tried to take my lunch money."

"Did you give it to him?"

"No."

"Good!" he says. "Who was it?"

I look away from Coach Callahan's peering eyes. "I don't want to get him in trouble."

"Who was it?"

I shrug.

"Anyone on this team?"

I shake my head.

"It's probably because you're the new kid and you're little," he says. "He doesn't know how tough you are. Doesn't know you're on the football team. And no one messes with anyone on the football team."

I nod dumbly, then it suddenly registers what Coach Callahan has said. *On the football team.* Could he really have meant what I think he just said? A Fourth of July fireworks display explodes inside my head, loud, and bright in every color of the rainbow. I try to stop the grin broadening across my face.

"Did you just say what I think you said?" I ask.

A grin forms at the corners of Coach's mouth. "What do you think I said?"

"That I made the team?"

He answers by fishing inside his desk and pulling out a white binder with BULLDOGS PLAYBOOK in black magic marker across the front. He tosses it at me, and I catch it.

"Guard it with your life. Have it memorized by Monday."

"Yes!" I say, whooping for joy, holding the playbook against my chest.

"You're still on probation." Coach Callahan points to the playbook. "If you'd dropped it when I tossed it to you, I'd have asked for it back."

My stupid grin fades only the slightest amount.

"Now get ready for practice and don't make me regret this decision."

"Yes, sir!" I say, almost in a shout, and turn to leave.

"Oh, and by the way, if the kid who gave you that shiner touches you again, you tell him that Coach Callahan will bring the entire football team to that bus stop and make him wish he was never born."

*

Coach Callahan may have wished he'd waited one more practice to make his decision. With a helmet that actually let me see the ball as it was coming to me, I was doing much better catching passes. Not quite as good as in the backyard with no equipment on at all, but pretty good.

But the same "run to daylight" drill that got me in trouble yesterday gets me again. And once again, it's Jessie Stackhouse who proves that he's a man, and I'm just a little boy.

The first four times through the drill, I get through untouched, twice because the offensive lineman opens up a huge hole that I run right through, and the other two times because the defender gets a shot at me, but I fake him out and get past him unscathed.

But the fifth time, I'm up against Jessie Stackhouse, and my blocker isn't one of the two or three guys who at least has a chance to control him.

Sure enough, just like yesterday, he tosses his blocker aside with little effort and then as I unsuccessfully try to fake him to the outside, he drives his helmet into my chest. I've got the ball pinned hard to my ribs, determined not to fumble again, and I succeed in that respect, but he drives me backwards while picking me up off my feet, and then slams me into the ground so hard he not only rattles every bone in my body, he knocks the wind out of me.

Uhhhhhhhhhhhhhhhhhhhhhhhhhh.

That's the sound escaping from my mouth, one constant, agonized exhalation.

Uhhhhhhhhhhhhhhhhhhhhhhhhhh.

I stare up at the clear blue sky and fight back the panic as I yank out my mouthpiece. I struggle to draw in a breath, but can only continue the sound of exhaling even though there's no air left in my lungs.

Uhhhhhhhhhhhhhhhhhhhhhhhhhh.

Coach Callahan suddenly appears over me, blocking out most of the sky. I'm ready for him to yank my helmet off and give me mouth-to-mouth, his whiskers scraping against my skin as he blows air back into my lungs.

Then he'll probably call me a baby and tell me to get off the field. But I won't care. I just want to breathe.

Uhhhhhhhhhhhhhhhhhhhhhhhhhh.

Instead, he grabs me by the front of the jersey, lifts me off the ground, and drops me. My teeth slam against each other; my mouthpiece flaps

OFFSIDE

against the helmet's facemask. I lie there stunned, my panicked brain trying to process what the coach has just done.

Then, as he reaches for me again, I suck in a quick gasp of air. And then another and another, each one a bigger gulp to fill my tortured lungs.

I can breathe!

Relief floods through me even as my chest awakens to the agony of the hit, pain radiating out from my ribs. Groaning, I climb unsteadily to my feet, shake my head to clear the cobwebs, and slip the mouthpiece back into place. Its dull, plastic taste once again fills my mouth.

Jessie Stackhouse towers over me, concern etched on his face. "You okay?"

I nod, not quite ready to speak yet, just happy I can breathe again, at least momentarily grateful for that most basic bodily function.

"Sit out the rest of this drill," Coach Callahan says and turns away.

Embarrassed, I feel as though I've let the coach down. He showed his faith in me, giving me the playbook and telling me I've made the team, not to mention his offer of protection against Smitty at the bus stop, and what do I do? Lie on the ground making little baby noises because The Big Guy hit me too hard.

I'll be lucky if he doesn't ask for the playbook back after practice.

CHAPTER 25

After practice, I shower and head out to the front of the building where my mom's light blue Ford Fairlane is parked at the far end of the half circle extending in from Goodrich Street. There's a late bus every afternoon for students who get detention or are involved in less time-consuming extracurricular activities than athletic teams, but it's long gone by now. More than twenty cars are lined up in the half circle, most of them with a mother at the wheel, although there is the occasional father. It's a good thing our family has two cars; if I had to wait for my father, I'd be walking three miles home each night.

I toss my gym bag in the back seat along with my books and slide into the front seat. My mother looks up from the book she's reading, *Tai-Pan* by James Clavell. She flashes an automatic smile, and then shrieks.

"What happened to you?" she says, wide-eyed, her hands thrown up to her face. She shakes her head. "This football obsession has got to end. You're just too small. When your father gets home—"

It takes me a few seconds to remember my black eye—even though people have been staring at me all day—and figure out what my mother is reacting to. Since it's the left eye, it's facing right at her in all its purple-and-black glory.

But I no sooner realize why she's so horrified than I react in the exact same way to her words. Back in Plainfield, I was the best athlete in every sport I played. But just three days into football practice, she's saying I'm too small. My heart sinks. And calling football an obsession? Well, maybe she's right about that, I think with a bit of a wry grin that tries to take some of the sting away from her words.

"I'm okay, Mom," I say. I smile. "It looks worse than it is."

"What happened?" she asks again. She leans closer for a better look and her fingertips graze my puffy flesh. She smells of talcum powder, her hands of lemon detergent. "How could this happen with a facemask?"

"It didn't happen at football," I say, and realize that I haven't figured out a script I'm going to follow when telling my parents about the fight on the bus. But right now, my attention is elsewhere. "And I'm not too little. I made the team."

"You did?" She wraps her arms around me. "Well, of course you did! You're Rabbit Labelle! Congratulations!"

She pulls away, confusion replacing the happiness on her face. "But what happened to you? You look awful!"

"Can we wait to talk about it until Dad gets home?" I ask, in part so I only have to explain things once, but also to give me time to figure out what I'll say.

Disappointment and hurt clouds my mother's face. She purses her lips. "Why can't you just tell me?"

And I figure she's right.

Let my father be the last to know.

*

When we get home, I look in the mirror and have to admit I'm a sight to see. My black eye is more purple than black, but it circles the eye socket and fills the eyelid. I can see fine, which is a bit surprising because the eye is so puffy, but I sure am ugly. Jeff Goodwin was right. If I ever went to a dance looking like this, no girl would get within a hundred feet of me.

But my dad doesn't even notice right away. He comes bustling in at 8:30, walks right past me in the front room, where I'm sitting in the middle of the sofa, studying my playbook while listening to the Red Sox on the radio. Dad continues on to the dining room where I hear him set his briefcase on the table.

"Did you see Rabbit?" my mother asks, making me look up from the Halfback Right Option page in the playbook.

"No, not really," my father says. "I'll catch up with him in a second, but I'm famished. It actually was tough getting out of work this early. I'll have to run back in tomorrow, and maybe Sunday, too. There's just so much to do. My new boss is impressed, but it's like I'm doing the work of three people. It'll be worth it, but—"

"You need to see your son," my mother says firmly.

"Yeah, sure," my father says in a tone that sounds annoyed that she interrupted his play-by-play of his work day. "Just give me a second."

In a bit, he pokes his head around the corner. "How the Sox doing?"

With George "Boomer" Scott already on second base, Rico Petrocelli rips a liner into left field. We both stare wordlessly at the transistor radio I've propped on the arm of the sofa as Ken Coleman announces that Scott has scored easily and Petrocelli has pulled into second base with a double.

"That ties it up, 2-2," I say tonelessly, and my father nods.

"What inning?"

In fairness to him, my black eye is facing away from him, so he probably can't even see it. But it also feels so typical for him.

Mom enters the room and glares at my father, hands on her hips. "Andre, look at your son."

I turn to my father so there's no missing the ugliness of my black eye.

"Oh my God!" he says. "Who did this to you?" He looks at me with fire in his eyes. "It was the *niggers*, wasn't it?"

"Andre!" my mother exclaims. "There's no need for that!"

"They're savages!" my father says, his breath suddenly heaving. "That's what they are. There's no need to sugarcoat the truth." He shakes his head. "I did *everything* I could to avoid—"

"It was a white kid," I say.

The words stop my father in his tracks. For a moment, he's speechless.

I want to tell him—the cruel, angry part of me wants to tell him—that it wasn't a black kid or a white kid who did this to me.

It was my own father.

My dear old dad just couldn't say no to his beloved promotion, so he's tossed me out into the jungle of Smittys and all the other kids who don't like me for reasons I can't comprehend. And if I'd seen even a single switchblade or heard the terrifying click of its blade opening, I'd say it. But since Lynn hasn't been quite as bad as I had expected—I still hate it with all my heart, but it's no New York City with its Mau Maus—I don't let fly that verbal dagger to my father's heart.

"A white kid?" my father says. "Why?"

He says it as if he'd understand completely why a black kid would beat me up, but he finds it incomprehensible that "one of our own kind" would do it.

"He wanted my lunch money," I say.

"Next time, just give it to him," he says. "It isn't worth it."

"I did that the first day, but it was never going to stop."

"What's his name?" my father asks, his jaw set. "We'll take care of this." He looks at my mother. "I'll go in to the school and talk to the principal about it. Get the kid thrown out or at least suspended. The principal is a reasonable man. I'm sure we can work this out."

Then he shakes his head in frustration. "But I can't do it on Monday or Tuesday. I have early meetings that I can't miss. They're just crucial. Marie, for now you'll need to bring Rabbit to school. There's no need to subject Rabbit to this violence."

"I'm taking the bus," I say, and my father almost gets whiplash turning back to stare at me. Barely realizing I'm doing it, I clench and unclench my fists. "My football coach has a message for the kid that I need to deliver."

"What's that?"

"That I made the team and he'd better leave me alone."

My father's eyebrows shoot up and a look of happiness flashes over his face. "You made the team? Congratulations! And they're all going to stand up for you? That's great! I knew this would all work out."

I sigh. This is why I wouldn't have even told my father the good news if I hadn't already told my mother. I'd have kept it from him until I had no choice. Because now he's using it as proof that sacrificing his family for his almighty promotion was really quite reasonable and now we're all going to live happily ever after.

If I didn't love football so much, I'd almost wish I hadn't made the team.

*

The Red Sox lose to the Yankees that night, 5-2, to end a three-game winning streak and fall a half game behind the Minnesota Twins and Detroit Tigers. But to tell the truth, I barely pay attention to the game unless the Sox or the Yankees get a couple runners on base.

Mostly, I stare at the playbook, digesting the differences between a "Red Screen Right" and a "Gray Power Left." I'm supposed to learn the split end and flanker positions first, which are pretty similar except that the flanker doesn't set up on the line of scrimmage like an end does. Then, once I've got the wide-out positions down pat, I'll add halfback. Coach Callahan thinks I'm too little to play running back—he thinks that this little Rabbit will get torn to shreds by the other teams' huge greyhounds—but he wants me to learn it just for some possible emergency.

What I think, though, is that you don't really understand a play until you know what *everyone* is doing. It's not enough to know that as a split end I'm supposed to run ten yards and then cut for the post if in one play that's to serve as a decoy and draw my defender out of the zone so the running back can break a big gain, but in other play that same post route is an actual passing play with the split end as either the first or second option.

So I give myself the extra time as I study each play to make sure I understand what's really happening at the other positions. I hope to have every position memorized by the end of the weekend, know the playbook so completely that if one of the offensive lineman says in the huddle, "What am I supposed to do?" I'll be able to tell him.

But I need to learn my own position first, so I concentrate on split end and flanker as I flip through the one-hundred-plus-page playbook.

I read the play, then close my eyes and quiz myself on what my responsibilities are for that play and the one before it, and the one before that. When the Red Sox game is over, I turn off the radio, and head up to my bedroom, where I keep studying some more until my eyes just won't stay awake any longer.

I lay the playbook on my nightstand and set the alarm so I don't miss Saturday's ten a.m. practice.

*

It's a good thing I did all that studying, because most of Saturday's practice is spent going through the plays. The varsity plays its first game next Friday night, and the JVs play three nights later on Monday. Except for the big Thanksgiving Day game against cross-town rival Lynn Classical, the varsity plays on every Friday night and the JVs on every Monday.

So now the percentage of drills designed to simply improve our skills has dropped off, as has the participation of the backups, so the team's starters can get their timing down. As a result, a lot of us spend most of the practice standing around watching until finally the JV players are sent down to the far end of the football part of the huge open field. Not all the way to where the soccer team is practicing, but to the far football goalposts.

All the JV players except Jessie Stackhouse. He's no longer one of us; he's been promoted to play full-time with the varsity. He may only be a freshman, but he's no five-nothin', hundred-nothin'. He'll be slamming his 170 pounds of rock-hard muscle into someone else.

Even though I've been thinking of new fakes to use on Stackhouse, I can't say that I'll miss him.

CHAPTER 26

On Monday, I walk to the bus stop full of confidence despite my shiner having reached the peak of its ugliness: a mix of purple, black, yellow, and even some red. I'm going to settle things once and for all, but do so in a graceful, diplomatic way. There's no way Smitty can keep beating on me when I've got the entire football team on my side, but I don't want to humiliate him and earn another enemy for life.

I just want to be left alone.

So I walk past Cassidy and the other kids, who snicker at my looks, and walk up to Smitty, where he's standing with three of his tough-guy friends. They're all seventeen or eighteen and are smoking cigarettes, their biceps bulging as they cross their arms and wait for me.

"Smitty, could I talk to you privately?" I ask, my voice shaking despite my best efforts to keep it even.

Smitty narrows his eyes. "Who you calling Smitty?"

"I..." I swallow hard and lick my lips. "I thought that was your name. I thought someone called you that."

He takes a long drag on his cigarette. The tip glows brightly, then he blows smoke in my direction. "My friends call me that," he says. "A little piece of turd like you doesn't call me Smitty."

I nod and try to relax my breathing. My heart is hammering worse that at the end of a full session of wind sprints at practice.

"I'm sorry," I say. "I didn't know."

"There's a lot you don't know." His eyes bore into mine.

"Could I speak to you? Speak to you privately?"

He shakes his head, no. He runs a hand through his thick red hair, then spits on the ground, coming within inches of my shoes. "You got something to say? Say it."

I realize with a sudden sick, sour sensation in my gut that this is going to blow up in my face. There's no way I can say anything to protect myself in front of his friends without humiliating him.

Why hadn't I seen this coming? *Of course* he wasn't going to talk privately to me. Thinking he still held the upper hand, he was going to dish out the humiliation for his buddies' enjoyment.

I swallow hard again. "This was a bad idea. Sorry, my mistake. Maybe another—"

Smitty takes two quick steps toward me, grabs me by my short-sleeved blue shirt, and lifts me off the ground. "What you got to say to me, squirt?" he says as my shirt begins to tear. "It better be, 'Here's your money, sir!'"

Smitty takes two more steps and pins me against a telephone pole. A rough splinter slides into the skin of my back. My books clatter to the ground. I can barely breathe.

"What you got to say to me, kid?" Smitty asks, gritting his teeth. His nostrils flare. He smells of stale sweat and smoke. His eyes are on fire.

"I made the football team," I manage to blurt out. "And the coach told me to tell you to leave me alone. Or else, he'd get the entire team here to protect me."

Smitty drops me to the ground and pins his knee against my chest. Then the sound I've been fearing since Randall's story around the campfire explodes in my ears.

Click!

The terrifying sound is both soft and loud at the same time. Then I feel warm, sharp steel against my throat.

Smitty's eyes are crazed. "What do you think I am, stupid?"

I can't say a word.

"I'm asking you!" Smitty says, his face contorted in fury.

"No," I manage to croak.

A girl's high-pitched scream shatters the surrounding silence.

"Don't try to tell me that a freaking midget like you made the football team," he says. "I ain't stupid. Don't talk to me like I am."

My eyes feel like they're bugging out of their sockets. I can't speak a word.

"I don't see no football team, do you?" Smitty says.

I just stare into his crazed eyes and hope Smitty doesn't increase the switchblade's pressure on my throat.

"*Do you?*" he screams.

"No," I say in a hoarse whisper.

"I didn't think so," Smitty says.

An adult voice yells, "What's going on?" from what feels like far, far away.

In one quick motion, Smitty stands up and spits in my face.

I climb unsteadily to my feet and look about. Everyone is staring at me, including the man who may have saved my life. Broad shouldered and in his twenties, he's standing beside a rusted-out, gray box-shaped car with dents all along the side closest to me. It's a car that may even be uglier than my black eye, but to me it looks as attractive as a Corvette.

"Are you okay?" the man asks, and I foolishly look around to make sure he's talking to me. How stupid can I be? Who else could he be talking to?

I look at Smitty, who appears calm and relaxed, as if nothing has happened, except that his red hair is askew. He's hidden the switchblade and doesn't even have a cigarette between his lips anymore.

Just waiting for the bus, sir, is how he looks.

I lick my lips, nod to the man dumbly, and bend over to pick up my books.

"Are you sure?" the man says.

I look at how close Smitty remains—just two strides away—and I'm not sure of anything. I take one step back, then two.

And then I whirl away and make a mad dash back to my house, separating my books into my two hands. It's like I'm carrying two footballs as I race for the end zone.

Only this isn't for six points.

This is for my life.

I glance over my shoulder and see that no one is coming after me, but I don't slow down. I reach the brick walkway to our house, bound up the steps, and burst through the front door.

My mother emerges from the kitchen, wide-eyed and looking like she wants to scream.

"I need a ride," I say in jagged breaths.

"What happened?"

"Every day," I say. "Every morning, I'm going to need a ride."

So much for settling things once and for all.

*

It was all my fault. I handled it all wrong and inadvertently provoked the whole incident. But that's what happens when you put a country bumpkin into Lynn, Lynn, City of Sin.

In fact, I'm just like the characters on the *Beverly Hillbillies* TV show: Jed Clampett, Jethro, Granny, and Ellie Mae. A bunch of dumb yokels trying to fit in where they don't belong.

That's me. Only unlike the TV show, this isn't funny.

By the time I change my shirt and we get in Mom's car, I'm not sure if I know up from down anymore.

I'm not even sure anymore that Smitty had a switchblade. I never saw it. Sure, I heard the *click*—or thought I heard the *click*—but maybe that was just the same hyperactive imagination that has expected Nicky Cruz and the Mau Maus on every street corner along with all of Lynn's prostitutes, none of which I've seen.

And that warm blade against my neck? From the passenger seat, I turn the rearview mirror to look at my neck, but see no puncture wound, not even the slightest scrape.

"Rabbit!" my mother says in what's close to a holler. "Talk to me!"

I realize that she's been saying this over and over for a long time.

I look into her eyes, choke out, "I hate it here!" and bawl my eyes out like a little baby.

*

Was there really a switchblade up against my throat?

Of course there was.

But maybe there wasn't. Maybe it was really all in my head, planted there by Randall McLeod around that campfire with the flames sparkling high and the sweet smell of pine in the air, back in the days when I had friends and my biggest worry was whether we could get enough guys together for a backyard football game.

This is what I spend most of the day thinking about. I manage to avoid looking foolish in English, but in History and Math I get called on and don't even know what the question is.

"Could you repeat the question, please?" I have to say, but even when the teacher repeats the question, I have no idea what she's talking about. I'm going to have to work extra hard tonight on my homework to make up for this, but I wonder if my concentration will be any better then.

Why would it?

I wonder how long it will take me to get busted down to Jimmy Keenan and, as he called them, the other "dummies."

*

Fortunately, the mental fog I've been in all day lifts when I enter the locker room to get ready for practice. The music blares and its pounding, pulsating beat gets my heart pumping. I've learned enough about music these last few days, escaping my total ignorance, to know that this is the Rolling Stones that are playing, their lead singer is Mick Jagger, and the song is "I Can't Get No (Satisfaction)."

I have no idea why Mick Jagger can't get any satisfaction, but the song has got me so pumped up I'm ready to run through a brick wall or take on Jessie Stackhouse. Which, I guess, are kind of the same thing.

It's crazy, of course, but that's just how I feel. Perhaps my mother's concerns that rock 'n' roll is of the devil are right. But I like how it makes me feel.

No, I *love* how it makes me feel.

The locker room smells awful and wonderful at the same time. It stinks of stale sweat and unwashed equipment, but those odors also have become familiar and comfortable.

More like home than home itself.

So I get dressed with a smile on my face, basking in the knowledge that I'm a member of this football team, the Lynn English High School Bulldogs. JVs, of course, but I'm only a freshman. In a couple of years, I'll be in the varsity starting lineup, maybe catching the game-winning pass to beat Lynn Classical in the Thanksgiving Day game at Manning Bowl.

A dozen or so of us head outside at the same time. We walk carefully down the stairs, our cleats making it feel like we're on ice, then we exit the building and our cleats clack on the asphalt rhythmically until we reach the grassy field.

I'm a part of this. I'm really part of the team.

As it turns out, Jimmy Keenan and I get matched up against each other almost the entire JV part of practice. He's first-string flanker and cornerback, and I'm second-string. So when the starting offense is running through its plays, I'm at cornerback, covering Keenan.

At first, I struggle. The first few plays are runs, and Keenan blocks me with ease, using his size advantage—six inches and at least forty pounds—to knock me to the ground with gusto.

"Still think you're too good for us?" he says the first time, and then, "You suck!" the second.

But then the offense switches to some passing plays and I seize the upper hand. I give Keenan one quick bump at the line of scrimmage and then I'm stride-for-stride with him as he runs his route. The quarterback, Chris Higgins, tries to hit him on a post play, but I easily knock the pass down. Same thing with a fly pattern where Keenan just runs straight as fast as he can. And when Higgins tries to hit him on a quick out, I step between them and pick off the pass. In a game, I'd easily run the interception back for a touchdown, but here I just run ten yards before Coach Callahan blows the whistle.

I flip the ball back to Higgins, a smile forming on my face. No one else can see it behind my facemask, covered up as it is by my mouth-piece, but it's there, growing wider and wider.

A glow of satisfaction fills me. I can do this. I can be good at this.

"You can't throw that pass!" Callahan yells to Higgins. "What are you, stupid? If the man isn't open, check down!"

Coach Callahan turns to Keenan. "And what's your problem?" Callahan yells. "Can't get any separation on the midget?"

It isn't the first time I've been called a midget and it won't be the last. It's music to my ears.

"Go again!" Callahan yells.

The next five passes all go to the other receiver, a black kid named Charlie Watkins, and three are completed. When Higgins comes back to my side, I'm ready.

Keenan blasts out, anger and frustration in his eyes, and cuts to the post. I'm with him all the way. As the pass floats down, the two of us go up for the ball, but I've got inside position and I pull the ball down and tuck it into my gut as we fall to the ground.

Another interception.

The whistle blows.

"Keenan!" Callahan says in a taunting tone of voice. "Looks like Labelle owns you!"

Jimmy Keenan shoves me from behind and when I turn to look at him, I see clouded eyes filled with hatred. He pulls his mouthpiece out so it just dangles from his facemask.

"Keep your head up, squirt," he says. "This ain't over."

He gets some revenge on a running play, a sweep, where he buries me, lowering his shoulder into my chest and driving me into the ground so hard it seems he's trying to slam me not just into the turf but a few feet beneath it.

But he's far from even, based on how he looks at me when Coach Callahan calls out, "Okay, first team defense, now!"

Keenan lines up at cornerback while the rest of the players who aren't defensive starters line up. Coach assigns us positions on this makeshift offense, and I start at flanker, matched up with Keenan.

But with Higgins going to starting safety, that leaves Russell Blake as our quarterback, and he struggles. Including the three quarterbacks on the varsity, he's fifth-string overall, and he shows it.

I beat Keenan several times, but Russell just can't get me the ball. Once, he so severely underthrows me on a fly pattern when I've got ten yards on Keenan that Keenan is able to pick off the pass. Coach Callahan blows the whistle and Keenan spikes the ball and yells, "Take that!"

But Coach Callahan steps in the next play as quarterback himself and hits me in step on a post pattern and I pull it in and with a two-step lead on Keenan, I race away until Higgins converges from deep safety and takes me down.

I run back to the huddle, flooded with euphoria, ready to go at it again. I flip the ball to Coach Callahan and he gives me a nod. But it's his last throw today as the quarterback. He's proven his point, or found out what he needed to know.

He gathers the defense together and says, "If you guys can't play any better than this, you're in real trouble." He looks at Keenan. "Some of you may not be starters much longer."

CHAPTER 27

Coach Callahan makes the switch on offense the next day. I'm now practicing with the first team.

But so is Jimmy Keenan.

Coach has demoted the split end, Charlie Watkins. The black kid.

I can't understand it. I've faced Charlie in drills and think he's much tougher to defend. Keenan's got a couple inches on him, but Charlie is quicker, makes better cuts in his routes, and in a one-on-one situation makes some of the best fakes on the team. It makes no sense to me at all.

He's got a big Afro, but he's quiet. I've never heard him speak. And he says nothing now, but the look of anger in his eyes rings loud that this isn't fair and he won't take it lying down. He's getting his job back and beware anyone who tries to stop him.

I can't blame him. I'd feel the same way.

Keenan is all smiles, of course, clapping his hands and popping out his mouthpiece and yelling, "Let's go boys!" and "Big game coming up!" as if he's the team captain instead of someone who should have gotten busted down to second string. He even grins at me for a second, as if he's forgiven me for threatening his starting job, until he remembers who I am and looks elsewhere, claps his hands, and yells some more.

But instead of me covering him tight, he's got Tommy Nordstrom, who's too slow to play cornerback, even on JVs. Tommy would have trouble covering his grandmother on a fly route. So Keenan beats him easily, time after time, catching passes, and looking like a star.

Looking better than me.

Because I'm lined up against Charlie Watkins, who may not be a starting split end anymore but is still the best cornerback we've got. When I try beating him with pure speed, he's right there with me. I'm just a tiny bit quicker, but not enough to make a difference.

Or at least I don't know yet how to make it a difference.

Charlie keeps breaking up passes sent my way.

"Get separation, Labelle!" Coach Callahan yells, and I can almost hear him add, "or you'll be back with the scrubs where you belong!"

So I try to make my fakes just a little bit better, run my routes just a little more crisply. And with one or two fakes, I get just a little more separation.

Until I get Charlie to bite on what he thinks is a simple out route, where I run straight for seven or eight yards and then cut for the sideline. Charlie cuts in for an interception as Higgins goes to throw, Charlie certain he's going to pick it off and in a game, run it back for a touchdown. But Higgins just pump fakes, and I break off the sideline route and go deep. I'm wide open when the ball nestles down in my hands and not even the deep safety can get to me.

A touchdown.

Only in practice, to be sure, but after Charlie's stifling coverage, it feels great to have broken one.

"'Bout time you got loose, Labelle!" Coach Callahan yells as I trot back to the huddle and flip him the ball.

Charlie is furious, of course, and slams into me right at the line of scrimmage on the next play. I can't blame him. His coverage had been almost perfect until the one big play. But that's all he can think about.

So after he breaks up the next pass sent my way, I say, "I beat you once, but you're still the best we've got."

He stares at me for a second, then nods.

*

"How's football going?" Mom asks when she picks me up after practice. She always asks this. It's part of a routine we've settled into. I put my gym bag and books into the back seat of the Ford, slide into the front seat, and take the sandwich in the brown paper bag that she hands me. She's made one for me each day this week since I told her on Saturday how famished I felt after practices.

So I unwrap the sandwich from its wax paper and see what it is that I'll be wolfing down while answering the three standard questions, of which "How's football going?" is the first. Today, the sandwich is a fluffernutter, peanut butter with marshmallow fluff.

After swallowing a mouthful, I say, "Great," and take another bite. I don't say any more than that, like tell her whether I'm on the first team offense or defense, because for now, it's enough that I made the team. If I get knocked down to second team split end or flanker, it'll only disappoint her if I've told her I'm on first team, plus I'll have to talk about something that has me depressed. Best just to say, "Great," like I've done every other day.

"How were your classes?" she asks, which is always question two. It's really question one for her, what she really cares about, but since she's only there because of football practice, it's natural for her to ask about that first.

"Fine," I say, and to make her happy, I add, like most every other day, "I've got a bunch of homework, but I'll be able to get it all done."

"Good," she says in a way that, without actually saying it, adds, "Keeping up with your schoolwork is more important than sports."

"Any problems?" she asks with an almost indiscernible quiver in her voice. This is the third automatic question, one added just yesterday, the result of me begging her yesterday morning to drive me to school and never again make me take the bus, the result of me bawling and saying how much I hate this place.

She's been trying to get me to talk about what happened at the bus stop, about Smitty and his switchblade—if there really was a switchblade, because I never really saw it—but I've stuck with what I told her then, which is that a big kid was going to beat me up and take my money.

Which is all she needs to know.

She doesn't need to know about the switchblade, either real or in my imagination thanks to Randall McLeod, Nicky Cruz and the Mau Maus. It'll only worry her and if she tells my father, it'll make him furious that I'm making up such nonsense to sabotage his big promotion.

So like I did yesterday afternoon, and like I'll do every time she picks me up and asks the new automatic question number three, I say, "Nope."

No problems. None at all.

"Rabbit," she says in a tone that sets off all my alarms. "Are you sure you're all right?"

"Yeah," I say. "Sure."

She falls silent for a short while. The only sound is the rustle of the wax paper as I eat my fluffernutter.

She points to it and says, "You know, they make that here."

I frown. "The sandwich?"

"Fluffernutters," she says. "I mean, they make Fluff right here in Lynn. On Empire Street. They invented the fluffernutter to increase sales. It worked, don't you think?"

I shrug. "I guess so."

"So," she says with a hopeful smile, "Lynn isn't all bad, right? Home of the Fluffernutter."

I feel like saying that now I never want another fluffernutter as long as I live, but I don't want to make her angry, so I say nothing.

"How are the Red Sox doing?" she finally asks. She doesn't really care, I don't think. At least not very much, not like me. This is just her way of making conversation.

"They were off yesterday, but they killed the Yankees over the week-end, 7-1 and 9-1."

"Don't say 'killed.' That isn't appropriate," she says, and before I can protest, she asks, "Are they still in first place?"

"A game out, behind the Twins," I say. "The Tigers are two games behind and the White Sox two and a half."

"Two and a half? How can a team be half a game behind?"

I explained this just a week ago, but clearly she didn't get it. "Chicago has played one less game."

"That hardly seems fair."

I look out the window and shake my head. She really didn't get it. "It's just the way the schedule works. They'll all play 162 games by the end of the season."

She nods, satisfied with the explanation, but I wonder if I'll get the same question again in another week.

She bites her lower lip and then asks the question she seems to have been wanting to get to all along. In an overly light and casual tone, she asks, "Are you making any friends on the football team?"

It occurs to me that I've made an enemy in Jimmy Keenan, but I really haven't made any friends yet, perhaps because of Keenan's popularity.

"You've been with them a week now," she adds hopefully.

"Nah, not really," I say.

"It's so unlike you," she says. "I would have thought you'd have friends coming over for supper by now."

"It's not the same as in Plainfield," I say in what must be the understatement of the century. "Maybe because the team had been practicing for two weeks before I showed up. Guys made friends then. I'm the new guy." I almost blurt out about Keenan's resentment even before I took his starting position, but hold my tongue.

"I just notice that some of your teammates share rides home," she says. "If you make some friends on the team—I mean, *when* you make some friends, because I'm sure that you will—then I can talk to their mothers and we can take turns driving you boys home."

I nod. *Yeah, friends would be nice.*

We drive in silence through Wyoma Square, which really isn't a square at all. It's an intersection that must have been designed by a drunk. Broadway branches off in an exaggerated Y-shape, remaining

Broadway on the right while the left side becomes Lynnfield Street. Halfway down the base of the Y, a hard left becomes Parkland Avenue. We pass a TV and electronics store on the right, then both Fauci's Pizza and Nickey's Pizza on the left. On the right, we pass the Tai Hong restaurant in another quarter of a mile and then a small fried clam stand that fronts Sluice Pond, which as ponds go is huge, just like everything else in Lynn, extending for about two-thirds of a mile.

"It's hard for you down here, isn't it?" she says.

I shrug. "Kinda." A few seconds pass, then I add, "I'm okay."

I crack my window open as we drive past St. Mary's Cemetery on the left, massive enough to take up more space than three football fields. Behind it, I spot a foursome walking down the fairway on the Happy Valley golf course. I hear the thwack of a tee shot and then a very loud curse.

Mom hears it, too. Our eyes meet, and we laugh, softly and sadly.

"I love you, Rabbit," she says, and a tear leaks out of the corner of her eye.

"I love you, too, Mom."

"I'm sure everything will work out fine," she says.

I look out my window and say nothing.

CHAPTER 28

The next day at practice, Jimmy Keenan isn't so happy. No more clapping his hands, yelling, and smiling. Coach Callahan busted him down to second string on offense.

Where he belongs.

Charlie Watkins is back starting at one split end and I'm starting at flanker. I'm glad for the team, because this is our best lineup, and I'm glad for Charlie, because this is what he deserves. But I'm a little disappointed that I won't be going head-to-head in these drills with Charlie. Actually, a lot disappointed. He was making me a better player, forcing me to figure out ways to get free other than just pure speed.

I don't even get a chance to go against him when the first-team defense is practicing. He's our top cornerback and Keenan is the other, but when I'm playing flanker on the scout team offense, Coach Callahan is putting me out on Keenan's side, not Charlie's. I hope it's because Coach thinks I might be better than Keenan at cornerback, too, and wants to see us go head-to-head. If so, I'm making a good case for myself because I get free most of the time, even if Russell Blake, the scout team quarterback, can't throw the ball long enough and accurately enough to take advantage of it.

But even though it's fun to go up against Keenan and maybe give myself a better shot at starting on defense, too, it's not like trying to beat

Charlie Watkins. You want to test yourself against the best and when you fall short, you figure out how to get better. How maybe some day you can be the best.

I'm tempted to ask Charlie if he'd like to do some one-on-one drills with me after practice, but to be honest, I'm afraid to try. I've never spoken to a black person before, other than my brief sentence to Charlie after I beat him yesterday, and that was no conversation. Janice Downing, a black girl, is in all my classes except French and Shop, but she's quiet and I don't sit next to her at all. We've never even said hello to each other. Mike Williams, who's also black, is in three of my classes, but I've never spoken to him, either.

Just like with the Puerto Ricans. I haven't spoken to Angela Santos or Wayne Sanchez or Carmen Vasquez. Actually, I don't think any of them really are Puerto Ricans even though that's what my father calls anyone who's Spanish, unless they actually come from Spain. I think Angela's family originally came from Argentina, Wayne from Mexico, and Carmen from one of those other countries in Latin or South America, I can't remember which, but certainly not from Puerto Rico.

Why haven't I spoken to anyone in my classes except the white kids? Has my father's fear of blacks and Puerto Ri—of blacks and *Spanish people*—polluted my own thoughts? Maybe they don't want to talk to me. They probably don't. But why haven't I tried? Has my father's assumption that they hate us filtered into my own thoughts? I don't think so, but I resolve to break the ice with someone who isn't white as soon as I can.

What about Charlie Watkins? Will he think it weird if I ask to do one-on-one drills with him? Will he think I'm not worth his time? Does he hate me just because I'm white?

I decide to try. Not *because* he's black, but because he's such a great player and I think we can help each other get better.

When Coach Callahan blows his whistle and tells us practice is over, I take off my helmet and walk over to Charlie, trying to calm my pounding heart. He still has his helmet on, his mouth guard dangling from the facemask. I glance around to make sure Keenan isn't too close because I don't want him to become even more of an enemy than he already is.

"I'm glad you're back on the starting team," I say, after I see that Keenan is already headed inside.

Charlie looks at me and nods. I swallow hard, my mouth dry.

"But I miss going against you one-on-one."

"You beat me once," he says, his eyes cold. "Won't happen again."

I nod, unsure of how to recover. "What I mean is…I thought going against you was making me a better player. Because I couldn't beat you. It was forcing me to try new things to get loose. Pay more attention to my cuts and fakes. Things I didn't need to beat anyone else."

Charlie stares at me, apparently wondering where I'm going with this. He takes off his helmet. His huge Afro is compressed on the left side.

"I was wondering if you'd like to try some one-on-one drills after practices," I say. "Just for a few minutes. Nothing too long."

"So you can learn my moves?" he says skeptically.

"So I can get better. You're the best cornerback on this team and the best split end, too. Nothing's going to change that. But if I can practice against the best cornerback we've got and learn how to make my moves better, then I'll be better against the other team's top cornerbacks. And if I get a little bit better, then maybe that'll help you, too."

Charlie nods thoughtfully. "Maybe tomorrow," he says. "Let me think about it."

*

I look for Charlie on the way out to practice the next day, but Jimmy Keenan finds me first. We're clomping across the parking lot, our cleats echoing on the pavement, and halfway across the asphalt, he grabs my arm.

"You think you're hot stuff, don't you?" he says.

I don't know what to say in response to that, so I just slide my helmet on, buckle it, and keep walking.

We're not alone. Other teammates are also crossing the parking lot, as are members of the soccer team in their shorts and thin shirts, but none are close enough to hear our conversation.

"I'm talking to you, shrimp!" Keenan grabs my arm again, gripping it tight, his fingernails digging deep into my skin.

I try to pull away, but he doesn't let me.

"Answer me!" he says.

"I'm just doing the best I can," I say.

"You think you're better than me, don't you?" he says.

I do, but there's no point saying that to him. In fact, I don't *think* I'm better than he is. I *know* I am. I've only been practicing with the team for about a week—my first experience *ever* in pads—and I'm still beating him on a regular basis. What's going to happen as I get even more accustomed to all this equipment?

"You think so, don't you?" he says. "You're just a *midget* and you still think you're better than me."

"Let go of me," I say.

"Make me," he says, and squeezes tighter.

He's bigger and stronger than I am, but I'm quicker. And as he likes to remind me, I'm smarter, too.

So I whirl on him and bump him with my chest, surprising him. With my free hand I chop down on the hand of his that's holding onto my elbow. Before he can react, I try to get my face into his, but with our helmets on and him five inches taller than me, my facemask collides with his chin.

He steps back, startled.

"If you're so good," I say, and point to the field, "then prove it out there where it matters."

Keenan composes himself and shoves me in the chest.

"I will, you backstabbing pipsqueak," he says. "Don't you worry about it. I'll kick your puny little ass." Then in a mocking voice, he adds, "*Rabbit.*"

I'm tempted to reply that he wouldn't have said a thing to me if he weren't really afraid that I'm better than he is. I almost do, but I bite my tongue, turn, and keep walking.

I think about how this place forces me to cope with guys like Keenan and Smitty just to survive. Slowly but surely, it's forming a hard shell around me. I don't like the change. I don't like this place. In fact, I hate it.

But I do like football. I *love* football. So I push all the crap out of my mind and tell myself to have a great practice. To beat Keenan on every single play. Make it clear I should be starting over him on both offense *and* defense.

From behind me, Keenan gets the last word in. "That first day, I never should have told you about practice."

I smile and think, *well, he's probably right about that.*

*

On the field, I spot Charlie Watkins just before we begin calisthenics and he just gives me a curt shake of the head. *No.*

I nod back, disappointed but not exactly surprised, and slip into the routine of jumping jacks, running in place, pushups and crunches.

I'm still matched against Keenan when I'm going against the first-team defense, and although I don't beat him every time, I do so often enough that I've got to have Coach Callahan wondering about whether I should be starting over Keenan on defense as well as offense.

CHAPTER 29

I eat *two* fried egg sandwiches after practice because we're going to wait to eat supper until my father gets home.

"We need to eat together as a family," my mother said yesterday to my father when he came home at close to nine o'clock, hours after she and I had already eaten. "This isn't good for Rabbit or any of us. If you can be home at a reasonable time, we'll wait for you. But we can't continue the way we're going."

So he promised to be home by eight, and although it's 8:09 by the time he walks in the door, Mom looks pleased that we'll be together. She's pulled out all the stops. We're having a roast stuffed turkey with bread stuffing, mashed potatoes, gravy, corn, squash, and cranberries. It's like it's Thanksgiving, with the smell of turkey hanging in the air, making my mouth water before I even come to the table.

I'm sitting on the side of the table facing the kitchen with my parents sitting at the two ends, like usual, my father still wearing his dark suit and tie, Mom in a nice dark blue dress. I load my plate up with everything except the cranberry sauce. My drumstick's skin is cooked to a golden brown, its dark meat so tender it's almost falling off the bone.

"That drumstick's almost as big as you are, Rabbit," my father says with a chuckle.

Back in Plainfield, he could make dumb comments like that and laugh at them as if they were really funny, and I'd nod and grin. But everything's different now, even if we're finally eating supper together.

Now, that stupid chuckle of his makes me grit my teeth.

I ignore him and take a big bite out of the drumstick. It tastes delicious, the skin crunchy and the meat moist. Juice runs down my chin, warm and greasy, until I wipe it away with my napkin.

"That black eye of yours is almost gone," he says.

I nod.

"What's the latest on the Red Sox?" he asks while cutting the large slice of white meat drenched in gravy that's centered on his plate.

"Tied for first with the Twins," I say.

He nods, waiting expectantly. When I don't add what I'd say to anyone else—that the Sox just swept Kansas City, giving them four straight wins—a disappointed look comes over his face, and he shovels some turkey into his mouth.

On the wall behind me, the clock ticks softly and slowly.

Tick...tick...tick....

My silverware clinks on my plate as I eat.

Tick...tick...tick....

My father clears his throat. "Is everything working out with your mother driving you to school each morning?"

I nod.

Tick...tick...tick....

"No more problems?"

I shake my head and take another bite out of the drumstick.

Tick...tick...tick....

He glances at my mother, eats some mashed potatoes, and asks the question I know is coming next.

"How's football going?"

"Good."

Tick...tick...tick....

I take a bite of stuffing, prepared to continue the silent treatment I'm giving my father until he finally gives up and talks to my mother about the Vietnam War or the economy or whatever else is on the front page of the news these days.

But then I realize I can't keep it up. I want to, but I just can't help myself. Not with football.

"The first varsity game is tomorrow night and everyone dresses for the game, even the JV," I say. "But I'm just going to stand on the sidelines. I won't play no matter how lopsided the score is, so don't bother coming. You'll just be bored."

My father nods, looking relieved.

"But Mom told you about the first JV game, right? It's on Monday."

Surprise dawns on his face. "I think she, um...she said something about it." Then his eyes dart from me to Mom and back. He looks like a trapped animal. "Yeah, she did. I'm sure of it." He nods. "Good luck."

"Are you coming?" I ask.

It's the question the trapped animal has feared. He winces, then licks his lips. "What time is it?"

"The varsity games are on Friday night, but JV games are on Monday afternoon. As soon as the two teams can get ready after school. About four o'clock."

His face turns a little pale. "Four o'clock? I could never make that. That's right in the middle of the workday."

I nod. It's what I expected. In fact, it's what a part of me wants. The way I feel about him now, I don't want him there to see my games. If I score a touchdown or do something else impressive, I *want* him to miss it. Then Mom and I can talk about it, and he can feel bad about what a rotten father he is.

In a cautious, almost fearful, voice, Mom asks, "Is there any way you could—"

"No!" my father says in almost a shout. "Not at four o'clock! That's impossible! You know how late I'm working."

"Couldn't you sneak out early one day?" she asks timidly. "You're working so—"

The fiery glare my father sends her way stops her dead in her tracks. She blinks fast, then looks down at her plate and toys with a piece of white meat.

"How can you even ask if I can make a game at that time?" he asks, his anger rising. "Four o'clock? I'm buried in work. Maybe if the games were at six or seven like the varsity ones. But not four. That's out of the question."

He takes a deep breath, clearly trying to calm himself down. He gives me a weak grin. "I'd like to be there, you know that, Rabbit. But I just can't. Besides, you probably won't play much, at least this early in the season. Missing those two weeks of practice before Labor Day had to really set you back. I'm sure you're blaming me and you're probably right. But maybe I can get out for a game—*one* game—later this year when you're playing more."

I grin. He walked right into my trap.

I drop the bombshell. "I'm starting at flanker."

My parents' jaws simultaneously drop. Mom's fork clatters on her plate.

"What?" my father asks.

"Rabbit, why didn't you say something before this?" my mother asks. I can see she feels a bit hurt, maybe even betrayed, by all my one-word answers in the car, and I feel bad about that. So I try to explain.

"I wanted it to be a surprise," I say. "Besides, it changes around from one practice to the next, and I didn't want you to be disappointed."

"Well, that's wonderful!" my mother says. "Isn't it, Andre?"

"It's great," my father says, but he's wearing the look of a trapped animal again. "Congratulations, Rabbit." He smiles and reaches out to tousle my hair. "But I still can't be there."

*

Friday night's game against Gloucester is my first as a member of the Lynn English High School Bulldogs—my first real football game at all, actually. It's a thrill to pull my game jersey over my head for the first time.

I'm wearing number seven, the only single-digit number on the team. Keenan saw it as we got on the bus and joked that's because the jersey is so small they couldn't fit a second number on it. That got some laughs, especially from Luke Scanlon, who I'll bet gave me that number on purpose.

Let them laugh. I don't care. I'm proud of it. I'm proud of what I've done so far. I certainly don't care what guys like Keenan and Scanlon think.

But I soon find that it's hard to feel like a member of the team during varsity games. We bus together to the stadium already dressed in our uniforms, but inside Manning Bowl's cave-like locker room all the JV players are relegated to the benches farthest from where Coach McDonough addresses the team. When the team charges out onto the field, we're the last to go, except for Scanlon, who locks the door behind us. And on the field, we stand on the sidelines far away from the coaches.

We're there, but we aren't there. Almost invisible. The main thing is to just stay out of the way.

Even so, I'm glad we get to dress for the varsity games, especially this first one. I can't imagine playing in my first JV game without having a chance to experience Manning Bowl first as one of the useless scrubs. I find myself gawking at it, looking all around in wonder, like Randall McLeod's Uncle Art staring at the New York City skyscrapers, just a hayseed out of my element.

Manning Bowl is *huge*. No, not just huge. *Humongous*. It seats somewhere between twenty and twenty-five thousand people. Tonight there are probably only around a thousand or so with more than half of them on our side, but it's still hard to grasp a stadium that can seat that many people, even if it is old and ugly, constructed during the Depression, nothing but slabs of gray cement and beat-up wooden stands where the fans sit. There's even a section that's roped off on the Lynn English side because the wood has rotted out and it isn't safe to sit there.

But twenty-five thousand people!

My English teacher, Miss St. Onge, used the word "microcosm" in class today. It means a smaller representation of something large. Well,

Manning Bowl is Lynn, Lynn, City of Sin in a microcosm. It's ugly, crude, dirty, and falling apart. But huge.

Someone, I can't remember who, said that the Rolling Stones played here last year. The Rolling Stones! I may be a hick who's only now just learning about popular music, but it's hard to believe that I'm playing football in the same stadium where the *Rolling Stones* held a concert.

So I look all around me like a country bumpkin, and before I know it, we've scored a touchdown. In the stands behind us, the Lynn English fans are cheering, jumping up and down, clapping their hands, and whooping it up. Halfway between the sideline and the stands, a dozen pretty cheerleaders in very short red-and-gray skirts jump up, spreading their legs wide and throwing their hands high in the air, all while shaking their pompoms. From the press box atop the opposite side of the stadium, the person describing each play over the public address system adds extra enthusiasm for this one.

Scottie Joyce off the right tackle for three yards and a touchdown! Lynn English leads, 6-0!

We go for two—Coach McDonough isn't using a placekicker this year—and Joyce gets stopped short of the goal line.

Joyce off left tackle, stopped by Papadopoulos. The two-point conversion is unsuccessful. Lynn English leads, 6-0.

Up in the stands, the band breaks into the school fight song: "Roll on You Bulldogs" to the tune of "Roll out the Barrel." It seems like a strange choice. An old-fashioned polka, for crying out loud. I wonder what Mick Jagger and the Rolling Stones would make of it. Probably think it's as goofy as I do.

But I tell myself to get used to it. I'll be hearing it for four years, unless I somehow get rescued from this armpit of a city. Some of those times will be after I've scored a touchdown, so I'd better not just get used to it. I'd better like it. It needs to become sweet music to my ears even if it is just a goofy polka.

The offensive team starters come to the sidelines and the other varsity members congratulate them by smacking their shoulder pads and slapping their helmets, paying special attention to Scottie Joyce, who scored the touchdown.

"Way to go, Joycie, baby!"

"Atta boy!"

"Just the start, boys!"

But all of us JV players stand back. It's not our place to be part of this celebration, even though a few of us clap. None of the varsity heroes want to be congratulated by one of us. It's almost as if we've got a disease—the disease of not being big enough or fast enough or good enough—and they don't want to get infected.

We're here, but we're not here.

*

We win, 12-7. Or to be more accurate, the *varsity* wins, 12-7. There's no "we" involved. I didn't get in for a single play. I didn't break a sweat. I just stood there. Which is just what I expected.

They, meaning the varsity, won, thanks to a big fourth-quarter defensive stand near the goal line. I'm glad for them. Everyone on the varsity is happy and joking around, but I still feel like an outsider.

I may have dressed for this game, but I'm not part of this team. My game is on Monday.

CHAPTER 30

The JV team plays at Manning Bowl just like the varsity, but the similarity ends there. That Monday afternoon, darkness hasn't fallen yet, so the stadium lights aren't on.

There's no band, playing that silly polka, "Roll on You Bulldogs." No cheerleaders in their short red-and-gray skirts chanting when we're on defense, "Push 'em back, push 'em back, *waaaaaaaay* back," and then leaning waaaaaay back to show their red underwear. Or what is supposed to be a cheerleader's version of underwear.

Not that I was looking during the varsity game or anything.

No fans, other than parents and a few friends. My mother is there, so for me, at least, there aren't *parents* but at least *a parent*. And of course, no friends. What passes for my friends—Anna and Cindy, Jeff and Paul—will smile and talk to me between classes and I even eat lunch with Jeff and Paul, but no one here likes me enough to do anything outside of school with me, much less come to a game as unimportant as this one.

No PA announcer. It's mostly silent, or as silent as football games can get with the whistles blowing and pads slamming into each other and players grunting with the effort of their exertion.

No Coach McDonough or Coach D'Agostino. Either they're running practice for the varsity or JV games are a waste of their time. It's just Coach Callahan with Coach Harper assisting him.

So it's minor league in every way.

But that doesn't bother me. Because I'm part of this team. And I'm going to play, actually contribute. I hope to play on the varsity someday, but if you give me a choice between playing here in front of nobody and standing around and doing nothing under the bright lights of the varsity, just let me play.

*

It's halftime, we're trailing Lawrence, 14-6, and I still haven't caught a pass. Chris Higgins, our quarterback, hasn't even thrown to my side of the field. He's connected with Charlie Watkins twice, but mostly, we're trying to run the ball the first two downs and unless it's third-and-long, we're running on third down, too.

So I'm spending most of my time blocking the defensive back I'm lined up against, or sometimes a linebacker. The defensive back, number twenty, is bigger than I am by several inches and thirty or forty pounds. The linebacker, number fifty-one, is an even bigger mismatch. He isn't quite a Jessie Stackhouse, but he's got to outweigh me by at least seventy pounds.

When you're five-nothin', hundred-nothin', you learn pretty fast that you can't block those kind of opponents chest-to-chest. If you try, like I did the first few days at practice, you just get knocked on your butt. You have to block them low and take their legs out from underneath them. Play after play, I line my shoulder pads up with their thighs and, especially if they're already running fast, I take them down almost every time.

"That's cheap," the towering linebacker says after I cut his legs out from underneath him the first time. "Play like a man."

But if I try blocking him "like a man," I'm going to be on the sidelines and Jimmy Keenan will be in the lineup instead. In fact, it would have been surprising that Coach Callahan didn't start Keenan ahead of me, considering the run-oriented game plan, if not for my success in blocking during practices by hitting low.

The defensive back never says a word to me, but the next time the linebacker picks himself off the ground, he slams into my shoulder pads with his big, meaty hands, and says, "Stay away from my knees, you little runt! Play like a man!"

I realize that he thinks I'm trying to hurt him, give him some kind of knee injury. Or at least that has him worried.

I feel a lump in my throat, but still manage to say, "I'm not playing dirty. I haven't hit you in the knees once," and then I trot back to the huddle, where Chris Higgins, our quarterback, calls another running play that has been relayed to him by either Mark Evangelista or Joey Carbone, the two running backs who rotate each play.

I'm not always blocking on the running plays, just most of the time. Sometimes, I go out on a fly just as fast as I can or on a post pattern, just clearing out the area by acting as a decoy. But the defensive back is paying less and less attention to the decoy plays. I want to tell Coach Callahan that this is the perfect time to fake another decoy play and actually throw to me because I'll be wide open, but one thing the coaching staff has made very clear is who's running the team. The coaches call the plays, the quarterback announces them in the huddle, and everyone else keeps their mouths shut. Suggesting plays is not an option.

But at the end of the half, minutes after he gave up a big touchdown pass to give Lawrence the lead, Jimmy Keenan says something anyway, making me think that he really is as dumb as he pretends to be. I'm walking off the field when he spots Coach Callahan, who's ten yards ahead of me, and runs up beside him.

"Coach, I'm a better blocker than Labelle," Keenan says. "He's too small. Take a look at him. If we're gonna run the ball, put me in there."

Coach Callahan stares at Keenan, and for a second, I think he's going to hit him. Instead, he grabs him by the facemask. "When I want your worthless opinion, I'll ask for it. In the meantime, try not to trip over your own feet and give up a forty-yard bomb."

Callahan shoves Keenan with all his might, and Keenan stumbles backwards and lands on his backside, looking up from the ground while a few players reflexively snicker. Callahan whirls and heads for our cold, cement locker room beneath the Manning Bowl stands.

Midway through the third quarter, Keenan gives up another touch-down when he bites on a fake, slips, and can't recover. Lawrence misses the two-point conversion, but now we're down, 20-6.

Coach Callahan yells at Keenan when he comes off the field, and then adds a few more words for Higgins, the safety, who couldn't get over in time to stop the long gainer from becoming a touchdown. Then he hollers for me.

"Labelle! Get over here!"

I run to his side.

"On defense, you're going in there for Keenan," he says. "You think you can stop number eighty-two?"

There's only one answer to that question.

"Yes sir!"

Eighty-two is the Lawrence receiver who just beat Keenan for the touchdown and he might be the guy who also beat him in the first half. But I'd have said the same thing even if number eighty-two is Boyd Dowler of the Green Bay Packers.

"Then do it!" Coach Callahan says.

First, though, the offense goes out there, and now we're down by two touchdowns. We don't abandon the run completely, but we finally start passing the ball. The first two go to Charlie Watkins, one of which is badly overthrown, but the other connects for a twelve-yard gain and a first down.

The next one comes my way, on the right side of the field, and it's almost as if Coach Callahan heard the words I wanted to speak in the first half. My defender has gotten lazy, cheating to play the run since a pass hasn't come our way the whole game. So when Higgins fakes a handoff to Mark Evangelista on first down and I take off to go deep, my defender goes two steps with me, then heads for Evangelista, sure he's going to stop him on the sweep play behind the line of scrimmage. By the time he realizes it's a fake, I've got ten yards on him.

I raise my hand to make sure Higgins sees me, but it isn't even necessary. I'm his primary target and he's staring at me, seemingly paralyzed for a moment because he can't believe how open I am.

Throw the ball, I think, and then I add, *just don't overthrow it!*

He makes sure he doesn't overthrow it, throwing a cautious pass that I have to slow down for, but it floats into my hands and I take off. The defender closed the gap while I slowed down for the ball, but he's still not close enough. He dives and although I feel his hands tug at my left ankle and I stumble for a step or two, I right myself and keep going.

Now, it's just me and the safety, who's converging from the middle of the field. He's got the angle on me and in just a few more strides he'll be able to force me out of bounds.

But my mind goes back to all the times like this in the backyards in Plainfield, when we were only playing two-hand touch and I was still able to score.

I feel myself start to grin.

Instead of continuing to race down the sideline, like the safety expects, I stop and cut back sharply toward the middle of the field.

The safety overruns me, his arms flailing, grabbing briefly onto my facemask with one hand, jerking it for a moment until it slips free.

He tumbles to the ground and I'm racing for the end zone with no one in sight.

Just like back in Plainfield.

The defensive back from the other side of the field makes his best attempt, but he never gets close.

I run sixty-three yards for a touchdown.

I never slow down. Not even when I reach the end zone. I keep going until I'm out of the end zone, almost ready to run all the way out of the stadium, up the ramp to Western Avenue and beyond.

My heart feels like it's about to explode. But in a good way. I turn back into the end zone and I'm jumping up and down as my teammates rush to join me. They hug me, slap my shoulder pads and my helmet. Slap me on the back. Slap me on the butt.

Euphoria floods over me. We're yelling and whooping it up and even though the stands are almost empty, it feels like 25,000 people are cheering. Then Moose Mahoney, our lumbering 210-pound tackle, for whom it's been an effort to run more than sixty yards down the field, grabs me by the legs and lifts me up, and I laugh, thinking that for him I'm no more difficult to pick up than a juicy cheeseburger and fries.

This is why I love football most of all.

We line up for a two-point conversion, and Joey Carbone slams off-tackle, keeping his feet churning while bouncing off three defenders who try to drag him down but he keeps moving until he topples into the end zone. Now it's a 20-14 game.

I come back to the sideline, all smiles, and even Coach Callahan grins. He slaps me on the helmet and says, "Good move, kid!"

I'm so pumped up, I almost forget to go out with the defense after the kickoff. Fortunately, I see Jimmy Keenan moping around on the sideline, head down, kicking at tufts of grass and muttering, and this reminds me better than a kick in the head to get out there. I race onto the field and take my place in the defensive huddle.

Right away, Lawrence runs two sweeps to my side. I'm sure its coach saw the little runt—me!—come into the lineup and decided to take advantage. On the first play, the flanker who lines up on my side, a black kid who's maybe 5-5 and 140 pounds, blocks me far off the line of scrimmage, driving me backwards so fast I backpedal until I fall flat on my butt. I'm sure I look ridiculous, but even more importantly, I've left a gaping hole for the runner to scamper down the sideline. Fortunately, our outside linebacker, C.J. Powell, fights off the pulling guard and drags down the runner after only a two-yard gain.

I dodged a bullet on that one.

They come at me again on the second play. This time, I dodge the flanker and am waiting for the running back, cutting off the outside lane, until one of Lawrence's massive linemen, a brute who's got to be close to two hundred pounds, draws dead aim on me and though I try to sidestep him, he drives his massive shoulders into me and slams me down.

I feel as though I've been hammered into the ground and for a moment, I fear that I've gotten the wind knocked out of me again. How humiliating it will be to just lie there going *aaaaaahhhhhhh!* until Coach Callahan runs out and drops me on the ground until I can breathe again.

But my fears are unfounded. I can breathe just fine, even if the monster who slammed me down also seems to have shaken loose every bone in my body from where it's supposed to be. I peel myself off the ground and see that someone, probably C.J. Powell, bailed me out again. The referee spots the ball. Third down and five.

This time, Lawrence tries a pass to my side of the field. Three-for-three in attempts to go after me.

But this time, I hold my own. The flanker cuts across to the middle of the field on a quick slant pattern. The quarterback tries to hit him just past what will give them a first down, but I'm step-for-step with the receiver and bat the pass away.

Fourth down.

I trot off the field as the punt units come on. I feel good about the pass I've just defended but know that I've got to do better on running plays.

Jimmy Keenan meets me on the sideline and voices his agreement.

"You suck against the run," he says. "You can't do anything. You're awful! I don't know what Coach sees in you, but you aren't going to be in there for long the way you're playing."

I push away from Keenan, even though I mostly agree with him, and even as I get ready for the next offensive series, I mull over how to better handle defending the run.

The punt is a weak one and we take over at our forty-five, just five yards from midfield. It's great field position, but we lose it on the first play. A Lawrence defender drills Mark Evangelista just as he takes a handoff from Higgins and when helmet meets ball, the ball pops loose. It takes several funny bounces, and then gets scooped into a Lawrence defender's arms.

Back on defense.

I decide to play the run more aggressively, at least for a play or two, figuring that my contributions can't possibly get any worse.

Sure enough, Lawrence tries running another power sweep to my side. This time, I don't hold my ground, letting the blockers come to me. I read a running play right away, dart past the flanker's attempt to block me, and race into the backfield while the blockers are still pulling out of their positions.

One lineman dives to get in my way, but I swerve around him, close in on the running back, and drive my shoulders into his thighs with a loud crash. The two of us grunt at almost the exact same time as I wrap my arms around his legs and pull him to the ground.

A five-yard loss!

Powell yells his encouragement. "Attaboy! That's how we do it!" He whacks me on the shoulder pads as we walk back to the defensive huddle.

I wonder briefly if my play was really that big a deal or if he was just delighted that I finally hadn't left him on his own. I think that during the previous series, I should have been yelling about his big tackles and slapping him on the back.

But mostly I grin in satisfaction and hope I can do it again.

The next two plays are passes to the other side of the field that Charlie Watkins knocks down with ease.

Fourth down.

Keenan comes nowhere near me this time when I come to the sideline. I take a sip of water and get ready to go back out on offense. That was a big defensive stop, especially with Lawrence starting in our half of the field, but we've got a long ways to go. We're still down by a touchdown, and the third quarter is almost over.

After the punt, we take over on our eighteen-yard line. With us so close to our own end zone, Coach Callahan goes ultraconservative again, calling one low-risk running play after another. We pick up one first down, switch ends to start the fourth quarter, and then stall after he calls a sweep on third-and-six.

We punt, stop Lawrence on three downs; then, back on offense, have another series where we only get a single first down and then have to punt again.

Time is ticking away.

Fortunately, we stop Lawrence again on three downs, all runs, two to my side. One time, I assist Powell with the tackle. The other time, I'm no help at all, but he comes through anyway.

After the punt, we take over on our thirty-nine yard line with three minutes and forty-seconds left. A run up the middle gets only two yards.

The clock ticks down. I want to scream.

We're running out of time. We need to throw the ball.

Coach Callahan calls another run, but this one is the exact opposite of the colorless off-tackle plays we've been using. Higgins hands off to Joey Carbone sweeping left, then Joey laterals to Charlie on what looks like an end-around reverse. But as he comes sweeping around to the right side, he hands off to me.

A double reverse.

I take off, leaving behind the defenders who'd been over-pursuing Charlie. They flop around like fish out of water, flailing hopelessly for me, but I'm past them. I shift the ball into my left arm and see only one defender between me and a wide-open left sideline. And between me and the defender is C.J. Powell, our tight end, who's almost as good of a blocker as our linemen. Powell closes in on the defender, who's back-pedalling and tries to rid himself of Powell with no luck.

This is our basic "run to daylight" play from practice. I close in on the two and read which way Powell is forcing the defender. He's got the angle to be forcing him to the sideline, so I cut inside and as Powell shields him away from me, I take off for the end zone.

The safety is racing after me, but I've got a two-stride advantage. Shame on me if I let him catch up.

If there's an extra gear, I shift into it; if I'm only going at ninety-nine percent speed, I draw on that reserve.

I pull away from the safety. Three strides. Four strides.

And then I'm running into the end zone, my lungs about to burst.

But so, too, is my sense of overwhelming joy. I throw the ball over my head and jump up and down, filled with happiness as my teammates greet me. Almost as if in replay from the previous touchdown, they shout and slap me, and yes, Moose Mahoney chugs his way into the end zone, huffing and puffing, and again grabs me by the legs and lifts me up, whooping and hollering.

It's a great moment. About as sweet as it gets.

But we're still only tied. We need to convert the extra point and then hold off the Lawrence offense one more time.

We line up for the two-point conversion, and Higgins relays the call from the sideline. Quarterback option right. Higgins will run to the right and have the option of running it in or throwing a pass. I've spent most of the offensive passes lining up on the right side, but for this play Charlie Watkins and I flip-flop. He's our top receiver and this play only needs a couple yards. The play is designed for him to get free in the corner of the end zone while one of the running backs goes straight through the line and, with luck, gets open in the middle. I'm the last option, cutting across from the left to the right. A pass to me will be the farthest one, the one with the most risk of an incompletion.

Which is fine with me. I don't care who catches the ball or if Higgins runs it in himself. We just need *someone* to get the ball into the end zone.

Higgins moves off to the right, and for a split second it looks like he's going to cut through an opening and take it in, but the opening closes. Higgins drifts further right, sees the running back covered in the middle, and floats a jump ball to Charlie in the end zone.

Charlie leaps up, gets his hands on the ball, and pulls it into his body even as the defender tries to swat it away.

"Touchdown!" I yell, which isn't right at all. It isn't a touchdown, but it feels like it. We've scored on the conversion to make it 22-20.

We all swarm around Charlie and I'm yelling with all the rest of them and slapping him on the back.

"Way to go, Charlie! Great catch!"

Moose Mahoney doesn't try to lift him up, but Charlie's a bigger guy. Moose may only do that for me, the runt, the one guy on the team he knows he can lift without pulling a muscle in his back.

We trot to the sideline and everyone is slapping Charlie and me on the backs and whooping it up.

Only one guy isn't joining in on the celebration.

I turn away from Keenan in disgust as Coach Callahan's voice cuts through the air. "Still more than two minutes left, boys! Still gotta stop 'em."

Which we do.

We get a good kickoff and coverage, then stop them on four downs straight. Back on offense, Higgins takes the hike, and touches his knee down for a couple plays and the clock runs out.

A big comeback win in our first game. It feels so good. And I've proved that I belong.

Yeah, I love football best of all.

CHAPTER 31

M om can't stop talking on the drive home.
"You were amazing, Rabbit!" she says. "Amazing! You single-handedly won the game!"

I bite into a cheesesteak sub that she bought for me and my taste buds are overwhelmed. I've never tasted anything this delicious before. I'd never even heard of a cheesesteak sub until Jeff mentioned it in the lunch room the other day.

A pretty simple idea. Cook thinly sliced pieces of steak on a grill, and then put them on top of a bed of cheese inside a submarine roll. The hot steak melts the cheese and the whole thing melts in your mouth.

So Lynn doesn't just have football going for it. It also has cheesesteak subs, which my mother had to get because I'm famished and it'll be hours before Dad comes home, and she couldn't make something like ham and cheese or chicken salad before the game because it might go bad by the time I ate it.

Thank God she was out of peanut butter.

I sink my teeth into the sub and savor the gooey melted cheese. I can't make up my mind whether to wolf it down in record time because it tastes so good, or eat it slowly, savoring each bite.

If I weren't so hungry, I might slowly savor it, but my stomach has been growling since the end of the game, so I attack the sandwich like there's no tomorrow.

"You really were amazing," Mom says.

In the half second between when my mouth is empty and I take another bite, I say, "Thanks."

"It was just like back in Plainfield," she says. "When you were playing baseball or basketball. You dominated the game!"

I think she's overstating the case a bit, but my mouth is full so I don't argue the point.

"And you've never played football before!" she says. "But you were still the best player out there."

I swallow the latest mouthful and feel enough guilt to slow her down, at least a bit.

"Mom, there are a lot of really good players on that team," I say. "I'm not even the best receiver. Charlie Watkins is. But because he drew the coverage of Lawrence's top defensive back, that opened things up for me. I scored the touchdowns, but trust me, he's a lot better than I am."

"Charlie is the black kid?" she asks. "The one with the huge Afro?"

"Yeah," I say, this time with my mouth half full. "He's really good. I get better just practicing against him." I decide not to mention my ill-fated attempt to practice one-on-one with him. There's no advantage to bringing it up.

My mother nods thoughtfully. After a while, she asks, "Do you have any problems with the blacks on the team?"

"Nope," I say, which is the truth. The only people who've given me any trouble at all so far have been white. But I'm not going to start talking about that, either, or how the blacks on the team seem to stick together, mostly talking to each other.

She drives the car through Wyoma Square. "That's good."

We get home, and I run right upstairs to get working on my homework. I'm tempted to listen to the Red Sox game on the radio—they're starting a big two-game series against the Tigers—but I've got tests in History and Math tomorrow so I don't dare do anything more than quick checks on the score every fifteen or twenty minutes.

Later, my father gets home and we sit down to eat, and Mom recites all my exploits. He becomes all smiles and slaps me on the shoulder.

"I told you everything would all work out, didn't I?"

I think of how many times he used to say to me that life isn't all about sports, but now that sports has become the one good thing about this place—other than cheesesteak subs, of course—now suddenly it's okay for life to be all about sports.

Because sports makes good old Dad look good. Lynn isn't the armpit of the universe as long as I can score a couple touchdowns.

Man, I really love football, but I really can't stand my father.

*

"That was quite an exciting game," Anna says before Math the next day. I've just set my books down on my desk, and she gives me a warm smile. We're both in the third row from the front, with me on the far right closest to the door and her desk beside mine.

"Yeah, it sure was," I say with a big grin, pleased that she heard about it. A warm glow fills my chest. "It was quite a comeback."

Her face clouds. "Weren't we ahead the whole game?"

I stare at her. She looks as confused as I feel. "We were down, 20-6 in the third quarter," I say. "It was a *huge* comeback."

She cocks her head as if trying to figure out a difficult math problem. "It was 12-0 at the half. I'm sure of it because I was staring at the scoreboard during halftime when we played." A frown forms on her face. "I saw you on the sideline. Number seven, right?"

The warm glow in my chest evaporates, replaced by a sour feeling in my gut. Anna was there for the varsity game because the band played after touchdowns and marched during halftime. The band ignored the JV game. Like everyone else.

"You're talking about the varsity game on Friday night," I say. "I was talking about the JVs. Last night. I actually got to play in that one."

"Oh," Anna says and puts a hand to her mouth. Her cheeks flush. "I'm sorry. I just assumed…"

"It's okay," I say, although it doesn't really feel okay. It had felt so special to think briefly that she'd been paying attention to how I'd been doing when, in reality, she was just there as a band member. It had been about her, not about me. Which was okay. Perfectly understandable.

But I want her to be interested in *my* football team, the JVs, not the team of the juniors and seniors who ignore me and won't even let me use the real showers.

"How did the JVs do?" she asks, looking sheepish that she doesn't know.

"We had a big comeback," I say and she laughs.

"Let me guess," she says. "You came back from two touchdowns."

A smile creeps back over my lips. "So you were listening."

"Sherlock Holmes, here."

"Yeah, we were down, 20-6, but came back and won it on a two-point conversion, 22-20."

"That's great! I wished I'd seen it."

"So do I," I say, letting those words slip out before I realized it.

She laughs, a soft, feminine laugh that sounds so pleasing as it fills the air. "Let me guess. You had a good game."

I shrug nonchalantly and try to suppress, with no success at all, a big grin that spreads across my lips. "I did okay."

"Tell me what happened!" Anna says, but the bell rings.

Mr. Robinson steps to the head of the class and there's no more talking. But Anna gives me a wink that fills my chest with a glow far warmer than the one she started to put there a minute or two ago.

We'll just have to talk about it on the way to the next class.

CHAPTER 32

That afternoon, I see Keenan in the hallway between classes, walking in the opposite direction. He's elbowing Jerry Soucy, his best friend, and they're laughing as they walk behind a cluster of girls. Most of their attention is focused on Wendy Sawyer, a popular, redheaded senior with a big chest that she accentuates by wearing tight sweaters and tops almost every day. It's hard not to notice.

Today's sweater is light blue. Very tight.

But when Keenan sees me, walking with Jeff and Paul, his demeanor changes, like a sunny summer sky suddenly turned pitch black, filled with thunderclouds and bolts of lightning shooting to the ground, the roar of thunder crashing every few seconds.

"Hey, look, it's the superstar, *La-belly*!" Keenan says, elbowing Soucy, then moving to block our path. "*Belly, belly, belly.* Doesn't do a thing for almost the whole game, but gets lucky at just the right time. Now he thinks he's the hero."

Jeff, Paul, and I have stopped walking, but Keenan steps right into me, bumping my chest.

"First, he thinks he's too smart for the rest of us, then he thinks two lucky plays make him the hero." Keenan gives me a shove. "But everyone on the team still hates him. Doesn't have a single friend on the team, isn't that right?"

A solid lump in my throat keeps me from replying.

"At least no white friends," Keenan says. "He's so desperate, he has to make friends with the darkies." He nods his head and stares at me. "Yeah, I saw you with Charlie Watkins." Keenan glances back to Soucy. "He's gone over to the dark side. Get it? The *dark* side?"

Soucy laughs as if it's the funniest thing he ever heard.

"I'm calling a penalty," Keenan says with a big grin. "Offside! Fifteen yards!" He goes to mimic a football referee pointing in the direction of the infraction, but instead of pointing at me, he cuffs me hard across the head.

Soucy laughs some more. "Too late to decline that penalty now," he says, and laughs at his own joke.

Keenan leans close to me, and in a low, rasping voice, he says, "You're gonna get what's coming to you, you little turd. Count on it!" He gives me a one-handed shove, clenches his fist, and looks around.

Mr. Tempkin pops out of a classroom, and though he isn't looking at us, Keenan steps back quickly.

"Count on it," Keenan says again, then he and Soucy head in their original direction, laughing at their brilliant wit.

"What's that all about?" Jeff asks.

I just shake my head.

There's no excusing Keenan's comments about Charlie. No defense for that at all. But I can understand at least some of Keenan's anger at me. It can't be easy to lose first your starting job on offense and then on defense. I'd be pretty sad if that happened to me.

And it might sting extra bad if the guy who beat me out was someone who I told about the team, someone who might not have made the team if I'd kept my mouth shut.

I get that. I understand and, in many ways, I feel bad for him. I get no pleasure from seeing Keenan unhappy.

But Coach Callahan has to start his best players. We aren't seven-year-olds. This isn't like T-ball where everyone plays the same amount of time. If Keenan isn't one of the top eleven players on offense or the top eleven on defense, he doesn't deserve to start.

And he isn't. Not anymore.

That has to hurt. But there's no excuse for being a bad teammate. You don't pick fights. You don't pout when the team does well just because you're on the bench. Keenan has made it clear he'd rather be the star while we're losing 50–12 than be a forgotten player during a win. And you certainly don't make racial insults about your teammates.

Simply put, Keenan is a bad teammate. But I've got to deal with him no matter what. And I've got to figure out why almost no one on the team likes me.

"What did you ever do to make him hate you like that?" Jeff asks, breaking the silence.

I shake my head again, glumly, and just say, "Nothing."

*

Keenan starts in again as we head out to the practice field, our cleats clicking on the hot asphalt of the parking lot behind the school. Others are also headed out to the field on this sunny day, warm and humid for September, and my helmet smells of stale sweat as I slip it on, but no one is particularly near me. I may have played well in our first game, but the varsity players probably don't even know that we won and certainly don't care even if they do know. And even among the JV players, I'm still the new kid who has no close friends on the team. So no one makes a point of walking out with me.

No one but Keenan.

From behind me, above the clatter of the cleats, I hear his voice, a soft, sneering whisper.

"What's the hero going to do today?" he says. "How many touchdowns will *La-Belly* score this time?" He then launches into a mock cheer based on one the cheerleaders shout during the varsity games. "Rabbit *La-Belly*, he's my man. If he can't do it, no one can!"

I had tried to get out here before him, rushing to get dressed and hurrying out the locker room exit. But like all bullies, Keenan has no interest in leaving me alone and must have kept an eye on me and followed close behind. I've taken away his starting job and he's going to make me pay. I want to whirl around and shout at him, but there's no way to do that without sounding like a whiny baby.

"Leave me alone!" he'd surely say, mocking whatever words I might use, making them seem like those of a sobbing four-year-old girl.

To be honest, what I'd really like to do is clench my fist and smash it into his face—if his helmet is off, that is. With any luck, I'd break his nose and send blood streaming down his face until it dripped off his chin.

I never used to think like that, never mentally applauded violent images forming in my brain. It sickens me that I've changed this way, been *forced* to think even momentarily like an animal just to survive in this jungle. But then I remind myself that I'm one of the lowliest members on the food chain. If I allow images of a bloodied Keenan to linger for long in my brain, I'll get *my* nose broken and *my* blood spilled.

At my size, only a fool gets into fistfights.

So I push the ugliness out of my mind and just ignore Keenan. I keep walking as if I can't hear a thing.

That's when Keenan spits on the back of my neck.

He hocks a loogie, and then I feel it on my warm, already damp skin. It's wet, slimy, and disgusting. Only half believing what's happening, I reach back my hand to touch it, to confirm the vile truth, even as his spit begins to trickle down my neck.

My fingertips come away moist. My stomach lurches. My anger flares. My fingers reflexively clench into a fist.

But I don't turn around.

"Go ahead, do it," Keenan urges, taunting me. "I'll even give you the first punch, you little pussy. A little turd like you couldn't hurt a flea. Go ahead, take your best shot."

His voice reminds me of the cobras, Nag and Nagaina, in *The Jungle Book* that I read when I was little. The cobras hissed their taunts to the mongoose Rikki-Tikki-Tavi, trying to trick him into looking in their paralyzing eyes.

And right now, I'd like to be a mongoose. I'd attack the cobra, clamp my teeth on its wide neck, and hold on while it shook me to and fro, trying to kill me even while I had its life within my own teeth.

I want to be Rikki-Tikki-Tavi. I've taken enough abuse. I want to fight.

But I tell myself that isn't the answer. I take a deep breath and turn slowly, my arms out with fists unclenched, prepared to say, "Why are you doing this?"

Keenan takes one step closer, glances back, and drives his fist into my gut.

Light flashes before my eyes. I double over in pain. Gagging, I fall to the pavement.

As I crumple to the asphalt, I see Keenan's smile of victory, the cold hatred in his eyes…and no one near us who could have seen him sucker-punch me. Those ahead of us, closer to the field, had their backs turned to us, and no one else has followed us yet out of the locker room exit. Not even any soccer players. Which is what Keenan saw before he attacked.

I roll on the ground, arms wrapped around my stomach, barely noticing the jagged rocks on the asphalt digging into my skin. For all I know, it's glass and every sideways motion is tearing up my skin. All I can think of is the blazing pain in my gut, radiating down into my abdomen and into my legs and upwards into my chest and arms. I can barely breathe. The taste of vomit fills my mouth.

Keenan looks back to the locker room exit and waves frantically. He yells, "The little kid is hurt. Something's wrong with him."

Then he bends over until his face is close to mine. He whispers, "This is only the start, you little puke. If you know what's best for you, you're quitting this team. You hear me?"

Then he turns back to the school and yells, "He says someone hit him."

CHAPTER 33

Coach Callahan appears over me, hands on his knees, legs spread wide, concern etched on his face.

"What happened?"

I groan, the pain decreasing a little, but it still grasps hold of my gut in its fist and clenches until I can barely hold down what I ate for lunch. My legs feel weak, my fingers cold and clammy.

I look from Coach Callahan to Keenan, who is trying to look angelic and confused for everyone else even while his cold, hard eyes bore in on me. Eyes that say *Don't even think about telling on me. I'll hurt you worse than you can ever imagine. You don't want to mess with me. Don't even* think *about it!*

I recoil from the look in those eyes. I love football, love it so much. Even while my body spasms in pain, my mind replays the indescribable feeling of delight when I faked the defender who had the angle on me and then cut back, forcing him to overrun me, the thrill of then racing for the end zone. The pure joy at taking the double reverse and sprinting down the sideline for the touchdown that tied the game and gave Charlie the chance to catch the winning two-point conversion. And yes, the warm smile in Anna's eyes as I told her about it.

I love all that.

But the look in Keenan's cold eyes reminds me that there are limits to everything, even my love for football. His words come back to me, harsh and biting. *This is only the start, you little puke. If you know what's best for you, you're quitting this team. You hear me?*

If this is only the start, what next? I love football, but do I love it enough to endure whatever Keenan has in store for me, even if that means more of this, even if that means…even if it means more of what Smitty promised me…even if it means an audible *snick* and a cold, sharp blade pressed against my neck, the pressure increasing and increasing until a trickle of blood—my blood—slides down the blade.

I don't love *anything* that much.

My choice is obvious. The surrender forms inside my head. It takes the shape of words exonerating Keenan, agreeing to his story, to the idea that someone, but not him, sucker-punched me.

"I'm not…"

Keenan sees my surrender, knows the words—*I'm not sure who hit me*—before I speak them. His face softens. It may be my imagination, but I can almost see him start to grin.

He's beaten me.

I've taken away his starting flanker position. I've done the same at cornerback. But this is Lynn, Lynn, City of Sin, and it's a jungle. Keenan may not be the king of this jungle, but he might as well be as far as I'm concerned. He's the lion, fresh from the kill, blood still dripping from his mouth.

What does that make me?

A gazelle, I guess. Quick and graceful, but the smallest and weakest of the herd. The one the predators always single out for the easiest kill.

Yeah, that's me.

And I think, where does it all end?

This is only the start, you little puke. If you know what's best for you, you're quitting this team. You hear me?

The end is pretty clear.

Smitty chases me away from ever taking the school bus again. Keenan scares me off the football team, taking away the one thing I love in this godforsaken armpit of the universe.

What's left?

Nothing but the weakest gazelle, no longer racing joyfully through the jungle but instead hiding, terrified of what predator will strike next. Wounded and bleating, now the juiciest of all targets. The smell of its fear making even the most satisfied predators hungry for this easy morsel.

That's what I am.

Pathetic.

But it doesn't have to be that way. I don't have to give in. Maybe Keenan will beat me, perhaps he's got a switchblade that will soon be against my neck. But I'm not going to let him take away the one thing that has made this place at least slightly livable.

I'm not going to surrender.

Keenan is not going to win.

Lynn, Lynn, City of Sin. Never come out the way you go in.

Maybe I'll leave this place in a coffin. Maybe Keenan puts me there. Or maybe Smitty. Or some thug I haven't yet met.

But I'm not going to crawl in the coffin myself.

If Keenan is going to win, he's going to have to take it away from me. I'm not giving it away.

New words form on my lips.

"I'm not…" I lick my lips. "I'm not going to lie for you, Keenan."

Keenan's eyes widen in shock as I snatch away his certain victory.

"Keenan sucker-punched me," I tell Coach Callahan. "Then he told me, 'This is only the start, you little puke. If you know what's best for you, you're quitting this team. You hear me?' And it isn't the first time he's threatened me."

Coach Callahan looks even more astonished than Keenan. Hands on his hips, he turns to Keenan, who takes a step back.

"He's crazy!" Keenan says. "I didn't touch him."

"There wasn't anyone near us," I say, propping myself up on one elbow, wincing at the sharp pain in my gut. I force myself to keep talking. "The only other guys out here were way ahead of us. They were already on the field. It was just the two of us. I was walking alone, he said something and spit on my neck. When I turned around, he sucker-punched me in the gut."

"I did not," Keenan says, holding his hand up as if he's in court taking an oath. "So help me God. I swear it on my mother's soul. He's either making all this up or he hit his head and he's hallucinating. Or something like that."

"Hit my head?" I say. "I've got my helmet on."

Keenan flushes. "Okay, then he's making it up."

Coach Callahan looks back and forth between us, Keenan standing and me lying on the ground, still partially doubled over.

"I thought you were the one who said someone hit him," Coach Callahan says to Keenan.

"I, I—" Keenan stammers. He glances at me, frozen for a moment, then shakes his head as if to clear the cobwebs. "I was just repeating what he said. He said someone hit him."

"Really?" Coach Callahan says, sounding as if he doesn't believe it at all.

"He lies about everything," Keenan says. "You should have seen him the first day of classes, back when he was taking classes with us dummies. He comes in almost at the end of class and gets away with it, telling Mr. Sipowicz that he accidentally went to his Monday class instead of his Tuesday class. Then afterwards, he tells all the rest of us that he was smoking pot in the boys room."

Coach Callahan's eyes widen. He turns to me.

"I did not! I—"

"He's probably stoned right now," Keenan says. "That would explain why he's hallucinating." His face brightens. "Maybe he's on LSD."

LSD? What is that?

Coach Callahan turns to me. "Rabbit, get up, take your helmet off and look at me."

I painfully get on all fours, then rise to stand before him, my legs a bit wobbly. I remove my helmet.

Coach Callahan leans so close I can smell old cigarette smoke on his sweatshirt, gray with red letters spelling out "LEHS Bulldogs." He sniffs, then leans back.

"You do drugs, Labelle?"

The question shocks me. "No! Never!" I say. I can't believe he's swallowed Keenan's story. "I was late for class that first day because I went to my Monday class, but everything else is a lie. I've never done drugs."

Coach holds up a hand in a stopping gesture. "I didn't think so."

A half dozen other players have filtered out and gathered around. Coach gives them a hitchhiking motion, pointing his thumb to the field. "Keep moving, guys. Move along. None of your business here. Move it!"

They obey, until I blurt out, "I don't even know what LSD is!" The players' heads whip back around so fast they almost get whiplash.

"Did I tell you to keep moving?" Coach Callahan yells, and they all walk quickly away, their cleats clopping loudly.

When they've gotten a good distance away, Keenan starts in again. "He's lying! I swear it! Ask anyone. He lies about everything!"

Coach Callahan stares at him. "You're going to have to do better than that, Keenan." Coach points at me. "Look at him. You expect me to believe he *made up* a story about getting hit? *Nobody's* that good of an actor, not even Marlon Brando. He got hit, all right. And it seems quite the coincidence that all this happens the day after he takes away your starting job."

Coach Callahan takes a menacing step toward Keenan. "You slugged him because you're pissed off you aren't starting anymore, didn't you?"

"No," Keenan says, shaking his head. "I swear it!"

"Either that or else you're trying to intimidate him in some way that forces him to quit the team. Just like he said."

"No!"

"I believe you did exactly what Rabbit says you did," Coach Callahan says. "You slugged him and thought you could get away with it. And you might since there don't seem to be any witnesses. If I knew for a fact you did it, I'd kick you off the team and try to get you kicked out of school besides. There's no place for that."

"I didn't! I swear it!"

"Keenan, shut up before I hit you myself."

Keenan blinks.

"Labelle, are you okay to practice?" Coach asks.

I nod. The sick sensation in the pit of my stomach lingers, but I'm pretty sure I'll be okay.

"Are you sure?"

"Yes."

"Then get out there," he says, pointing to the field, "and get loosening up. If you can't, get dressed and see the nurse before she goes home."

"You!" He turns to Keenan. "We're going to talk to Coach McDonough."

*

Five minutes later, none of the coaches have come out of the building so Jake O'Meara starts the calisthenics, beginning with jumping jacks, running in place, and pushups. Everyone counts off the exercises, "One…two…three," just like usual, but there's a distracted air throughout the team. Everyone but O'Meara has their backs to the school building and it looks like we've all noticed the coaches' absence, so there's lots of glancing around and covert looking out of the corners of our eyes.

I feel queasy and even stop halfway through the pushups because I think I'm going to puke. But I'm sure I'll be okay and join back in on the quad stretches.

O'Meara has cycled through all the calisthenics and started back in on jumping jacks when all of a sudden he stops. In unison, the team turns to see the four coaches, all of them wearing gray LEHS Bulldogs sweatshirts with red lettering, step onto the field and gather next to the near goal post. Behind them walks Keenan, who's putting on his helmet.

All the coaches look unhappy. Frowns crease their brows. But Coach McDonough looks like a volcano ready to erupt, his red-faced fury to remain bottled up for only another few seconds as he strides a few steps closer to the team and then stops. He crosses his arms, sets his jaw. His silver whistle dangles from a black cord around his neck.

"Labelle, get over here!" he bellows.

As I sprint over, he blows the whistle and yells at O'Meara, "Did I tell you to stop?"

The team starts in on more jumping jacks, counting out in unison but sounding softer than before as if everyone still wants to listen in.

Keenan stands to the left of Coach McDonough. Lined up behind them are the three assistant coaches with Coach Callahan on the right. He shifts uncomfortably on his feet and looks away.

"Now let's get one thing straight," Coach McDonough says. He glances at Keenan, then bores his eyes in on me. "One of my rules is that freshmen will be seen but not heard. Your role on this team is to stay out of the way until you're big enough and good enough to help the varsity. Neither of you two is good enough *or* big enough. Labelle, you're probably *never* going to be big enough. God knows why I ever let you even have a shot on this team."

"Do you think my priority—" he stabs his index finger in his chest "—is settling disputes between two frigging freshmen who can't play football worth a damn? Or do you think it's spending time on the *varsity,* which is the only team this school cares about, which has players who aren't a bunch of goddamned whining babies that I need to babysit all the time?" Spit flies from his mouth on the word *babysit* and lands halfway between him and me.

I can't believe what I'm hearing, words that are blaming me equally with Keenan. As if it was my fault he attacked me. Somehow, he's convinced Coach McDonough that I'm the guilty one. I glance at Coach Callahan who looks down at the ground, embarrassed, and bites his lower lip. A momentary silence fills the air, broken only by the players behind us counting off their calisthenics.

"I can't hear you!" McDonough roars, his face growing even more red with anger.

"The varsity, sir," Keenan says quickly.

I shake myself into action and echo Keenan's words. Behind the helmet's facemask, he grins. Because he answered more quickly? Or because he knows he's won? I'm afraid it's the latter.

"I will not tolerate distractions caused by a couple of goddamned freshmen," McDonough says, words that presumably are meant for both Keenan and me, but he's pointing angrily at me. "If the two of you can't get along, I'll cut you both and I'll do it in a heartbeat. Do you understand?"

"Yes sir!" I say, this time beating Keenan by a split second.

"Now I want you two—" as McDonough speaks, Keenan lifts his hand to his mouth "to shake like men on it and I don't ever want to hear another word from either of you. Do you understand me?"

"Yes sir!" we both say in unison.

I no more want to shake Keenan's hand than kiss his cleats, but McDonough has made it clear I have no choice. I've got to make up with the same guy who ambushed me just a few minutes ago. I try to think of it as the empty handshake between two hated rivals in any sport, like football captains after the coin toss has decided who will receive the ball, but even those handshakes are based on mutual respect and sportsmanship.

How can I have any respect for Keenan after what he's done, not just sucker-punching me but then somehow turning the head coach against me? And where's the sportsmanship?

Keenan steps forward and extends his hand. His eyes are sparkling, his white mouthpiece visible in the most wide-mouthed grin.

I reluctantly put my hand forward and Keenan grasps it.

A thick layer of warm spit covers my palm and I now understand why Keenan was raising his hand to his mouth just as McDonough was about to issue our shake-hands-and-make-up ultimatum.

The sensation disgusts me, just as it disgusted me when spit flung by Keenan clung to my neck minutes earlier. Apparently, spit is his signature.

He rubs our palms together just in case I'm too dumb to realize what he's done, and then he clenches my hand as hard as he can, as if he's trying to break every bone in my fingers. I try to retaliate, but he's stronger than me.

Suddenly, he releases his grip and when I let go, too, he gives me a light slap on the side of the neck that probably looked to McDonough like a good-natured, hey-let's-get-along gesture, but I knew its real purpose.

To smear the last bit of spit on his palm onto my neck.

CHAPTER 34

After practice, I walk out to where my mother is waiting in her Ford Fairlane at the beginning part of the half circle that bends toward the Lynn English front entrance. I'm not going to tell her about Keenan's attack. She'd just worry and maybe even try to get me to quit the team. It's best that she doesn't know. Best for her and for me.

I toss my things in the back seat and grab the brown bag that holds my chicken salad sandwich. My stomach may still be churning, but not enough to stop me from eating. I unwrap the wax paper and take a big bite of a chicken salad sandwich. It tastes delicious, the white slices of Wonder Bread covering the small squares of chicken and little bits of crunchy celery mixed in with mayonnaise.

Mom navigates the half circle, having to stop multiple times for cars pulling out of their parked spaces, then pulls onto Goodrich Street, heading for Chestnut Avenue. As we near the corner, we pass Charlie Watkins walking on the sidewalk, his gym bag slung over his shoulder, holding two books in his other arm.

I frown. There are a couple guys on the team who live in walking distance and don't bother with rides. I see them walking home all the time, but never Charlie.

My mouth is full, but I still manage to say, "Stop. I think my friend might need a ride."

Mom's face brightens. She raises her eyebrows. "A friend? That's great!" She begins to pull over, then glances in the rearview mirror, sees Charlie and his huge Afro, and freezes.

She swerves back, almost cutting off another car, probably one that emerged from the half circle in front of the high school seconds after us.

"He's…he's black," she says.

"So what?"

"You're *friends* with him?" Her face has turned ashen, her lips pale.

"Kind of. Well, not exactly friends, but he's on the team."

She pulls to the stop sign on the corner. "You really want me to give him a ride?" she asks, incredulous. "Where does he live? Anywhere near us?"

"I don't know, but yes, if he needs a ride we should—"

"I'm not driving into the ghetto."

"*The ghetto*? Mom, he lives here in Lynn. There's no ghetto—"

"You know what I mean. There are good sections like where we live and bad sections." She doesn't say it, but I can finish the sentence that my father has spoken several times: *bad sections where the blacks and Puerto Ricans live.* "I'm not driving into a bad section of the city for someone you barely know."

A horn honks behind us and she turns right onto Chestnut Avenue. Away from Charlie.

"Mom, please stop." I've long since stopped eating my sandwich. This has suddenly become very important.

But she doesn't.

"He's kind of my friend…we've talked a couple times," I say, stretching the truth a little. "He caught the pass on the winning extra point, remember? He's the split end and the other cornerback." When she says nothing, I decide to try to humor her. "It's like we're twins."

She glances over and gives a sour look. "I hardly think that's funny."

"Like Brooks and Frank Robinson on the Baltimore Orioles," I say about the white third baseman and black outfielder.

She keeps driving, lips pursed, and I become angry. We get to the stop light at Western Ave. My anger burns hotter and hotter until it boils over with sudden vengeance.

"You're just as bad as Dad," I say.

"What's *that* supposed to mean?" she snaps.

"He says all these awful things about black people and you act all outraged but what are you doing right now? You're acting just like he would. You're no different."

Her face flushes. "If I weren't driving, I'd slap your face."

Slap my face? Like that's going to scare me after dealing with thugs like Smitty and Keenan. She can slap me all she wants. If I'm not backing down to Keenan, I'm not backing down to her either.

"If you're different than Dad—if you're not just a *phony* who says one thing and then does something else—you'll circle around the block and go back and pick up Charlie."

She keeps driving, gripping the steering wheel so tightly with both hands her knuckles are white.

"He might live three miles from school just like me," I say. "That's a long way to go with a heavy gym bag and books."

She slows down for the light at Maple Street, and I recall one trick she's used a couple times on my father. I try it.

"You will if you love me," I say.

She looks at me hard, the fury in her eyes trying to bore holes in me. I look back at her with all the same fury.

And she looks away.

She takes a deep breath and exhales loudly.

Without a word, she turns right when the light glows green instead of staying straight, and circles back to the school.

*

We find Charlie walking in the opposite direction on Chestnut and Mom, eyes darting left and right, pulls to the curb. I roll the window down.

"You need a ride?"

Instinctively, he takes a step back, then I poke my head out farther and he recognizes me. He takes cautious steps towards the car and peers inside.

"Is this your mother?" he asks.

"Yeah."

He hesitates. "My momma couldn't pick me up today, but…"

"Hop in," I say. "We'll take you home."

"I don't know…" He hefts his gym bag higher on his shoulder, as if trying to compare its weight with the dangers of taking a ride with us. Strangers, kind of. Not totally, but kind-of strangers. White strangers.

"Where do you live?" I ask.

"You're probably not going my way."

"We are now," Mom chimes in with a sudden and surprising cheerfulness. "You can tell me about your game-winning catch. I saw it, but I'd like to hear you tell me about it."

Charlie smiles. "I guess so. If it's not too far out of your way."

"Hop in," Mom says, and he climbs in the back seat, pushing my bag and books to the driver's side.

He gives her an address but she doesn't recognize it. Nor does she recognize the street it's off of. A tinge of color creeps up her neck and cheeks. "We've only lived here for a few weeks and I don't know my way around town," she says sheepishly. "Can you direct me?"

Charlie tells her to keep going on Chestnut, then take a left on Essex. I look down in my lap and see my chicken salad sandwich with one diagonal slice untouched and the other half eaten.

"Want half of my sandwich?" I ask, grabbing the half-eaten side in one hand and holding out the other in the wax paper wrapping. I turn all the way around and lift the sandwich over the back of the car seat that runs straight across the front. "I get hungry after practice so my mom makes me a sandwich. It's chicken salad."

He stares at it with a hungry look, but shakes his head. "I'm fine, thanks."

"Are you sure?" I keep dangling the sandwich in the air. "It's really good, but I'll have to wrap it up and eat it later if you won't take it,

---

because my mom won't let me eat in front of you. You know, bad manners and that stuff."

"Rabbit!" my mom scolds.

"Go ahead and eat it," Charlie says. "I'm fine."

I keep trying to persuade him, finally saying that I'm not hungry enough to eat the whole thing so I'll just have to throw it out.

"Well if you're going to throw it away..." he says with a grin, and reaches for the sandwich.

Mom asks him again about the game-winning catch, but he doesn't answer right away. I turn around and my suspicions are confirmed.

"She does the same thing to me, too," I say. "She waits until my mouth is full and then asks me a question."

Charlie nods with a broad grin and Mom gives me a playful swat on the arm.

When he's finished with that mouthful, he says, "Your son scored the two touchdowns. I just got the two-point conversion."

"But that won the game for us," I say.

"It looked like quite a catch," Mom says. "Describe it for me."

Charlie recounts the play and my mother praises his ability. He thanks her, then the car falls silent until the inevitable question is asked.

"So how did practice go today?" she asks.

"Fine," I answer, and hope Charlie doesn't say anything more.

He doesn't.

We ride in silence, and after a right turn followed by a left and another right, I'm quickly lost. The streets are lined with tightly packed, three-story, three-family houses in various states of disrepair. Peeling paint. Partially detached gutters dangling in the air. No lawns, just dirt and pavement extending from crumbling concrete sidewalks. Laundry hangs from clotheslines extending off sagging side porches. I never thought of our house as anything special, but it's a mansion compared to most of what's here.

Charlie finally breaks the silence.

"You came back for me, didn't you?" he says.

I glance at my mother, who opens her mouth but no words come out.

"You turned right onto Chestnut Street, heading toward East Lynn," Charlie says, "but you came back to give me a ride to the other side of town. That was very nice of you, Mrs. Labelle. Thank you."

My mother nods, and after a brief pause, says, "Rabbit insisted. He practically tore the steering wheel out of my hands."

*

"I don't usually believe in keeping secrets from your father," Mom says after we drop Charlie off and head home. "But he's got a lot on his mind these days and he doesn't handle some things very well. Let's keep this just between the two of us."

"Sure," I say. A warm glow radiates out from within my chest. "Thanks for turning around. I didn't think you were going to."

"Neither did I," she says with a sidelong glance. "That big Afro kind of scared me. But...you made me do the right thing."

From the bottom of my heart, I say, "Mom, I love you."

CHAPTER 35

Charlie and Jessie Stackhouse walk out to practice with me the next day. The two of them appear out of nowhere as I'm checking out the exit, trying to make sure Keenan isn't about to leave the locker room at the same time. At first I think it might be a coincidence, them just happening to show up at the right time to join me. But there they are the next day, ready to head out just as I slam my locker door shut.

"Jessie plays hockey, if you can believe that," Charlie says as we walk carefully down the stairs, our cleats click-clacking noisily. "Every other brother I know plays hoops during the winter, but he's out on the ice scoring hat tricks."

"Hat tricks?" I ask, unfamiliar with the term. What could a hat trick possibly be? Hockey players must be the dumbest athletes in the world if they let an opponent hide the puck in their hat and then, at the right time, pull it out and score with it. I tried to pull off a hidden ball trick all through Little League and Babe Ruth and never got it to work once.

"It's when you score three goals in a game," Jessie says, making me breathe a huge sigh of relief that I didn't say what I'd been thinking and expose what a total imbecile I am.

"He set a scoring record last year," Charlie says. "As good as he is in football, he's ten times better in hockey."

"Twenty," Jessie says, and they both laugh while I try to decide if ten times better than him is even possible.

"Says he might even give up football in another year or two so he can concentrate on hockey. Thinks he's going to play in the NHL some day."

"It could happen," Jessie says with a hard look in his eyes.

"Why not?" I say. "What's to stop you if you're good enough and you work hard?"

"What's to stop me?" Jessie says with a look of incredulity, then turns to Charlie. "Is he unbelievably naïve or just plain stupid? He better be one or the other, 'cause if he's making fun of me—"

"I'd never make fun of you," I say, stunned at the very thought. "Why would you think that?"

"'Cause there isn't a single black player in the NHL," Jessie says. "Only been one, *ever*. And you ask what's to stop me, like it's no different than if it was you?"

I feel bad now, and for a moment I don't know what to say. "I'm just a dumb hick," I finally manage, and then to prove my point, I actually tell them what I had thought a hat trick was.

They explode into gales of laughter.

"You thought..." Jessie begins, but he can't even finish the sentence, he's laughing so hard. He and Charlie bump sideways into each other, holding their stomachs. Tears stream down Jessie's face. I join in on the laughter even though it's at my own expense.

"You really thought that?" Jessie finally says, shaking his head in disbelief. "Hide the puck...under a hat?"

I nod.

"See, I told you white people is just as dumb as us," Jessie says to Charlie and they both laugh.

"Hard to believe he's in accelerated English and French," Charlie says. "Smart but dumb."

Jessie looks at me. "Really?"

I nod.

"I'm in accelerated History, Algebra, and Biology," he says.

"Put the two of you together and we'd have an Einstein," Charlie says.

"But one who tries to score goals by hiding a puck under someone's hat," Jessie says, and we all explode in laughter again.

*

In the following days, if I'm ready and Charlie and Jessie aren't, I wait for them near their lockers, which are one row closer to the outside door than mine.

The white guy and the two blacks. An odd three musketeers.

We get funny looks, even from Coach McDonough, but only Keenan makes a comment. He waits until one practice when most of us JV players are just standing on the sidelines watching the varsity players run through plays. I'm alone with no one within five yards of me, when he sidles up to me.

In a low voice, barely more than a whisper, that no one else can hear, he says, "Nigger lover."

I can barely believe my ears. In fact, I refuse to believe them. I stare at Keenan.

He removes all doubt by leaning forward until our two facemasks click together and I can smell his sour breath. He says it again. "Nigger lover."

I stumble backwards a step, reeling, and then another, windmilling my arms to steady myself. A sense of unreality overwhelms me. I feel as if I'm in a dream, my brain foggy, my mouth so dry I can't speak.

A sharp whistle—one of the coach's—cuts through the fog. Coach McDonough yells and curses at some player. I blink rapidly and shake my head to clear the cobwebs.

Keenan looks around and steps back beside me. "All of your own kind hate you. So you have to kiss ass with the darkies."

A ball gets deflected and bounces wildly toward us. At the last second, Keenan sees it, steps smartly aside, and it hits me in the thigh and bounds away.

"Pay attention over there!" Coach McDonough screams. "Quit sleeping!"

I jog to the ball, pick it up, and toss it to Jake O'Meara. The varsity starts practicing another play. I keep my eyes on the action in front of me so I don't get hollered at again, but I think about what Keenan has said, or at least part of it. It's something I've wondered myself even before Keenan brought it up the first time.

Why haven't I made any other friends on the football team? Why no *white* friends?

It feels strange to be so wildly unpopular when I had so many friends in Plainfield. And not just any friends. *Great* friends. Ones I spent all my time with. One who would do me favors if I only asked, and I'd do the same for them.

The upperclassmen won't even consider being my friends just because I'm a freshman. They won't even let me use the good showers. If I ever make it to my senior year here, it's not how I'll treat the under-classmen, but at least I don't feel singled out. The upperclassmen treat all the other freshmen and sophomores the same way.

But what about the other freshmen and sophomores? Other than Charlie and Jessie, of course. I figured a lot of my teammates would remain resentful for a while that I'd missed the Summer Suicides, but I thought they'd come around eventually as long as I proved I was a good player. And I thought for a while after Monday's game things would be okay. Guys slapping me on the back, whacking my shoulder pads hard so they'd give off that crunching sound.

But then two practices later, Keenan sucker-punches me and eve-rything goes back to how it was at my first practice. I'm still an out-sider, the hayseed from Aroostook County, so dumb I'm messing with Keenan, the fair-haired boy with the flowing, golden locks, taking his job away, and then accusing him of cheap-shotting me.

I realize a lot of these guys played with Keenan at Pickering Junior High and the others at least played against him. And maybe they were on the same baseball or basketball teams.

A popular kid like him? Friends with everyone? Then the kid who nobody knows shows up, skips practices, and takes away his starting job.

I'm the enemy to all of them. The bad guy.

At least the white players. Maybe even the blacks, unless they've heard Keenan's real view of them.

This could be a very long season if I can't turn my teammates around. And I haven't the slightest idea of how to do it.

*

At our next JV game, I get to run back kicks for the first time. It's something I've only practiced a few times, so my gut is in knots before the opening kickoff, but I tell myself that at least it isn't one of Coach Callahan's mile-high punts. Those seem to rise higher and higher, never stopping, up into the wispy, white clouds. I have trouble finding the football and when I do, I can't tell whether I need to backpedal or come in quickly. It leaves me feeling a little dizzy, wishing for the first time that I'd played outfield in baseball, that most boring of positions, just so I'd have practice for those kicks.

I had seemed to be coming around on the punts in practice, and the lower-hanging kickoffs had come naturally right from the beginning. But it's one thing to do okay in practice; another when it counts. And I want to do more than just okay. A fair catch or simply not fumbling is okay, but I want to hit a big-gainer. Call me greedy, but isn't that what it's about?

I'm hungry for more touchdowns.

It's another home game at Manning Bowl, this time against Swampscott, which according to the buzz of locker room conversation is always one of the top powers in the state. Swampscott proved it three days ago when its varsity destroyed ours, 51-12. Its third stringers were playing by the start of the fourth quarter, otherwise it would have been even worse.

We win the coin flip and elect to receive. I trot back to my position and look at my ten teammates in their white uniforms arrayed in front of me. Then I survey the Swampscott players in their navy blue uniforms lined up for the kickoff, each of them looking bigger than the Lynn English player assigned to block him. I begin to wonder if Swampscott has fielded thirteen players instead of just eleven and actually begin to count them when the referee blows his whistle. The Swampscott kicker runs up to the ball and puts his leg into it.

The ball flies high into the air, off to my right, and for a sickening instant I think it's going to fly over my head, but I position myself under it and let the rough, rawhide surface settle down into my hands.

I catch it against my stomach, tuck it under my arm, and dart forward, looking for a hole. Ahead of me, my blockers take on the coverage team, loud grunts filling the air as thundering collisions explode, pads slamming into pads. A bitter taste forms on my tongue.

For an instant, it looks like a hole has opened up. I veer to my left, shifting the ball into my other arm, cradling it up against my body so it can't be easily stripped away.

I hit the hole with as much speed as I can, my heart hammering as I see open space in front of me—

And a beast that must weigh close to two hundred pounds slams into me from my blind side. Swampscott's version of Jessie Stackhouse. He practically separates my head from my torso. My head snaps sideways. My teeth dig into the plastic mouthpiece, without which I'd be left looking like a Halloween lack-o'-lantern.

The beast keeps his legs churning, lifts me up off my feet, and slams me into the ground with a jarring crash. It's as if he's tried to drive me through the ground so hard that my head will pop out somewhere in China.

For a second, I think he's knocked the wind out of me, but the surprising and wonderful sensation of air flowing into my lungs quells that fear. A thin strip of sod almost the length of a football is wedged sideways into and around my facemask. I pull most of it loose, but a dollar-sized segment remains in the facemask even as I use one hand to pick clumps of dirt away from around my eyes and the back of my other hand to wipe it away from my mouth. Mostly, though, I just smear it.

Without a word, Charlie takes hold of my facemask and yanks out the remaining sod. I mutter, "Thanks," and try to shake out the cobwebs.

I finally see the beast in black—really see him—for the first time. He wears number fifty-one, which seems only fitting. He's like Dick Butkis, the Chicago Bears' fierce middle linebacker. The toughest man in pro football wears number fifty-one, and this number fifty-one seems as tough as they come.

After three quick, unsuccessful plays—two runs and an attempted pass that becomes a sack for Swampscott's big number seventy-one—it's time to punt.

That's about how the whole game goes. I don't have to worry about a sky-high punt that I have to field cleanly because our defense never once forces a punt. Swampscott does fumble twice, which sends the Swampscott coach into a fury, throwing his clipboard to the ground and screaming at the offending player, but other than that, the Big Blue, as they're called, score every time. They don't try many passes—Charlie and I minimize the damage there—but they just grind us up with their running game, just like the Green Bay Packers.

We have no answer for them at all and lose, 65-6. I score our only touchdown on a kickoff return, freezing number fifty-one with a fake and then taking off, outracing him up the middle. C.J. Powell throws a nice block to take out one of the two remaining defenders, and I fake out the other one and race into the end zone. But by that time we're losing, 42-0. It's hard to get excited when you're still down 42-6 and the other team has been knocking the stuffing out of you all day and it sure looks like they'll keep doing it until you surrender.

We don't surrender but we sure get embarrassed.

*

When it's time to break up into varsity and JV squads the next day at practice, Coach Callahan gathers all of us JV players into a big circle down at our end of the field. As his LEHS Bulldogs pullover jacket flaps in the brisk, cool wind, he looks around the circle until he spots Jimmy Keenan on the opposite side and then me. His eyes narrow and he purses his lips.

"How'd you boys like getting your asses kicked last night?"

No one answers. I stare at the ground. My ears burn, not because of his words but because of the look he's giving me and Keenan.

"It wasn't fun was it?" Coach Callahan asks, looking all about the circle of players.

I shake my head, as do many others. Some mumble their agreement.

"It was damned embarrassing, that's what it was," he says. "It was a butt-whipping. An ass-kicking. We got humiliated!"

I stare at a triangle-shaped chunk of turf that's next to my right toe.

"I hope you felt humiliated. So humiliated you never want it to happen again."

I feel the coach's eyes burning into me and look up. I stare back at him. He glances at Keenan and then back to me, back and forth like a spectator at a tennis match.

"We have to play as a team," Coach Callahan says. "There is no 'I' in T-E-A-M. We can't play as individuals. We can't act like individuals. We have to all work together or we're going to fail. You don't have to like everyone, but we can't be fighting amongst ourselves and expect to have any kind of success. A house divided against itself cannot stand."

He keeps going a little longer, but to be honest, I tune him out. I believe in teamwork and always have. But this talk that we lost because of Keenan and me is so crazy I can't stand it. We got crushed by Swampscott because almost every team gets crushed by Swampscott. That team was going to destroy us even if Keenan and I were best friends.

But not only is it crazy to blame the loss on anything but a total mismatch in talent, it's also unfair to blame me at all. I don't deserve half the blame. And that's what Coach Callahan is doing when he singles the two of us out from everyone else and then talks unity.

Try having someone sucker punch you in the gut and then talk to me about unity.

Is that having a bad attitude? If so, then I'm guilty. But I think it's just being human.

CHAPTER 36

The next night, Coach Callahan's words still sting, but not as bad. What really has me upset is the Red Sox. It's down to the final week of their amazing season. They've gone from a next-to-last-place finish last year to being one of the four teams that have stayed within a game or two of first since early August. It looked like two easy games against the Cleveland Indians would help put the Sox on top before they finish with two tough ones against the Twins.

So what happens? The Sox lose both games to Cleveland, a lousy team that's *sixteen* games out of first, including a 6-0 shutout this afternoon. Now, they'll have to beat the Twins in both games this weekend and hope the Tigers don't sweep the Angels.

Yaz has been amazing, he's battling the Twins' Harmon Killebrew for the home run title and if he wins it, he'll take the Triple Crown. With two games to go, he already has 43 home runs and 120 RBIs. And their top starting pitcher, Jim Lonborg, already has 21 wins.

But they're probably going to blow what sportswriters have been calling "The Impossible Dream" season with those two lousy losses.

And if Coach Callahan and the Red Sox aren't enough to get me in a bad mood, there's always Dear Old Dad. He comes marching into the house after 8:30, rests his tan briefcase next to the front room sofa where I'm studying, trying to concentrate while my stomach growls.

"I'm home!" he yells for Mom's benefit.

I feel like answering, "Congratulations!"

But he's not a fan of sarcasm.

Mom bustles into the front room, gives him a kiss, and takes his coat and hangs it in the closet. "I made American chop suey," she says, and since The King has arrived, we all head to the dining room table.

We sit in our usual places and I answer the usual questions about my school day and football, responding with the same one-word answer to both questions: "Good."

I could tell my parents that Smitty got expelled for punching a teacher, so now I could take the bus, but I remain silent. I'm not in a talkative mood. Besides, maybe one of his tough-guy friends has taken over the lunch money extortion business. I've never specifically told my parents about Smitty so they don't need to know that he's gone.

What they don't know won't hurt them.

A tense silence descends, broken only by the wall clock behind me.

Tick…tick…tick…

Tick…tick…tick…

Tick…tick…tick…

Finally, my father breaks it for good, giving up on me and talking to my mother.

"Did you hear about those women arrested outside the White House last week?" he asks her. Without waiting for a response, he says, "If they had their way, we'd hand half the world over to the Communists. I'm sure half of them are Commie sympathizers anyway."

"Andre, not at the supper table, please," Mom says.

"Well, it's the truth," he says, ignoring her.

Mom purses her lips and a slight flush comes to her cheek. "The WSP is not made up of 'Commie sympathizers.'"

"What's the WSP?" I ask, intrigued.

"Women Strike for Peace," my father says, as if spitting the words out. "They hold rallies against the war and try to help young men avoid the draft. They're a disgrace. Traitors."

"They're not traitors," Mom says. "They're mothers who are concerned about their sons dying in—"

"You don't think *my* mother was concerned about *me* dying in WW2?" my father says angrily. "If the WSP had been around back then, Hitler would rule the world today and we'd all be speaking German."

"Do you really think North Vietnam is trying to rule the world?" Mom says.

"Yes! It's all part of the Communist plan to take over the world. First, it's South Vietnam. Then it'll be Thailand and Cambodia. Next thing you know, it'll be the Philippines and Hawaii, all toppling one right after the other like dominos."

"That's your theory."

"It's fact!"

Mom closes her eyes for just a moment and shakes her head. "Let's not argue about it during supper, okay?"

I eat some American chop suey and look at my suddenly angry parents, first my mother, then my father, back and forth like at a tennis match. They say nothing. The clock ticks loudly.

"What about when I get drafted?" I ask. It's something I really haven't thought about because it seems so far away. It also occurs to me that we've rarely discussed the topic as a family; at least, it hasn't been discussed in front of me, even though my parents clearly disagree.

"You won't get drafted because you'll be in college," my father says. "Young men in college get a deferment and don't have to serve."

"What about after I graduate from college?"

"We'll have won the war by that time, I'm sure," he says. "And if not, you can go for a graduate degree."

"What if I don't want a graduate degree?"

"You'll want a graduate degree if the war is still going on."

Mom leans forward, looking like she desperately wants to say something, but somehow is holding her tongue.

The clock ticks off a few seconds.

"What if we can't afford college?" I regret the question as soon as it's out of my mouth.

"That's why this job of mine that you hate so much is important," he says. "I'm not working this hard for just me. I'm doing it for you."

I almost choke on my chop suey. *Yeah, right.* I want to roll my eyes and shake my head, but manage to restrain myself.

Suddenly, I think of Charlie. I don't really know how much money his family has, but I bet it isn't much. That shabby three-family house where we dropped him off sure didn't look rich.

"But what about those who can't afford it?"

"They're the ones who have to fight," my father says.

"That doesn't seem fair."

"It's survival of the fittest," he says. "The ones with the most brains and the most money live; the ones who aren't smart enough to get into college or can't afford it…well, those are the ones who are most expendable."

Most expendable.

I recoil at this explanation. It works to my advantage, so I guess I should be happy about it, but its unfairness seems outrageous.

"The lower classes have always done most of the fighting," my father says. "Always have and always will. It's the way of the world. Don't worry, Rabbit. We may not be Rockefellers, but we aren't scum from the ghetto."

Scum from the ghetto.

*

The next day, my father works late again even though it's Saturday. I'm in a good mood until he gets home because the Red Sox beat the Twins, powered by Yastrzemski's three-run homer, to set up a winner-take-all game tomorrow. Unless the Tigers sweep the Angels in their doubleheader to force a one-game playoff, either the Sox or the Twins will be headed to the World Series.

But my mood turns sour when I'm summoned to the dining room just because he's finally arrived. I'm tired of not knowing when we're going to eat just because of him and his stupid job, tired of waiting and waiting until he shows up, tired of it all. I trudge down from my room, thinking, *yes, Your Highness, thank you for gracing us with your presence so we can finally eat.*

He's standing next to the dining room table, a big grin covering his dopey-looking face. "Rabbit, what do you have planned for tomorrow?"

I shrug. "Nothing."

"Nothing? What about the Red Sox?"

"Yeah, they won." I give him another shrug, unwilling to share my joy and excitement with him, not even about Yaz hitting his forty-fourth homer. "So I'll watch the big game tomorrow on TV."

"No you won't!" he says, his grin getting even bigger.

My eyes widen and I prepare to explode. I hate him for dragging me to this place and how all he thinks about is his job and how he doesn't care at all anymore about me, but all those reasons for my hatred fade into insignificance if he takes this game—the biggest one in my lifetime—away from me. He can't possibly do it. It just wouldn't be fair.

"Because..." he says, pushing his glasses to the bridge of his nose and sounding like a daytime TV game show host, *"we're going to the game!"*

My jaw drops.

"Yes, to Fenway Park for the big game!"

The explosion of anger that had been welling up in me seconds ago turns into an explosion of euphoria.

"You're kidding!" I scream like a girl finding out she's going to a concert by the Beatles. "You're kidding!"

I jump up and down, my hands raised over my head, fists clenched and pumping in triumph. The look on my father's—okay, on *Dad's*—face is so full of happiness, as is Mom's, it feels like the old days, when I was happy and they were happy and I loved them both the way a kid is supposed to love his parents, and a family feels like a family.

I throw myself into Dad's arms and hug him fiercely. How can I hate him after this? I've been wrong about him. He really does care about me! I can't believe that he even *thought* of getting us tickets, much less actually get them somehow.

"Thank you! Thank you! Thank you! This is going to be great!" I pull myself away. "Did you hear that Yaz hit another home run today? A three-run blast, his forty-fourth of the season. Killebrew hit one in the ninth to tie him for the lead, but that one didn't mean anything."

It's not like Dad has brought back Donnie, Jimmy, Scooter, and all the rest of my old friends from Plainfield. It's not like he's removed Smitty and Keenan from my life and actually given me *friends*.

But the Red Sox playing the Twins in the final game of the season to see who goes to the World Series?

I have trouble getting to sleep because all I can think about is going to the game and seeing in person for the first time the Green Monster, Fenway Park's huge left field wall, painted in green with the scoreboard lettered in white. I wonder if I'll catch a foul ball for the greatest souvenir ever. But most of all, I hope to see the Red Sox complete their Impossible Dream season with a win to send them to the World Series.

They were *awful* last year, next to last in the league with a 72-90 record. Twenty-six games out of first place. A team they called a 100-to-1 long shot during spring training this year. No one gave them a chance.

But a team now one win away from the World Series. Unless, of course, the Tigers force a playoff.

For a brief moment, I compare myself here in *Lynn, Lynn, City of Sin* to the Red Sox. A 100-to-1 underdog. So awful the team manager gave me an ancient relic for a helmet. No chance at all.

Then I push that thought away. For at least tomorrow, I want to forget about everything that has gone wrong in the last couple months and just enjoy being at Fenway Park for the biggest baseball game in just about forever.

Thanks to my dad. Who really does love me.

CHAPTER 37

Turns out, Dad didn't tell us everything.

He's out in the driveway first thing in the morning, washing his car, scrubbing the exterior vigorously with a big sponge until the soap suds are running along both sides of our driveway out to the street and down the hill. He rubs a damp towel along the vinyl seats, then dries them. Mom offers to help, but he insists on doing all this himself. Finally, he runs an extension cord out the front door, plugs in the Electrolux, and vacuums it, double-checking every inch for a spot of dirt.

What he didn't tell us is that we're going to be joined by Mr. Jordan, Dad's boss at work. In fact, the four tickets are Mr. Jordan's, and we're his guests.

So Dad didn't go out and get tickets for me after all as the greatest surprise *ever*.

I guess I should have known.

But maybe he told Mr. Jordan about me. I bet one time Dad said something like, "I've got this great kid who'd just *love* to see the Red Sox play some time." Well, he'd probably be a little more subtle than that, just drop a little hint here or there and that hint now has us going to the biggest game ever.

I'm sure something like that happened.

"He's a very important person," Dad says as we load into the sparkling clean car, Mom joining me in the back seat to leave room for Mr. Jordan in front. She's wearing her light brown fall coat over a blue, flowered dress because it's cool and damp today. I'm wearing a jacket, too, along with school clothes, my Plainfield team's baseball cap and my glove, just in case I get a chance to catch the ball.

"I need you to make a good impression, so mind your manners," Dad says, leaning over the seat back to look me in the eye. He's wearing his usual starched white shirt, black suit, and tie, the tie being a thin red one today, perhaps in support of the Red Sox. "I don't want to hear any of the backtalk that you've been giving me lately or else…" He draws in a deep breath. "Well, if you do, you'll regret it. This is very important to me. To us." He glances at my glove, grimaces, looks about to say something about it, then seems to reconsider. He sits down, then turns around and pokes his head over the seat. "And if he tells a joke, laugh even if it isn't funny."

Mr. Jordan lives in Lynnfield, a community one town over that probably hates having the four-letter word "Lynn" at the beginning of its name. The lawns are larger and greener, the homes far nicer than even the best of them in Lynn, especially Mr. Jordan's. It's easily twice the size of ours, with a huge picture window in front, a two-car garage, and brightly colored flowers lining the paved driveway.

He bounds out of the house and down the steps, wearing a light jacket and dark slacks and carrying a small gym bag. He's tall and thin, maybe a little older than my father with what I've heard my parents call salt-and-pepper hair, which I guess means a mixture of black and white. He slides into the front seat, reaches over the seat back to shake Mom's hand first and then mine.

"Mrs. Labelle, you should sit up here next to your husband," he says. "Lord knows, I keep the two of you apart enough as it is."

"Oh no," she protests with a shooing gesture. "Go right ahead. I'm sure the two of you have plenty to discuss."

He reaches into his gym bag and pulls out a brand new navy blue Red Sox cap, the big letter "B" in bright red. He hands it to me. "You've got to be dressed appropriately for the big day, kid, what do you say?"

"Thanks!" I say, and take off my Plainfield cap and pull on the new one. "Who's your favorite player?"

"Yaz, of course!" I say. "He's going to win the Triple Crown, you just wait and see. He's going to finish first in batting average and runs batted in for sure. He's got those locked up already. And I bet he hits a homer today to give him forty-five so he beats out Harmon Killebrew."

Mr. Jordan chuckles and slaps me on the shoulder. He turns to my dad. "Andre, you didn't tell me your son was such a Red Sox fan. He knows more than I do, and I've got season tickets."

"Oh, he's the biggest sports nut I know," Dad says. "It's all he thinks about. Isn't that right, Rabbit?" He turns around, smiling, but quickly shifts his attention to Mr. Jordan.

All the air goes out of my lungs. I feel like I've been punched in the gut. My father hasn't talked about me after all. Not said a single word. He didn't go out of his way to get tickets to make me happy, to show me he loves me. That didn't even enter his head.

And as he and his boss launch into a discussion about some new project, I realize that today isn't about baseball to them. It's just about business and that crummy job.

I try to push it out of my mind. I tell myself that it doesn't matter if my father really doesn't care about me, after all. I'm still going to the Game of the Century. How lucky am I to be able to say that?

*

We've got amazing seats along the first-base line, just eight rows in back of the Red Sox dugout and just seven rows behind where Vice President Hubert Humphrey, who comes from Minnesota, and Massachusetts Senator Edward Kennedy are sitting in the front row, both dressed in dark suits and ties just like my dad. Mr. Jordan sits on the left, closest to home plate, followed by my father, Mom, and me. Mr. Jordan and my parents can't stop talking about the two politicians sitting so close to us, but that's nothing to me. Carl Yastrzemski, George "Boomer" Scott, and Rico Petrocelli are only eight rows away. Who cares about the Vice President?

We face the Green Monster and its scoreboard, where we'll be check-ing on the only two other games that matter, Detroit's doubleheader with California. The Sox have just *got* to win this one. They've just got to. You don't come this close to the Impossible Dream and then miss the World Series by a single game.

I say all this to Mom while my father and Mr. Jordan have their own conversation, then I add, "Yaz is hot as a pistol and we've got Lonborg pitching, but he's never beaten the Twins. *Never.* Even though he's 21-9, he's lost to them three times this year and is 0-6 against them in his career. And Dean Chance, the Minnesota pitcher, is also a twenty-game winner this year, including a 4-0 record against us." I shake my head. "What are the odds, 0-6 and 4-0?" I slam my fist into the well-oiled palm of my glove to make the point.

"Well," Mom says. "Sounds like we're due."

I grin, thinking *That's Mom for you.*

But it doesn't seem that way in the early innings. In the first inning, first baseman George Scott, normally an excellent fielder, takes a relay from the outfield and has the runner out at the plate by a mile but throws wild and high and Minnesota gets an unearned run. Minnesota gets another in the third inning when Yaz gambles on a hit by Harmon Killebrew, charging it to keep the lead baserunner from reaching third, and instead the ball gets past him and the runner scores.

Two unearned runs on errors by Scott and Yaz, two of the best field-ers in baseball. I shake my head. I expected Dean Chance to mow down our hitters with his sinkerball just like he's doing today because that's what he always does. But to be down, 2-0, going into the fifth inning because of those two errors doesn't seem right. How awful would it be for Yaz to win the Triple Crown only to lose this game on his error?

I start to say this to my father and Mr. Jordan, but they're involved in their own conversation. It's as if Mom and I aren't even there. I suppose I shouldn't be surprised. I suppose I should have expected it.

It stings, but I push those emotions away and again remind myself where I am and how lucky I am to be here. So what if my father didn't get the tickets as a surprise for me? So what if he's acting as though I don't even exist?

I'm here and that's what's important.

I tell myself that until finally I believe it.

*

The Red Sox rally in the fifth inning. Lonborg leads off with a perfect bunt down the third base line that catches Minnesota's third baseman, Cesar Tovar, by surprise. He's so frustrated, he pretends to take a bite out of the ball when he picks it up.

Suddenly, Fenway Park crackles with electricity. Everyone seems to sense that this is the key break and we all begin to clap our hands and chant.

"Go! Go! Go!"

Jerry Adair and Dalton Jones get hits to load the bases for Yaz. The crowd roars as he steps to the plate, and for a brief moment I dream about someday this many people cheering for me.

"Hit one out, Yaz!" I yell. "Hit a grand slam!"

Some guy behind me with a gravelly voice yells, "Hit a grand salami! A big kielbasa!"

It seems like a silly comment even though I know that Yastrzemski is a Polish name and kielbasa is a polish sausage, but I pound my fist in my glove and join in.

"Hit a grand salami! A big kielbasa!"

"Go! Go! Go!" the rest of the crowd chants, even my mom, whose face looks flushed as she cups her hands around her mouth.

I join them. "Go! Go! Go!"

My throat feels raw but a huge smile covers my face. It's going to happen. Maybe not a grand slam—or a grand salami, as the guy behind me called it—but Yaz is going to get some kind of hit. He's been so amazing this year. The whole ballpark knows he's going to come through again.

And he does.

Not with a grand salami, but a hard hit to center field to score two runs and tie the score. Fenway Park goes nuts. The crowd continues to roar. Streamers unfurl through the air.

The next batter hits a high bouncer to the shortstop, who tries to throw the runner out at home and isn't even close.

We lead, 3-2!

A relief pitcher comes in and uncorks not one but two wild pitches, sending another run across home plate and putting a runner on third. Pretty soon, Killebrew makes an error and we have a 5-2 lead going into the sixth inning.

We all stand and cheer as the Red Sox players take the field, the Fenway Park organ playing some happy tune that I don't recognize. 5-2! There's no way Lonborg is giving up this lead.

And he doesn't, although Yaz helps him out in the eighth inning, killing a rally by firing a throw into second base and catching a runner who thought sure he had a double.

It's 5-3 with one inning to go.

The entire ballpark is standing and cheering. The first batter hits a grounder to shortstop, but the ball takes a bad hop and hits Petrocelli under the eye.

The crowd groans. But the Sox turn a double play and now we're just one out away.

Lonborg is still on the mound. He's given up only seven hits and one earned run. And he's going to get the final out.

Pinch-hitter Rich Rollins lofts a soft pop-up to Petrocelli at short. Rico catches it and jumps up and down for joy.

I thrust my arms into the air. "We did it! We did it!" Mom, who is all smiles, gives me a hug. My father and Mr. Jordan slap each other on the back.

Fans spill onto the field to celebrate. They flood the aisles, rushing to vault over the waist-high fence and join in the jubilation. Fans already on the field lift Lonborg onto their shoulders and begin carrying him out to left field.

I hand Mom my glove, ready to become part of the celebration myself, but glance first at my father for permission.

"Oh, no you don't," he says.

Mr. Jordan chimes in. "Sport," he says, "a little runt like you would get trampled to death." He laughs and my father joins him.

A little runt like you.

And my father thinks that's funny, no doubt following his own advice to laugh at any joke the mighty Mr. Jordan tells.

Well *ha-ha-ha*. If I laugh any harder, I just might pee my pants.

"We should leave now and beat the traffic," Mr. Jordan suggests, and we do just that. While everyone else celebrates, turning Fenway Park into one huge party, we skip out to save a few minutes.

*

At home, I lie on my bed and listen to the Tigers lose the second game of their doubleheader, clinching the pennant for the Sox. They really are going to the World Series.

But as I drift off to sleep, I wonder if what I'll remember most about today will be Mr. Jordan saying "a little runt like you," and hearing the awful sound of my father's laughter.

CHAPTER 38

As it turns out, the World Series breaks the hearts of Red Sox fans all over New England, mine included. Yaz bats .400 for the series and Lonborg throws a one-hit masterpiece in game two and a three-hitter in game five. But he has to pitch on only two days' rest in game seven against a fully rested Bob Gibson, the Cardinals' ace, and Lonnie just doesn't have it. The Impossible Dream season remains a dream come true, but the Sox fall one game short of being world champions.

If it weren't for football, I'd have considered getting "Red Sox fever" during the Series, faking some kind of sickness so I could stay home and watch one or two of the weekday afternoon games. But as much as I love to watch the Red Sox and other sports teams, I love to play even more. Especially football.

And football is getting even more fun.

We win four games in a row and I score a total of nine touchdowns, including at least one on either a kickoff or punt return in each game. After the fourth straight win, Coach Callahan pulls me aside and says he may shift me to running back, at least part of the time, to get my hands on the ball more often. I stifle the urge to be a smart aleck and ask if I'm still hurting the team by playing as an individual—the unfairness of that accusation following Keenan's attack still gnaws at me—but I just smile and say, "Sure!"

That night, I think of all the best fakes and cutbacks made by players like O.J. Simpson at USC and Gale Sayers on the Chicago Bears. I try to mentally practice those moves so I'll be ready when the time comes. The excitement keeps me awake for a while, but it's a good excitement—a *great* excitement!—and when I slide out of bed the next morning, I feel full of energy.

But I'm not so full of energy or excitement by the end of practice that day. I feel sore all over. At halfback, you get hit on almost every play. It's a lot tougher than playing split end or flanker. I'm not sure if I'll even have enough energy to eat the sandwich Mom has waiting for me when I get out to the car.

I'm also embarrassed, at least a little, about one play. I suppose it's nothing to be embarrassed about, but I feel myself getting hot in the face just thinking about Coach Callahan shaking his head and laughing about it.

Laughing about *me*.

The call is for a halfback option. I take a pitch from Higgins, our quarterback, and roll out to the right with the option to run with it or pass. At least, that's how it would be in a game. I can pick whichever option is most wide open.

The first time we ran the play, I didn't really look to pass at all. I just took off with it. So this time Coach wants me to pretend to consider the run, but pass it no matter what.

It can be a very effective play, especially if a defense is coming up fast to stop a runner who's having a big game. I've seen it work for big gains and even touchdowns in the college and pro games I watch on TV. Lots of times, the receiver is wide open. No one is within ten or fifteen yards of the guy so the halfback just has to toss it. It's the easiest pass in the book.

But it doesn't turn out that way this time.

I roll to the right, at first with the ball under my arm as if I'm going to run with it and then I look for the receiver who's supposed to be wide open. It should be Keenan, who's back in the starting lineup with me at halfback.

But I can't see him. Even though he should be wide open right in front of me and probably is. I also can't see the other receiver, Charlie, who should have cut diagonally across from the other side of the field.

I can't see either of them.

I can't even see their defenders, who I find out later have cheated and ignored the run entirely because they heard Coach order me to throw it.

But that isn't even the problem.

I can't see the receivers or the defenders because all I can see are the backs of Moose Mahoney, Russ Wheatley, and Matt Gallucci, the three linemen on that side of the ball. They're all big kids who tower over me and with them standing upright and blocking the defensive lineman, I can't see a thing except their numbers: 71, 74, and 66.

This play is impossible if you're five-nothin', hundred-nothin'.

But I have to throw it. Coach told me to throw it no matter what. I can already hear him yelling at me if I don't.

I wind up and realize if I don't lob it over the linemen, I'm just going to hit one of them in the back of the head. So I give it my best shot. I float my best attempt over the linemen to where I'm guessing Keenan is.

Next thing I know, a defender is racing past us, running the other way with what would be an interception return for a touchdown in a game.

Coach Callahan blows his whistle and comes rushing at me, his face almost purple with rage. "Did you do that on purpose?" he hollers, spit flying out of his mouth.

I'm speechless. It was an awful pass. You can't do worse than throw an interception for a touchdown. But on purpose?

"Did you do that just because Keenan was the receiver?"

My jaw drops.

"Did you?" he yells, standing over me.

I finally find my voice, although it comes out in barely more than a squeak. "I couldn't see."

Coach stares at me, not comprehending.

"I couldn't see anything," I protest. "When Moose, Russ, and Matt stand up, I can't see over them. I can't see a thing!" I point to them now, standing five feet away from me, an impenetrable wall.

Coach blinks, and like air from a burst balloon, his anger disappears. He shakes his head and laughs. "Okay, strike that one from the playbook when you're at halfback."

Keenan appears from behind Coach, his hands flailing in the air. "He did it on purpose! He did it just 'cause it was me!"

"Keenan, shut the hell up," Coach says, and calls another play.

*

That Saturday night, I walk into the gym wearing my usual school clothes: dark pants, a dark blue shirt, and dress shoes. It's the Halloween dance, the school's first of the year. On the stage at the far end, a college-aged guy in a wild, tie-dyed T-shirt splashed with every bright color, neon-striped bellbottom pants, and hippie-style granny glasses carefully places the next 45 rpm record to play on one turntable while the other plays the Beatles "All You Need Is Love."

Loud but not too loud.

Halloween streamers of orange and black hang from the gymnasium ceiling. Black figures of witches on brooms and gray cobwebs cover the wall. The basketball hoops at both ends have been retracted to the ceiling where more orange-and-black streamers hang from the glass backboards along with a white sheet bunched up to look like a ghost. The four white fiberglass backboards remain in place on the two sidelines—they aren't retractable—and the stands have been folded back to the walls. The girls line the right side, going from the entrance to the refreshment table beside the stage. The boys line the left side, and the couples huddle along the far wall opposite the stage.

I worry that none of the girls will dance with me because the two I know and like the best, Anna and Cindy, have boyfriends and are off-limits. I also worry that I'll have no one to stand with.

But neither worry proves well-founded. I spot the other girls from my classes and dance with gossipy Sue Fitzgerald, shy, quiet-as-a-mouse

Ellen Sweeney, and smiling Joyce Mulcahy; actually dance three times with Joyce, whose green eyes sparkle with fun.

Charlie Watkins and Jessie Stackhouse cluster together with other black students at the end furthest from the stage. I know better than to join them. That would be fine with Charlie and Jessie but really awkward with the others. Charlie's averted eyes let me know this, so when I'm not on the dance floor, I'm standing with Jeff and Paul and a bunch of the other guys from my classes. Jeff warns me that Keenan is going to spike the punch at the refreshment table, and since "everyone knows midgets can't hold their liquor"—as he puts it—I'd better watch out. But I don't think anything's happening to the punch, not with the way Coach Callahan, who's one of the chaperones, is casting his eagle eye over everyone.

When the DJ says he's going to take a short break, all of Keenan's friends—which seems to be just about everyone but me—start chanting for him to sing.

"Keenan! Keenan! Keenan!" they yell, pumping their fists.

It doesn't take much to get him onto the stage, grinning broadly as he and his band quickly set up. It's clear that they expected it, probably even arranged for the "surprise" since all their instruments are already at the back of the stage.

But when Keenan sets his guitar onto its stand, lifts the microphone, and starts to sing Frankie Valli's hit "Can't Take My Eyes Off You," I'm forced to admit that Keenan sounds pretty good.

Maybe even great.

His voice sounds silky smooth and he makes eye contact with every girl in the building. One after another, they get this dreamy-eyed look on their faces as they gaze at those golden, curly locks of his, and you can just tell they're worshipping the ground he walks on.

Especially Anna.

I want to rush over to her, shake her by the shoulders, and tell her what a total jerk he is and that he doesn't deserve her. But even though I'm a dumb hick, I'm not *that* stupid.

After wild applause for that song, Keenan picks up his guitar and he and the band launch into "Light My Fire." Couples flock onto the dance floor, but more often than not, the girls are facing Keenan, their faces flushed.

Anna's, too.

I didn't know much about popular music when we moved down here. In fact, I didn't know anything. But I've been listening and even *I* know that this song isn't about romance. It's about s-e-x. So it's no surprise that Coach Callahan—I guess it's Mr. Callahan outside of football—leaps up onto the stage when the song is complete, slings an arm around Keenan, and engages in a heated discussion.

Keenan nods and Mr. Callahan hops down.

But when Jimmy Keenan and the band launch into the Rolling Stones' "Let's Spend the Night Together" Mr. Callahan races to the back of the stage and rips electric cords out of the outlets, silencing the band. He waves his hand in a cutting gesture and despite a thin chorus of boos, yells out, "Where's the DJ? Get him back up here!"

*

The DJ wins the crowd back pretty quickly with the Stone's "I Can't Get No (Satisfaction)" which is such a great dance song that even I can do pretty good at it. And then a slow dance with "Never My Love" followed by "Brown-Eyed Girl."

It looks like the fun night will end quietly until Marilyn Turner approaches me.

"Whoa!" Jeff whispers when Marilyn gets to within ten feet of me, because she's got a really big chest for a freshman and is wearing a white miniskirt that exposes her gorgeous legs all the way up to…well, close to up *there*. She smiles and brushes her dark hair off her face and behind her ear.

"You're Rabbit, aren't you?" she asks.

I can't imagine that this beautiful girl wants to dance with me. She's Jerry Soucy's girlfriend, and I never would have guessed that she even knew my name. My mouth is so dry, I'm not sure if I can speak. So I just nod.

It turns out that she doesn't want to dance. "You like Anna Levesque, don't you?" she asks.

I nod again, and then say with my voice cracking, "As a friend, I mean. She's going out with Jimmy Keenan." I look around for the two of them and don't see them anywhere.

"They got in a fight and she'd like to talk to you."

"Me?" The gym suddenly feels hot and muggy. "She wants to talk to me?"

Marilyn nods.

"Where is she?" I ask, looking around again.

"Out back on the football field."

By reputation, this is where couples sneak off to so they can neck in private. The thought of her and Keenan necking gnaws at my gut, but it sounds like I'll see none of that.

I thank Marilyn, who smiles, and I head out the back door at a jog that soon becomes a full sprint. Or as close as I can come to a full sprint in my dress shoes.

I see no couples making out. Only a single, solitary figure cloaked in darkness, leaning against the goalpost, illuminated only by moonlight and the slivers of light escaping from the high gym windows.

I rush to Anna and don't realize that something is wrong until I'm little more than fifteen feet away.

Keenan turns to face me.

With a baseball bat in his hand.

I try to stop, but I'm in dress shoes, not cleats. My feet slip out from under me and Keenan is on top of me in an instant.

I try to get up, but he puts his foot on my chest and pins me down. He waves the bat menacingly in the air.

"So you've come to take Anna away from me, too," he says, his breath reeking of alcohol.

I shake my head. "No, Marilyn just said..." I gulp hard. "She just said that Anna needed me...needed my help."

In the darkness, I see Keenan smile. "That's what she was supposed to say." I hear footsteps approaching and thick, heavy breathing. For a brief instant, I foolishly think that help has arrived.

Then I see the outline of two figures: Jerry Soucy and Luke Scanlon.

"You got him cold," Soucy says.

"He couldn't wait to come out and help her," Keenan says. "And I can guess what kind of help he had in mind."

"You've got it wrong," I say. "I even noticed while you were singing how...how...how smitten she was by you. We're just friends. She *loves* you."

I suddenly wonder if she was a part of setting this trap, but refuse to believe it. Not Anna, not in a million years.

"This isn't about her," Keenan says with dismissive shake of the head. "It's about you. And how you don't deserve to live another second."

Don't deserve to live another second?

A chill runs up and down my back.

I wriggle to get loose from beneath Keenan's foot, but he just drops his knee down onto my chest. It crushes me, almost knocking the wind out of me, and I gasp.

I look into Keenan's eyes, insane with hatred.

I struggle to get loose, but feel other strong hands pin me down.

"Hold him, boys," Keenan says, and when they have me tight, he stands up and smiles.

"Bet you can't score any touchdowns with a broken leg." He laughs and the other two boys laugh nervously along with him. "You won't be much of a hero then, will you?"

And with that, he spreads his legs like a woodsman about to split logs, winds up with the bat, and swings.

It thwacks hard against the side of my thigh. Pain shoots up and down my leg. I scream out.

"Cover the little girl's mouth!" Keenan commands, and Scanlon's big, meaty hand, smelling of alcohol, covers my mouth.

Streaks of light crisscross through the darkness as Keenan winds up again...

...and he flies through the air as a figure slams into him and drives him into the ground.

Mr. Callahan rolls off Keenan and flashes the beam of a huge silver flashlight at the other two boys, who break away from us and race back toward the school.

"This isn't what it looks like," Keenan says. "Tell him, Labelle. We were just goofing around. It was just a joke!"

But Mr. Callahan answers for me.

"Keenan, you're finished," he says, his face just inches away from Keenan's. "From the football team and from this school. You're suspended until the end of time. That goes for your buddies Soucy and Scanlon, too."

CHAPTER 39

I miss the next two games with a leg that I can barely walk on, much less run. We squeak past Saugus, 12-7, in the first one to extend our winning streak to five games, but get slaughtered by Peabody, 50-6, in the second. That drops our record to 6-2, which is the exact opposite of the varsity's 2-6. We both have two games left, finishing the season against our big cross-town rival, Lynn Classical. The varsity will play on Thanksgiving Day in front of the biggest crowd of the year, bolstered by all the alums that come back for that one game before heading to their parents' house for turkey and stuffing. For those of us on the JVs, we'll still be playing in front of only a few family and friends.

Or in my case, one family and no friends. Dear Old Dad still hasn't made it to any of my games. He was furious when he found out about Keenan's attack and even called the cops to try to get Keenan arrested, quieting down only after finding out that Coach Callahan beat him to the punch.

So it's not like he doesn't care at all. But he hasn't cared enough to get to a single game, and I'm sure he's not going to break that perfect streak this season.

But who cares? Certainly not me.

Although maybe Anna will attend even though the band, of course, won't be playing. She was pretty crestfallen about Jimmy Keenan getting arrested and thrown out of school, showing up for school with her eyes puffy and bloodshot.

For a while, I thought she even blamed me. But just a couple days ago, she apologized and has been especially nice ever since, talking to me before every class, asking how the JV team is doing.

I wonder if maybe some day she'll be *my* girlfriend. I think I'd like that.

*

Higgins, the quarterback, pulls me aside as soon as Coach Callahan blows the whistle, ending my first practice back following Keenan's attack.

"Got a minute?" Higgins asks, shifting his feet nervously and averting his eyes.

"Sure."

"How's the leg feel?"

"Not too bad," I say. "It's good to get back out here. Missing games isn't fun."

"Yeah," he says. He clears his throat and blinks his eyes rapidly. "Hey, I just wanted to say I got it all wrong with you. I didn't mean to be unfriendly." He shakes his head. "No, that isn't right. I *did* mean to be unfriendly. I believed what Keenan told me about you. He said not to trust you and made up all kinds of stuff." Higgins shrugs. "I guess most of it was lies. Hell, *all* of it was.

"There's a reason you didn't have any friends." He sees Charlie waiting for me and holds up his index finger, asking for a minute. "No white friends, at least. That's because we listened to Keenan. We went to junior high with him. Hell, some of us went to kindergarten and grammar school with him. He was our friend, and when he said you were a snake, we believed him."

Higgins stares down at the ground. "I always knew he was a little on the edge, but I never thought..." He shakes his head. "I always threw the best ball I could to you. I never missed you on purpose, although I suspect he would have wanted me to. I could never do that. But I wasn't a very good teammate to you." In a soft croak, he says, "I'm sorry."

"Thanks," I say, and extend my hand.

He takes it and we shake.

"I noticed that we have the same study period on Tuesdays and Thursdays," Higgins says. "Some of us use that period to lift. On the Universal machine, you know?"

I do know, even though I've never tried it. Housed in a separate room off the gym, the Universal consists of weights connected to pulleys so athletes can lift with less risk of injury than using free weights.

"Sometimes we skip it because we're too sore from the game," Higgins says. "And sometimes the seniors monopolize it, so we're just wasting our time. But other times we get a pretty good workout in. I've gained a lot of strength over the guys who only lift during the off-season. You might want to try it." He grins. "You're not exactly the strongest guy in the world."

I nod in agreement, but say that with my injured leg, I'd feel more comfortable waiting until the season ends. I don't want to take any chances with it right now.

"Sure, that makes sense," he says. "When you're ready, just let me know. I'll introduce you to the other guys." Higgins winces. "I mean, you already know them. They're all on the team. But you don't really know them, because they listened to Keenan, too."

Over the next few days, I get similar apologies from C.J. Powell, Russ Wheatley, and Joey Carbone. I shake all their hands and agree to forgive and forget.

I'm briefly tempted to only forgive, not forget, feeling a flare of anger at how they treated me. But then I think about how I would have reacted in Plainfield if Donnie or Jimmy or Scooter told me the new kid was rotten and not to be trusted.

And then I forgive and forget.

*

Coach Callahan pokes his head around the corner just as I close my locker and grab my gym bag to go home. I've been practicing without any problems with my leg this week and am ready to go for our next-to-last game on Monday. But I can tell that isn't why he's stopped by.

"Your mother's car broke down at the A&P," he says to me, waving the white slip used for all memos from the principal's office. "She says you'll need to either catch a ride home with someone else or walk. And help yourself to whatever's in the refrigerator."

I nod and Coach disappears. Next to me, Bruiser laughs, then proclaims loudly, "Tough luck, rookie. I'd give you a lift, but to ride in my car you've got to either have tits or hair on your balls. You ain't got neither."

From a nearby row, somebody calls out, "Bruiser's girlfriend has both," and raucous laughter erupts all around us.

Bruiser flushes, stands with his fists clenched, and then shoves me hard against my locker. I hit it with my right shoulder and fall to the ground. Somehow, it's as if I'm the one who said the remark about his girlfriend or was at least laughing at it, which I wasn't.

Towering over me, he swears, pointing his finger at me, then mutters, "Damn freshmen."

I don't get up and brush my clothes off until he whirls and leaves. I pick up my gym bag, heavy with my English, Math, and History textbooks inside because I've got homework in all of them, and head out of the locker room, swearing that when I'm a senior, I'll treat even the lowliest freshman like a teammate, not a punching bag.

Charlie catches up to me on my way out the front entrance. Like me, he's got his gym bag slung over his shoulder. Moisture glistens in his Afro.

"Hey, I heard you need a ride. Unless you already got one, my momma's here. We'll take you home."

"Would she mind?" I ask, hoping she won't. My gym bag feels heavy and I'm already exhausted from a tough practice. But I have to add, "It's on the opposite side of town. Almost all the way to Union Hospital."

"In that case…you should probably walk." Charlie breaks into a soft chuckle. He nods toward a rusty, gray Rambler off to our left, its shape box-like and unattractive. "Get in the car." It may be one of the ugliest cars waiting in the semicircle, but since it'll save me from walking three miles with a heavy bag, it's as good as a Cadillac.

Before we slide into the back seat, he turns and softly says, "You know, Bruiser's girlfriend really does have hair on her balls."

We get in, laughing, Charlie sliding all the way over to be behind his mom with me on the right. He introduces me, explaining that I'm the one whose mother brought him home and even though I live all the way on the other side of town, it's time to repay the favor.

"Of course!" she says. She has a warm smile and an Afro almost as big as Charlie's. "I've got to shake your momma's hand for bringing Charlie home. I called her on the phone and thanked her after you done that, but there's nothing like saying something in person."

I explain that my mom is probably still stuck at the A&P or maybe is at the garage getting the car fixed, but she almost certainly isn't home. So we talk about the football team and our upcoming big game, sounding like what my mom calls "a mutual admiration society" what with all our compliments for each other, until Mrs. Watkins stops at the light where Chestnut and Boston Streets merge to form Broadway.

An inlet of Flax Pond extends for a couple hundred feet along the right side of the road, bordered by a playground where a little girl in a pink dress pumps her legs to go higher and higher, and two boys bounce up and down on a teeter-totter.

Quiet and peaceful.

Until two Hells Angels pull up beside us, one on each side, their motorcycles roaring. The biker on the left has flaming red hair and a large potbelly; the one on the right has black hair and is thin. For both, their hair is long and tangled, flowing down to their shoulders. They have scraggly beards, and wear sunglasses but no helmets.

"Lock your doors!" Charlie's mom says, her eyes wide and her knuckles gripping hard on the steering wheel. "Now!" She reaches over her shoulder and locks her own as Charlie and I lock ours. She lunges across the empty passenger seat at the same time that I unbuckle my seat belt and lurch forward. We both hit the front passenger door lock at the same time, driving the button down hard.

The two Hells Angels rev the engines of their Harleys until they roar so loud I expect fire to shoot out of the chrome exhausts. On the backs of their black leather jackets are the curving red letters "Hells Angels" on top and "Lynn" on the bottom, forming a circle with the club's skull insignia in the middle. I stare at the skull, feeling cold all over.

From somewhere deep within, the thought bubbles up: *my Nikki Cruz drives a motorcycle.*

"Dear Lord, help us," Charlie's mom says, and repeats it over and over. "Dear Lord, help us. Dear Lord, help us."

Even with the windows closed, I smell the motorcycle exhaust, gasoline, oil, and leather.

The biker right outside my window looks more closely at us, then dismounts, sets his kick stand, and slams an open palm against my window.

"Nigger lover!" he screams, coating my window with spit. He says it again and now Charlie's mom is shrieking. The other Hell's Angel has pulled ahead and laid his Harley down in front of the car. He points to her and shakes his head, his message unmistakable: *Don't you* dare *drive over my bike.*

"Dear Lord, what do I do?" she shrieks.

The biker on my side leans back on one leg and tries to kick in the window, driving his hard metal boot against the glass. It rattles, but doesn't give way.

The other biker tries the same thing on the other side, first on Charlie's mom's window and then on Charlie's.

On my side, the force of a kick is so severe, the biker's sunglasses flop to the ground. I stare at crazed eyes with pupils dilated wide. Eyes filled with hatred, fueled by what I can only guess is some drug.

I whirl around, look out the back window. Two cars behind us have us blocked in.

I wave at them and yell, "Get out!"

As if in slow motion, they back up what seems like inches and then a foot and then another. I'm screaming at them. Everyone is screaming: Charlie's mom to Jesus, Charlie to something I can't understand, and the bikers at us. Another heavy boot slams against my window and it almost gives way.

Finally, the car behind us pulls out and around us. I see the driver, a businessman in his suit, eyes wide with terror. He isn't pulling out to help us. He's just getting away.

As does the car behind him.

I go to scream, "Back up!" but no words escape my mouth. I'm looking into the black barrel of a gun, held by the biker just a few feet away from me. His hand is shaking.

"Nigger lover!" he screams again.

His hand shakes some more. I stare at the gun barrel, frozen, unable to speak or move. All I can think is that I'm going to die.

Finally, I duck, and the words escape my mouth. "Back up!"

Charlie and I yell in unison. "Back up! Reverse!"

I reach for Charlie to pull him down with me as I drop to the floor, but he still has his seat belt attached and my fingers slip through his shirt.

Charlie unbuckles his belt just as the car shoots backward, slamming him against the back of the front seat before he, too, drops onto the floor.

The car zooms backward for what seems like forever, then screeches to a halt.

"Get down boys!" Mrs. Watkins yells unnecessarily, and the car swerves hard to the left and rockets forward. "Protect us, Sweet Jesus!"

*

I'm still shaking when we get to my house. We all are.

I stumble out of the car and stare at the side door as if in a dream. It's dented in three places, caved in by the biker's steel boot. It's proof that what just happened wasn't a nightmare. That crazed biker with his long black hair and scraggly beard really did try to kick in the door.

And he really did point that gun at me.

I can't get the image out of my mind of that black barrel lined up square between my two eyes. His hand shook as he pointed that gun at me. How easy would it have been for that trembling finger of his to pull just hard enough on that trigger to…

I try not to think of it. Try not to think of my head exploding as the bullet passes through it. Try not to think of my brains splattering all over the inside of the car. Try not to think of my life ended before I'm even fifteen.

My heart pounds so hard I can hear it echo inside my head. I'm covered in a cold, clammy sweat. A bitter taste fills my mouth. I tear my eyes away from the side of the car and my mental image of that gun pointed at me, and look over at Charlie.

He looks how I feel. Like he's in shock.

"Dear sweet Jesus," Mrs. Watkins says, and pulls Charlie into her arms. "Thank you for protecting us."

I suddenly wish my mom were here to hold me like Charlie's mom is holding him. I feel as if I'm about to start bawling like a baby.

As if she's read my thoughts, Mrs. Watkins motions me over, and I walk to her as if I'm in a trance. She wraps one arm around me and the other around Charlie and hugs us both tight. I bury my face in her arm. It smells of talcum powder and soap.

I want to let everything out, just burst out sobbing, but I don't want to embarrass myself in front of Charlie. I wonder if he feels the same way about me.

"Oh, Lord," Mrs. Watkins sighs.

After what seems like a very long time in one sense and at the same time not even close to long enough, Mrs. Watkins releases us. We stare at the car and I can see that the damage on the driver's side is about the same as it was on mine.

"We're okay," she says, as if trying to reassure herself that that's really the case. "Thank the Lord for that."

"What happened?" I say, which is a pretty stupid question, I guess. We all know what just happened. But Charlie and his mom seem to understand what I meant.

"I bet they were on angel dust," Charlie says.

"'Cause they're Hells Angels?" I say, confused, not even sure what angel dust is.

Charlie looks at me like I'm the biggest fool on the planet, which I suppose I am. "'Cause they were acting crazy. Out of their minds," he says. "Angel dust does that."

I nod dumbly, resolving next time to keep my mouth shut if I don't know what people are talking about. My mom sometimes says that if people think you might be a fool, there's no sense in opening your mouth and removing all doubt. I guess that's what I did. I'd feel embarrassed if the fist of terror weren't still clenching inside my gut.

"Maybe those two were on angel dust, maybe not," Mrs. Watkins says. "But they didn't need to be on anything to hate us. Hells Angels hate lots of people. Maybe they hate everyone who isn't a Hells Angel. But they got a special kind of hate for black people." She looks at me. "And white people who associate with us."

My head is spinning. I can't think of the right thing to say, so for a change I don't say anything.

"I'm sorry you boys had to see that," she says. "But I'm afraid it won't be the last time in your life you see the face of pure hatred."

We say our stunned good-byes and I almost forget my gym bag and books in their car, getting called back for them as I walk as if in a trance toward the front door.

I see the face of pure hatred again that night. I see it again and again, along with the black barrel of that gun, pointed at my head.

I see it as I toss and turn, unable to sleep.

And when I finally drift off, I see it in my nightmares.

The face of pure hatred. The crazed, insane eyes.

The black barrel of the gun rising to point right between my eyes.

And then I see that shaking hand and that trembling finger on the trigger pull just hard enough.

And then I see my brains splatter everywhere.

CHAPTER 40

I wake up the next day still feeling exhausted, as if I've gotten almost no sleep at all, which isn't surprising considering how often I awoke from that same nightmare. Each time I found my pajamas, tangled sheets, and pillow drenched in sweat.

At school, I struggle to concentrate in my classes and even get embarrassed in Math when Mr. Robinson has to repeat his question for me three times before I'm even able to respond that I don't know the answer.

In the seat beside me, Anna whispers, "Are you all right?"

She's frowning and looking all concerned, so I quickly nod, but it's a lie. I'm not all right. I don't know if I'll ever be all right.

But I'm sure of one thing. Lynn, Lynn, City of Sin sure isn't all right and it never will be.

I hate this place. Hate, hate, hate it.

When I walk with Jeff and Paul DiSimone to my next class, I listen to them discuss yesterday's Apollo 4 launch, but I might as well be on the moon.

"Did you see Walter Cronkite on the news?" Paul says. "That new rocket was too powerful for him. I thought he was going to pee his pants."

"Our building is shaking! Our building is shaking!" Jeff says, mimicking Cronkite.

Any other day, I'd be joining right in, but today the conversation seems to be happening far, far away of me. It fades in and out, the words barely registering. It's as if I'm sleepwalking as I wander from class to class and then at the end of the day to the locker room for football practice.

When Charlie and I head out for practice along with Jessie, he and I exchange a brief look that without saying anything tells me that he's going through the same thing. Maybe he's more used to things like what happened yesterday than I am because he's black. I don't know.

Just based on hearing the stupid things my father says, I'm sure Charlie faces prejudice and unfairness all the time. But I don't know about violence. I don't know about looking into the barrel of a gun, which I'm sure Charlie saw just like me.

But what I see in his face is that no one gets used to what happened yesterday. He may have seen more bad stuff than this country boy from Plainfield, but it still knocks you down like a left hook from Muhammad Ali.

I don't really wake up from this haze until the first time I get hit. It's the second play after we split into varsity and JV, a "Red Sweep Right," and a defender I don't even see bursts through the blockers, drives his helmet into my gut, and slams me to the ground.

That gets my attention. It pushes the ugliness of the outside world out of my mind and lets me think, at least for an hour or so, about nothing but football.

And that's a great thing.

That hit turns out to be the best thing that happens to me all day. The worst thing comes that night at dinner.

*

Mom is unnaturally quiet when she picks me up after practice, even skipping over all the usual questions except how school went, and she barely pays attention to my answer on that one. The talk on the radio is all about the Apollo 4 launch with its powerful rockets and whether or not we're going to beat the Russians to the moon. It keeps my mind off what happened yesterday for a minute or two, but then we have to stop at that same light where Chestnut Street merges with Boston.

I break into a cold sweat and can't help myself from looking all around for Hells Angels and the roar of their motorcycles. But none appear, and Mom doesn't say a word until after we get home and I run upstairs for a couple hours of distracted study.

It isn't until we're all seated at the dinner table, eating Mom's home-made chicken pot pie with big chunks of white and dark meat, gravy, peas, and the crust baked golden brown—its aroma filling the air—that she hits me with the question.

"Rabbit, is there anything you need to tell us?" she asks.

I freeze, my fork hovering in the air halfway to my mouth. I swallow hard. I slowly lower the fork to my plate, then drop it with a clatter.

I'd been afraid of this, hoping that somehow my mom wouldn't find out while knowing that she most certainly would. It had been a miracle that she hadn't asked if I'd gotten a ride and who I'd gotten it from. I'd been prepared to tell her Charlie's mom and hope that would be enough, but she'd never asked and found out anyway.

By the looks of her, she'd found out *everything*.

"I'll help you out," she says with a glance over at my father. She purses her lips. "Mrs. Watkins called me this afternoon."

She waits for me to speak, but I can only stare at her. I should have known. Mothers have a secret network they use to share information with each other. Even between races. Nothing escapes their attention.

"Anything happen that we should know about?" Mom asks.

I look down at my food, open my mouth to speak, and in an instant the floodgates let loose and I'm bawling like a baby. The wracking sobs are so bad I can't even speak.

Mom gets out of her chair, kneels down beside me, and wraps her arm around my shoulder.

"Why didn't you tell me?" she says softly, and I can tell from her voice that she feels hurt that I kept it from her. She understands why I didn't tell my father—why I *couldn't* tell him—but not why I couldn't say something to her.

It's not something I can explain. I guess it's just that I couldn't bear to relive it again by talking about it even though that biker's face—*the face of pure hatred*—has been threatening me all day, forcing me to relive it.

Except during football.

Mom recites the story as she heard it from Mrs. Watkins and I mostly just nod, sniffle, and try to keep from breaking out in embarrassing sobs all over again.

"That settles it," my father says when Mom finally falls silent. His jaw is set, his eyes flaming with anger. "You'll have nothing more to do with that boy! Him or any of the other Negroes at that school. Hanging around with *that kind* is just asking for trouble. It's too dangerous. Violence follows them wherever they go."

"Andre, I don't know if that's—"

"No!" I yell, shooting to my feet. "You can't—"

My father leans over and slaps me hard across the face. "You don't talk back like that, young man! I've had enough of it!"

"Andre!" my mother shrieks.

"How can you blame Charlie and his mom?" I yell at my father as Mom slips between us, shielding me from him. "It wasn't their fault."

"It—"

"It was *your* fault!" I yell, poking my head around my mom and pointing at my father. "You're the one who dragged us here."

"That's not fair," he says, rocking back on his heels, his face turning pale.

"Were there Hells Angels in Plainfield? No one was pointing a gun at my head up there! Were there kids beating me up in Plainfield?"

"What—"

"*Lynn, Lynn, City of Sin!*" I chant. "You knew it and you brought us here anyway." Fury fills my father's face, but I don't care, not even if it earns me another slap across the face or a tanning of my hide with his belt. Nothing is going to shut me up. "This city is the worst place on Earth and you dragged me here because the only thing you love is your job. It's all your fault and nobody else's. I hate your job, I hate this place, and *I hate you!*"

He recoils, his head snapping back. He actually staggers, like a boxer who's taken a big punch. He collapses into his chair, eyes wide, and grips its wooden arms.

"Rabbit! You don't mean that!" my mother scolds, and grips me by the elbow, her nails digging into my skin. "Apologize to your father!"

"For what? I meant *everything*!"

I break free of her grip and race up the stairs to my room, where I'm sure I'll soon face the wrath of my father's belt.

*

After what feels like an awfully long time, Mom comes into the room and sits beside me on the edge of my bed. I'm lying face down, my face buried in the pillow, wet with my tears. It smells of stale sweat, the sweat from last night's tortured nightmares.

Mom strokes my hair and tells me that both she and my father love me so much and they're sure everything is going to work out fine. I listen but don't listen. I hear the words and could parrot them back to her, but I don't believe them at all.

Sure, I believe that she loves me, but my father? What's that phrase that adults say to kids all the time but then ignore themselves? *Actions speak louder than words.* Well, my father's actions don't just say that I don't matter to him, they scream it. He loves only one thing—his job.

I *thought* that he loved me when it seemed he'd arranged for that amazing surprise of the Red Sox game. Just the idea that he'd cared enough to even *think* about it, much less actually get the tickets, filled my heart with love and gratitude. But his true colors showed soon enough when Mr. Jordan let slip that it had been his idea. My father hadn't thought about me at all. Hadn't even mentioned me to his boss. The tickets were just an accident. What a fool I'd been to think otherwise.

"Sit up and look at me," she says. "This is important."

So I do, my back against the bed's headboard and my knees drawn up to my chest.

She moves closer to me and rests her hand on my knee. "You need to apologize to your father."

The words sound like they're in a foreign language. "For what?"

She blinks. "For telling him you hate him."

I don't say anything.

"That's a horrible thing for a parent to hear. You hurt him very much."

I look down at my hands and think that maybe he deserves to be hurt. Mom lifts my chin so I have to look at her. "How about going downstairs to tell him right now?"

I shake my head and her shoulders slump.

"When?" she asks.

"I'll apologize as soon as it isn't the truth."

She winces. "You don't mean that."

I look her in the eye. "Yes, I do."

CHAPTER 41

The next ten days zip by in a blur. The "Cold War" between my father and me continues, like the United States and the Soviet Union, our bombs on the launching pad, ready to go at a moment's notice. And we both know it. We eat dinner in an awkward silence broken only by the clock on the wall behind me going *tick...tick...tick.*

Back in Plainfield, we would have at least reminisced about the Red Sox' magical season or talked about how the Patriots look like one of the worst teams in the NFL and the Giants aren't much better even with Fran Tarkington at quarterback. Or we'd have wondered aloud if Bill Russell and the Celtics can get the championship back from the 76ers after losing it last season for the first time in eight years.

But here in the City of Sin, it's only *tick...tick...tick.* Mom tries to start a conversation, but in no time, it's once again just *tick...tick...tick.*

The nightmares become less frequent. It's only been once or twice in the last week that I see that gun's black barrel pointed at me, and I watch it fire and splatter my brains all over Mrs. Watkins' car, waking me to a silent, choked scream and a gasp for air. During the day, I break into a cold sweat every time we stop at that light at Chestnut and Boston. And I can barely hold in the shriek when I hear the roar of a motorcycle.

But for the most part, I'm back in my usual routine. I don't need a big hit at football practice to snap me out of my daze. I'm not "over it" as Mom has asked a couple times, but I'm not a basket case. I'm getting by, doing okay in school, and in our next-to-last game against Marblehead, I pick up right where I left off, scoring three touchdowns, one on a pass, one on a kickoff return, and one on a punt return.

Which leaves only Lynn Classical between us and an 8-2 record, the best for a Lynn English JV team in many years.

*

A cold wind whips through Manning Bowl, stinging my skin as I trot back to take the opening kickoff. I blow on my hands to warm them. The last thing I want is any numbness in them when the ball comes floating down or, just as importantly, after I've gotten the ball and a tackler lowers his head into me.

As usual for the JV games, the stadium has a cold, cavernous feel to it with almost no one in the stands. I don't look up. I know all the Lynn English JV fans who are there because it's always the same fifty or sixty parents and friends huddled together, a few specks in stands that could seat twenty to twenty-five thousand.

I long ago gave up searching for my father's face among them. He isn't interested and I don't care. It doesn't matter to me. Not anymore.

I push any stray thoughts of him out of my mind. I don't want anything distracting me from my biggest football game ever. The Thanksgiving Day varsity game will have thousands of people in the stands, but I'll just be watching on the sidelines, no different than any of the fans except that I'll be wearing a uniform, one that won't get a single grass stain or clump of dirt on it.

So this is my Super Bowl.

The referee blows his whistle, and within a few seconds I'm watching the ball rotate end over end on its way down to me. I catch it in both hands, cushioned against my chest, and take off.

Zero to sixty in under eight seconds is what one of the car commercials advertises. In your mind, you can hear the squeal of the tires and smell the burned rubber. That's what I try for. Zero to sixty.

I sprint straight ahead, then veer just a little to the left as a possible gap opens up. I shift the ball to my left hand, cradle the tip against my bicep, and as the crashing of shoulder pads and the sound of grunts fills the air, I hit the hole at top speed.

A Classical defender grasps my jersey, but I break loose. Two more defenders bear down on me, one straight ahead and the other slightly to my right. I cut to the left and then as they veer to that side, I cut back hard to the right. They windmill their arms, but they're not going to touch me. The one on the right collides with the other and I'm off to the races. I fly down the field and, as I cross into the end zone, I glance back and see no one within twenty yards of me.

Now that's the way to start the game!

We kick off to Classical and although they get a couple first downs, they soon have to punt. It's a bad kick, a line drive that leaves the defenders more than twenty yards away when I catch the ball.

I run straight ahead, freeze the defense with a fake to the right and then cut back to left, using a perfect block by C.J. Powell to get free wide.

I'm racing down the left sideline and no one is going to catch me. Another touchdown!

I score one more touchdown on a nice pass by Higgins, but don't get any more chances on kick returns because they kick the ball away from me, angling it out of bounds on punts and squib-kicking it on kickoffs so it bounces along the ground and gets fielded by one of the blockers.

We're winning in a romp, leading 34-6 midway through the fourth quarter, so Coach Callahan begins to take out some of the starters, one by one. It's our last game of the year, and the move is one my Plainfield basketball coach used to do so the fans could cheer those players.

At first, I don't think it makes sense here in this huge, empty stadium. If anyone cheers, who will hear it? But when Higgins trots off, the cheers of the fifty or sixty fans are audible after all. The same for Charlie.

When it's my turn, I slap the hands of my teammates in the huddle and with my mouthpiece flapping loose on my facemask, I head for the

sideline. I hear the smattering of applause and an attempted chant of
"Rabbit! Rabbit! Rabbit!"

It's been a pretty good year. Despite the cold wind whipping at my
face, I feel a warm glow of satisfaction. Not bad for the five-nothin', hundred-nothin' kid who had to beg for a tryout.

"Great season, Rabbit!" Coach Callahan says, and shakes my hand.

I slap the hands of my teammates along the sideline. Charlie and I
exchange a quick but heartfelt hug. We're all whooping it up.

"Eight wins, baby!" Higgins yells. "And we crushed Classical!"

We all yell, "Yeah!"

When there's a break in our celebration, a girl's high-pitched voice
from the stands cuts through the air.

"Rabbit, you were amazing!"

Anna.

During a game, you never look into the stands. All your focus is
on the field. But with the game, and now the season, over, I turn and
find the source of that familiar voice. Her gloved hands are cupped to
her mouth, her blonde hair poking out from beneath a red ski hat, its
long, loose strands flapping in the wind, and her pretty face crimson
in the cold.

My grin goes a mile wide. I point to her and she flashes that bright
smile that warms my heart.

Maybe I have my first girlfriend.

Probably not. A shouted compliment doesn't mean she's madly in
love with me. I shouldn't get carried away.

But maybe she is.

I don't forget my mom, pointing to her, too, standing three rows up
from Anna.

Alone.

I look back to Anna and drink in that smile. I can't take my eyes off her.

Charlie, who has sidled over next to me, gives me a bump. With
a nod toward Anna in the stands, he says, "Great game, Romeo," and
we laugh.

*

The next day before Math class starts, Anna regales everyone seated in the nearby desks with my exploits. She's wearing a pretty yellow sweater over a white blouse and dark blue slacks.

"He was amazing," she says, and I see some of that starry-eyed look on her that she showered on Jimmy Keenan while he was performing at the Halloween dance. "I've never seen anyone run so fast. His legs were just a blur. I guess that's why he's called Rabbit," she says with a smile. "And the moves! He'd fake one way and the defender all but collapsed to his knees!"

Cindy, Jeff, and Paul glance my way. I'm a little bit embarrassed and I feel my face grow warm, but mostly I'm enjoying it.

Especially coming from Anna.

After class, we walk together to Science. Amidst the loud buzz of conversation and laughter, I ask her about the musical pieces the band will be playing during halftime of the Thanksgiving Day varsity game. She runs through the list with enthusiasm, and it occurs to me that she feels the same way about playing the flute that I feel about football.

"I wish I could hear you play," I say.

"We have a Christmas concert next month."

"December sounds like a good time for a Christmas concert," I say. "Better than October or July."

She laughs and swats me on the elbow. Her laughter, soft and melodic, puts a big smile on my face and makes me feel warm inside.

Before I chicken out, I ask her for her phone number, and she gives it to me, her eyes twinkling, and adds that she's in the phone book if I lose the number. I caution her that my parents keep a close eye on the telephone bill's message units so I won't be able to talk for long, but she says that's okay and flashes that brilliant, warm smile again.

It's a smile I can get very used to.

CHAPTER 42

The sun is bright, but the wind blows cold and biting for the Thanksgiving Day varsity game. Unlike the JV games, in which I stay warm because I'm active on every play, today I'll be rubbing my arms and blowing on my hands and even running in place because I'll just be standing on the sidelines.

It'll be exciting in future years when I actually play in these games because the band is playing in the stands behind us, the cheerleaders are cheering, the public-address system is announcing the plays, and there are thousands of people in the stands, making Manning Bowl, which feels like an empty tomb during the JV games, come alive. It's still just a lot of ugly concrete with a section of the stands that's closed because of the rotting wood seats, but it's alive with the sounds of football beyond just the slamming of bodies together and the grunts and the officials' whistles.

The cheerleaders are doing a cheer now where they each take a turn, praising a starting player. One of them starts with, "Willie Jenkins, he's my man. If he can't do it..." Another continues, "...Jake can! Jake O'Meara, he's my man. If he can't do it..." They go through the lineup and finish with "If he can't do it, no one can!"

It'll be cool to have a cheerleader cheer my name like that and cool to have the public-address announcer say my name after I make a play.

"That's a pass from Chris Higgins to Rabbit Labelle for twenty-three yards. First down!"

But mostly, it'll be cool to play for the varsity against the best possible competition and see how I do. I hope I start next year. Not many sophomores do, but the two starting ends and one of the backups are seniors, so Charlie and I could move our pass-receiving one-two punch right onto the big squad. That'd be fun.

But today will just be standing around and dreaming.

Classical takes the opening kickoff and drives for a touchdown. This could be a really long day. The Rams are 6-3 and our varsity only 2-7. The only thing that can save the season is to beat Classical, and right now it looks like we're going to take the whipping.

It gets worse on the following kickoff. Willie Jenkins, our top split end and kick returner, gets hurt returning the kick, taking a hit to the knee just as he plants his foot. He has to be helped off the field, his arms around two teammates, unable to put any weight on the knee. It doesn't look good.

We punt, and Classical again drives the field for a touchdown. The fans on the opposite field go wild, jumping up and down and clapping and pumping their fists. After the extra point, it's 14-0 and the first quarter isn't even over. The gray concrete and rotted stands may not be the ugliest thing in Manning Bowl today.

It gets worse.

On the following kickoff, Jenkins's replacement, Brian Costello, fumbles the ball. He trots toward the sideline, head down, angling toward all of us scrubs and away from the coaches. Coach McDonough runs after him, his face red with rage, and catches him just ten feet away from me.

"What's wrong with you?" he yells, throwing his arms up in the air in frustration. He crowds in, his nose inches away from Costello's facemask. "How many times do I have to show you how to protect the ball? How many laps have you had to run during practice because you can't hold onto the ball? What's it going to take to get through your thick skull?"

Costello stares at the ground.

Coach McDonough whirls around, still looking like his head is about to explode. "Callahan!"

Coach Callahan, clipboard in hand and hair flapping in the wind, rushes over.

"Who's that hotshot kick returner I've heard about on the JV team?" McDonough yells.

My eyes go wide and my heart begins to hammer. I slide the mouth-piece past my lips into my mouth and taste its sour plastic.

"Labelle," Coach Callahan answers.

"Where is he?"

I step forward and feebly raise my hand. Callahan points to me.

"The midget?" Coach McDonough says, incredulous.

"He's little, but he's good," Coach Callahan says. "He's really good. Outstanding, in fact. You should try him. He's worth the gamble."

"He ain't even a hundred pounds! He'll get killed out there!"

"Only if they catch him," Callahan says. A huge grin spreads across my face, but the coaches can't see it because I've got my mouthpiece in.

"How many fumbles this year?"

"None. And nine touchdowns in six games on kick returns alone."

McDonough does a double-take, his eyebrows shooting up. "Nine?"

"Yes."

McDonough gives me a hard look. "Kid, you better play bigger than you look."

I nod eagerly.

"You watch our kick returns during practice?"

It seems to me that the team practiced kick returns only a couple times early in the season and not at all since. Unless, that is, the varsity practiced it after the JV squad split off down to the far end of the field.

But there's only one answer to a question like that. I flip my mouth-piece out and say, "Yes, sir!"

"Okay, then. You're out there for the next kick. Let's hope it's a punt." He turns to walk away, then stops and shakes his head.

"How much do you weigh?" he asks.

I gulp hard, sure he's going to change his mind, but before I can answer he holds up his hand in a stopping gesture. "No, don't tell me. I don't want to know."

*

The defense stiffens on a game-saving fourth-and-two from our eleven yard line and we take over the ball.

"Attaway, boys!" some of the guys yell, and slap each other on the shoulder pads. The crunching sound echoes across the sideline. Falling behind by twenty would have been disastrous. But now we have to move the ball.

And we do. Perhaps Classical has eased up, deflated after failing to deliver the knockout punch, or maybe we've seized the momentum. Scottie Joyce breaks off a twenty-five yard run and then Jake O'Meara completes two quick passes and we're moving into the Rams' territory. Behind us, our fans finally start making some noise.

I feel ready to jump out of my skin. Adrenaline rushes through my body, but I've got nothing to do. There's no release. I do a few jumping jacks and run in place to loosen up. I yell out my encouragement to the offense, then walk to the orange water cooler and take a sip, wincing as the icy cold fluid goes down my throat.

I mentally rehearse my moves, giving a silent reminder to hold onto the ball. If I fumble, I might as well keep running right out of the stadium.

The offense pushes the ball into the end zone on a fourth-and-goal from the two yard line and though we fail on the two-point conversion, we're back in it, 14-6.

We kick off and after two first downs, the Rams have to punt. I run onto the field to about our ten yard line, wanting to get out there before Coach McDonough changes his mind.

"Fourth and three from the Classical 43 yard line," the PA announcer says, his voice tinny and loaded with static. "Classical drops back to punt."

There's a buzz in the crowd and subconsciously I can almost make out the words, "Look at him! Look at the shrimp!" They're coming from the English sideline. As I get to the midpoint between the two sides, I even hear a loud, raucous laugh.

But I push all that away. It all becomes like static on the radio. Now it's just me and the football.

It flies up high, higher than it went in the JV games, and it comes down against a background of blue sky and puffy white clouds. I give a quick glance to the onrushing defenders, then back up at the ball.

One defender on the left could hit me right after I catch it; I've got time with the others. The safe play would be a fair catch. Just lift my hand, catch the ball, and we take over from there. No return at all.

But this isn't the time for the safe play.

I keep my hands at my chest, position myself under the ball coming down end over end, and track it into my hands, not making the mistake of trying to do too much and run with it before I've got it secured. The rough surface touches my hands, cushioned against my chest, and I slide the ball against my right bicep.

I take two quick steps forward and the defender on the left who was bearing down on me flies past, his hand grasping momentarily at my jersey. He's overrun the play.

I fake to the right, freezing the defenders on that side, and then cut to an open lane left by defender behind me. I race through the opening, come to two more defenders, fake hard to the outside and cut back inside to the right. They stumble, reach out for me with flailing arms, and I'm off.

There's no one between me and the end zone.

But I'm taking nothing for granted. I've seen players on TV make great moves to get open and then ease up, thinking they've got the touchdown only to get caught from behind.

No one is going to catch me from behind.

My legs churn faster and faster. I don't dare look back. I just pretend that someone is on my heels and I've got to accelerate even more.

Faster.

Faster.

Faster.

And then I'm in the end zone, but I'm not even taking a chance on that. I keep running through the end zone before I stop, gasping, and turn around.

There isn't a single Classical Ram near me. Instead, only a wave of my teammates, arms spread out wide, rejoicing. I jump up and down and they pour all over me.

"What a run!"

"Yeah!"

"Way to go!"

I smell their sweat and the grass stains from their uniforms. They whack me on the helmet and on the shoulder pads, then swat me on the fanny.

"What a touchdown!"

Eventually, I run to the sideline, still carrying the football as if it's glued to my fingertips and bicep.

"That was a seventy-eight yard punt return for a touchdown by freshman Rabbit Labelle," says the PA announcer.

The band blares out the fight song, that "Roll Out the Barrel" polka that sounded so stupid when I first heard it, but sounds so sweet now.

Roll on you Bulldogs.

Show them how you got your name.

Roll on you Bulldogs.

Each game enhances your fame.

Fight on to victory.

You're not afraid of your foe.

The courage of the English Bulldogs,

Everybody knows!

Charlie comes over and slaps me on the shoulder pads. "Great run, man!"

We score on the two-point conversion to tie the game, 14-14, and everyone on the sideline is slapping each other's hands and bellowing out encouragement.

Coach McDonough comes over. He shakes his head, but smiles. "I thought you were gonna get killed on that play." He slaps me lightly on the side of the helmet. "Great run, kid!" He opens his mouth to say something more, and I get ready for him to say I should have taken the fair catch, but he just slaps me again and says, "Helluva run!"

CHAPTER 43

For a brief moment I think I can break the second-half kickoff for a long gainer, maybe even a touchdown to take the lead. We've charged out of the concrete locker room beneath the stands with lots of yelling and slapping each other on the backs and shoulder pads.

"Let's do it!" somebody bellows and we all answer "Yeah!" and "Let's get 'em!" as we run onto the field. The band plays the fight song, the fans shout and clap their hands, and the cheerleaders jump up and down, shaking their pom-poms.

The kickoff comes down to me, end over end, and everything becomes quiet. Just me and the ball. I take it and dart up the middle. I cut to the left, but there's no long runback this time. A Classical player lunges at me, extending his arms and catching enough of one ankle to trip me up. I stumble, try to right myself, and while I stagger at half speed, a huge brute of a defender comes at me at full gallop and drives his helmet into my chest. I feel all of what must be close to two hundred pounds as he slams me hard into the ground.

Ahhhhhhhhhhhhhhhh.

The air escapes from between my lips, but I can't breathe it back in.

Ahhhhhhhhhhhhhhhh.

My chest feels like it's been crushed. Pain radiates through my entire body, but all I can think of is…

Ahhhhhhhhhhhhhhhh.

...I can't breathe. Like what happened in that practice so long ago, I've gotten the wind knocked out of me. But my mind just wants to scream: *I can't breathe, I can't breathe, I can't breathe.*

Ahhhhhhhhhhhhhhhh.

The brute climbs off of me and stares down.

Ahhhhhhhhhhhhhhhh.

I feel like I'll die from lack of oxygen by the time the coaches and trainer get out here. Somewhere in the back of my mind, I know this isn't true. No one dies from getting the wind knocked out of them, but still...

Ahhhhhhhhhhhhhhhh.

I remember Coach lifting me up and dropping me flat on my back. I remember after the second or third time, the air rushed back into my lungs.

Ahhhhhhhhhhhhhhhh.

I stagger partway to my feet and like a fish out of water, flop backwards onto the ground.

Ahhhhhhhhhhhhhhhh.

Still no air.

I get back up and flop backwards again.

Ahhhhhhhhhhhhhhhh.

And again.

And there it is!

Air!

I can breathe! I suck in huge gulps and realize the players and officials clustered around me are looking at me as if I'm having some kind of epileptic fit.

Which I suppose is just what it looked like.

I draw in one last huge gasp of air and nod at everyone around me. "I'm okay," I say with great effort and begin to trot off the field.

Coach Callahan meets me halfway, two steps ahead of the trainer, Mr. Noyes, a short, balding man in his fifties. They both look very concerned.

"Wind knocked out," I say, every word still an effort. "I'm okay," and though the effort still hurts, I keep trotting to the sideline. I'm sore as hell. My chest feels like it'll be one gigantic black–and-purple bruise tomorrow.

Charlie moves up beside me. "You okay?"

I nod.

"You sure?"

"Sure."

"You looked like Jerry Lewis out there," he says with a cautious smile, referring to the comedian who gets some of his biggest laughs from slapstick humor that looks a lot like what I just did.

I nod and smile. "I'm okay."

Minutes later, Brian Costello, who I replaced as kick returner but is still starting at split end, drops what would have been a touchdown pass. His defender falls down so all Costello has to do is catch the easy pass and he could almost walk it in, but the ball bounces off his hands, then his chest, then his hands again, and falls to the ground.

Coach McDonough goes ballistic. Costello, a starter only because of the knee injury to Jenkins, hasn't done anything right. He's fumbled away a kickoff and dropped an easy touchdown pass.

McDonough yells for Coach Callahan and on the next play, they send Charlie in for Costello.

"Go get 'em!" I say.

Seconds later, Charlie makes his first varsity catch for a big first down. I cheer like crazy, knowing he's in there to stay. But the drive bogs down and after we punt, Classical moves back downfield for a touchdown. With the extra point, we're now down 21-14.

On the resulting kickoff, I almost break it for a long return, but two defenders angle me out of bounds at the Classical 42. We move down the field with Charlie making a nice catch to prolong the drive, but we get stopped short of the goal line. Classical takes over and responds in kind. The back-and-forth continues late into the fourth quarter, both sides driving deep into their opponent's territory only to turn the ball over on downs, so close to a critical touchdown but yet so far.

We're running out of time.

On what may be our last chance, a fourth-and-goal with only minutes left, our halfback, Scottie Joyce, gets stuffed at the line.

Rams' ball.

We may not get the ball back again. If they can get two first downs, that'll pretty much run out the clock and the game will be over. Making matters worse, Scottie is staggering off the field, cradling his shoulder, in a great deal of pain. He's one of our best players, both on offense and defense. His loss is probably the final nail in the coffin.

The Rams get one first down, breaking a long run for what would have been a touchdown if not for Jessie's game-saving tackle. But they don't get the second one that would ice the game.

With less than a minute remaining, I trot onto the field for what will certainly be our final chance. I need to either return this punt for a touchdown or come pretty close. There isn't time for us to score if I don't.

I slide the mouthpiece into place, blow on my hands, and let everything else fade into the background.

Just me and the ball.

Me and the ball.

When I see its flight, I groan loudly. I run for the left sideline as fast as I can. The punter has angled his kick for the sideline, intentionally trying to let it fly out of bounds to take away any opportunity of a return.

But it may not quite reach.

I urge my legs to move faster. The punt is going to land close to the sideline. Awfully close. Maybe out of bounds, taking the ball out of my hands. I glance at the defenders bearing down on me. Even if the ball stays in, I'm going to have almost no room to run. It's a great kick.

But not great enough.

I catch it just two steps from the sideline and face a wall of defenders trying to angle me out of bounds. I'm on our thirty-two yard line, and retreat as I try to run wide to the open side of the field.

I run back to the twenty-five yard line, then the twenty, trying to give myself room to run. If I fail now, I'll have left the offense with almost the entire length of the field to go and less than a minute to do it.

But I get a great block from Jessie that takes out one defender, I fake another one as I cut back to the fifteen, and then...

There it is!

An opening to the far sideline. Jessie's key block and my retreat has gotten me outside their far-side contain men, the ones responsible for keeping me penned in.

I freeze one defender with a fake, then burst around another one and streak through the opening.

Down the sideline.

Faster.

Faster and faster.

As I fly past the Classical coaches, my legs churning, some part of my mind hears one of them shriek, "No! No! No!" above the rising wall of cheers from the English side. But all that is deep inside my brain. All I'm thinking about now is that end zone and not letting anyone catch me.

From the far side of the field, I see one lanky figure angling after me...

...but he isn't going to catch me.

No one is going to catch me!

I fly into the end zone and keep going until I'm out of it before I fling the ball into the air in euphoric triumph. Gasping for air, I turn to see my teammates racing after me, arms waving and fists pumping.

We yell and slap each other on the shoulders and go crazy, especially Jessie and me.

"Great block!" I yell so loud my throat is getting hoarse.

"Great run!" he yells back along with several of the others.

We keep celebrating until we realize almost all at once that we're still behind by a point, 21-20. If we don't make the two-point conversion, we still lose.

The whistle blows and the lead official signals a Classical timeout. I run to the sideline, beaming. The band blasts away with the fight song. The fans yell and cheer.

"Labelle, get over here!" Coach McDonough yells.

I sprint over to him, sure I've done something wrong but I can't think what it might be.

"They tried to kick the ball out of bounds because they're afraid of you," he says. "They're terrified! We're going to use that against them. You've played some halfback, right?"

I nod.

"You know all the halfback plays?"

Just like with his question about kick returns, there's only one answer. "Yes, sir!" And to remove any question at all, I add, "I know all the plays from every position."

"Okay, get out there at halfback. Joyce is hurt and we need a play-maker. That's you. Sell the run and it'll be an easy touchdown. They'll come after you because they're scared of you. It'll be wide open. But you've *got* to sell the run." He takes me by the shoulders, turns me toward the field, and gives a little shove. "Now get out there. Quickly! Make sure the Classical sideline sees you're in there."

I race out onto the field as the quarterback, Jake O'Meara, converges on Coach McDonough to get the play to call in the huddle. I clap my hands and pump my fist to attract a little extra attention from the Classical sideline, then stand with my back facing the Rams' sideline.

I figure it's going to be some kind of fake handoff to me with the play going the other way. Coach wants me to sell the run, convincing Classical to tackle me. I'm the decoy. I resolve to follow through with the best fake in the history of football. So good I get tackled by half the Classical team.

But when Jake O'Meara steps into the huddle and calls the play, my blood runs cold.

"Halfback option right. On two."

For a split second, I freeze.

Halfback option.

I want to say, "But I can't see over the line!"

But I can't even speak.

And it's too late for that.

Ohmigod, ohmigod, ohmigod. What am I going to do?

Now I know what Coach McDonough meant when he said to sell the run. He figures the defense will all rush after me and leave the receiver all alone in the end zone.

An easy touchdown pass.

But only if I can see that wide-open teammate in the end zone.

Ohmigod, ohmigod, ohmigod.

Well, I tell myself, I'm just going to have to run it in myself or somehow get open enough so I can see someone open in the end zone.

Ohmigod, ohmigod, ohmigod.

I blow on my hands and take my position in back of O'Meara and off to the right, sure that the pounding of my heart will make it so I can't even hear the snap count. All my senses come alive. I smell the fresh grass, the soil, and all the sweat. I taste the plastic of my mouthpiece and the sharp, bitter tang of a speck of vomit at the back of my throat.

And I try to push it all away.

Just me and the ball.

On two, I break to the right and look back to O'Meara, who pitches the ball to me. I take it in stride and see a wall of our linemen and Classical defenders in front of me. I can't see a glimmer of the end zone. Just the backs of our jerseys and the fronts of theirs.

I run wide, looking for an opening.

There is none.

The Classical defense converges on me. I fight back the panic and fake a move toward the line of scrimmage.

I look. Can't see anything but the wall of players. Just like in practice.

I cut back to the outside.

Still nothing.

For a split second, the word *ohmigod* echoes inside my brain. I push it away.

I make my decision. I'm going for broke. I take a chance that I won't run out of room before the sideline arrives.

I tuck the ball into my arm and sprint to the outside to create an opening. As defenders converge and the sideline looms on the right, a gap opens and I look to the end zone.

Where Charlie is standing all alone.

I take aim and let the ball fly. It floats through the air, seeming to move in slow motion.

Floating slowly…

slowly…

slowly.

And then it nestles safely in Charlie's hands.

He grasps onto it and holds it aloft in jubilation. The referee signals the successful two-point conversion.

We all go crazy.

"*Yeaaaahh!*"

"*We did it!*"

We're all jumping around and yelling and I hear "*Ohmigod, ohmigod, ohmigod*" in my brain, only this time it's the celebratory version, not the panicked one.

"Two-point conversion successful for English," the tinny-sounding PA announcer says. "Pass from Rabbit Labelle to Charlie Watkins. English leads 22-21."

I hug Charlie.

"What took you so long to throw it, man?" he says, laughing. "I was open for *hours!*"

I laugh, too, and we all run for the sideline with the fans in the stands going nuts and the band playing that wonderful polka fight song.

Roll on you Bulldogs.
Show them how you got your name.
Roll on you Bulldogs.
Each game enhances your fame.
Fight on to victory.
You're not afraid of your foe.
The courage of the English Bulldogs,
Everybody knows!

After the kickoff and three plays by Classical, the final whistle sounds. The wind stings my face, its gusts cold and nippy, but I've never felt a warmer glow inside me.

Yeah, I definitely love football best of all.

CHAPTER 44

W e bus back to school, shower, and change, the adrenaline only beginning to fade, the warm glow still radiating as strong as the sun. People who don't play sports don't get it, won't ever get it, but this happiness is sweet and pure.

Bruiser even offers to give me a ride home if I need it. I don't, but imagine that.

I step outside, the wind cold on my wet hair, and see my father in his car, the silver Plymouth Fury, parked in the semicircle in front of the school. It makes sense, I suppose. Mom is working on the turkey and all the fixings, and my father can't be at work today, no matter how much he might want to, because it's closed for the holiday. Still, it feels strange to see him here.

I slide into the front seat, my stomach already craving one of Mom's sandwiches or something else to tide me over until we eat. I guess I'm no different than Pavlov's dogs that we studied in school.

My father doesn't start the car right away, waiting until he sees other teammates emerging from the big red doors at the front entrance and streaming past to other cars. He pulls out of the semicircle, but instead of heading out to the main drag, Chestnut Street, he turns onto Clovelly, a side street, goes halfway down it, and pulls to the curb.

His eyes begin to water and his lips tremble. "I'm not very good at saying I'm wrong, maybe because I don't do it very often," he says in a shaky voice. He clears his throat. "But I've got a lot of making up to do on that front." He takes a deep, shuddering breath. "I am *so* sorry. I watched you today and you were...you were amazing!"

"Thanks." I hadn't realized he was coming to the game; I hadn't even considered it. I didn't think he'd bother because I didn't expect to play.

"Did Mom come?" I ask, afraid that the Thanksgiving Day meal had kept her away.

My father snorts. "She said she'd risk the turkey overcooking and burning the house down before she missed your game."

I smile. That's Mom.

"She's a lot smarter than I am," he says, his voice choked. "I've been such a fool." Tears stream down his face. He wipes them idly and shakes his head. "My job, my career, is important to me. It always will be. It's..." He shrugs. "...it's part of what makes me tick." He looks at me and strokes my hair. "But somehow I let it become the only thing that made me tick. I lost sight of how being *your dad* was also a big part of what makes me tick."

Walls inside me begin to crumble.

"I'm sorry things have been rough here for you in Lynn," he says. "And I'm sorry I can't undo that. We're going to have to make the best of it here until some other position becomes available somewhere else. The way things work, that'll probably have to be a promotion in some other division in a couple years. Until then, maybe we can just buy a house in one of the other, nicer communities around here. I thought I'd found a good neighborhood here away from the..."

I tense.

"Well, I'm not really sure what I know anymore," he says. "Watching you and the black boy, Charlie...Charlie, what's his name?"

"Watkins."

"Yes, that's it. Charlie Watkins. Watching the two of you hug makes me think that perhaps I'm wrong about all that, too." He shakes his head. "I don't know.

"But I do know this. I'm sorry I've…" He sniffles, takes out his handkerchief, and blows his nose. "I'm sorry I've failed you as a father." He begins to weep. "When you said that you hated me, I was very hurt and felt you were being very unfair.

"But you were right. I hate me, too, right now. I hate the me that I've become. I'm going to be different. I can't promise I'll make every one of your games from now on, but I sure intend to make most of them. Watching you out there today…" He shakes his head. "What was I thinking?"

The dam bursts and my eyes flood with tears. I try to wipe them away but there's no stopping them.

Dad throws his arms around me. "Can you forgive me?" he asks. "I love you with all my heart. I'm going to change. Can you love me again?"

I don't need to think twice. Football coaches ask some questions that have only one answer; sometimes dads do that, too.

Acknowledgements

Thanks to my Lynn English High School classmates, Tom Howland and Chris Mullen, for all their help in getting the details right. Also to Mary Winston McCarriston for her enthusiasm and publicity.

To my team of first readers, who once again provided me with great insights, and to my editor, Dayle Dermatis, whose expertise caught countless mistakes. Any typos or errors that remain are entirely my own fault.

To my friends and family, for their love and support, especially to my brother, Steve, whose frequent flier miles have gotten me to Oregon for so many writing workshops.

To my son, Ryan, and his fiancée, Stephanie, and to my daughter, Nicole, and her husband, Greg. I love you dearly.

And to the Best Wife Ever and the love of my life, Brenda, whose support borders on the insane. I am so very, very lucky.

About the Author

DAVID H. HENDRICKSON's first novel, *Cracking the Ice*, was praised by Booklist as "a gripping account of a courageous young man rising above evil." He has since published *Bubba Goes for Broke* (writing as David Bawdy), *Body Check*, and many short stories. His fiction has appeared on multiple Kindle bestseller lists in several genres.

He's been honored with the Joe Concannon and Scarlet Quill awards for his coverage of college hockey.

For more information about his writing, visit him online at www.hendricksonwriter.com, where you can sign up for his mailing list and be notified of new releases.

A Special Request from the Author: Word of mouth is crucial for any author to succeed. If you enjoyed this book, please consider leaving a review where you purchased it. Even if it's only a line or two, it would make all the difference and would be very much appreciated.